CENTRAL

WITHDRAWN

PENNY TOWN JUSTICE

PENNY TOWN JUSTICE

A. L. McWilliams

CONTRA COSTA COUNTY LIBRARY

Five Star
Unity, Maine

3 1901 02817 0175

Copyright © 2000 by A. L. McWilliams

All rights reserved.

This novel is a work of fiction. Names, characters, places, and incidents are either the product of the author's imagination, or, if real, used fictitiously.

Five Star First Edition Romance Series.

First Edition, Second Printing.

Published in 2000 in conjunction with The Seymour Agency.

Cover design by Brad Fitzpatrick.

The text of this edition is unabridged.

Set in 11 pt. Plantin by Elena Picard.

Printed in the United States on permanent paper.

Library of Congress Cataloging-in-Publication Data

McWilliams, A. L. (Audra LaVaun)
Penny Town justice / A.L. McWilliams.
p. cm.—(Five Star first edition romance series)
ISBN 0-7862-2812-1 (hc : alk. paper)
1. Arizona — Fiction. I. Title. II. Series.
PS3563.C927 P46 2000
813′.6—dc21 00-057307

To Mary Sue Seymour,
with thanks for being my agent and friend.

CHAPTER ONE

Arizona Territory, 1886

Though she had prepared herself for this moment, Christina Cates' hands trembled as she tipped up the half-pint glass bottle and poured a measure of arsenic into a teaspoon. She gazed down at the little pyramid of white powder, drew a long, slow breath, and dropped the spoon into the cup of tea on the counter in front of her.

Except for the clinking of the spoon hitting against the sides of the cup, the house was silent. Still stirring, Christina left the kitchen and padded down the darkened hall in slippered feet to the parlor. She climbed the stairs gracefully, her white, silk gown sweeping the steps behind her, and crossed the landing to the second door on the right. It was ajar.

Christina peered through the crack at her husband, feeling her body sway with the hard, pulsating beat of her heart. Robert Cates was sitting up in bed with his French briar pipe tucked in the corner of his mouth and today's newspaper spread across his lap. Brow furrowed in concentration, he turned his head slightly, reading the headlines, and a silver-streaked sideburn glistened in the light from the oil lamps.

His nightly routine never varied. First his pipe, then a book or a newspaper, and lastly a cup of chamomile tea to help him relax.

He looked up as she pushed the door open.

"It's about time."

Eyes lowered, Christina crossed the room to the bed. "I'm sorry. I spilled water on the floor. I had to clean up."

"That's what the maid's for."

"I gave Rosa the afternoon off. She wanted to visit her sister."

Glancing up, she saw her husband's jaws knot as he folded the *Arizona Star* in half and pitched it to the floor. Christina flinched in spite of herself. She held the steaming cup with both hands. "You gave her the afternoon off."

"Yes."

"Tell me something, Christina. Who pays Rosa's wages?"

"You do."

"Yet I'm the last to know what's going on in my own house. Next time ask me before you give the maid a day off."

Christina nodded. "You're right, of course. I don't know what I was thinking." She looked at him finally, looked him square in the eye, and held the cup toward him. "You should drink your tea before it gets cold."

He took the cup from her hand, and Christina turned and sat down in front of her dresser. She gazed at herself in the mirror a moment, at the green-tinged bruise surrounding her left eye and the darker, more recent one that marred the clean curve of her cheek, reminders of why she was following through on this act she had contemplated for so long. It was the only way out. Robert Cates had given her no other option.

She looked past her image in the dresser mirror to that of her husband and watched with dark, expressionless eyes as he lifted the cup to his lips.

It was too late to back out now . . . even if she wanted to.

Picking up her brush, Christina ran it through her hair and saw the light play upon the long, glossy waves. She was a young woman and attractive, but she felt ancient at times, and it was only when she expected a visit from Jim Mitchell that she cared for her looks any more. He would be here any minute now.

She reached for her face powder, hoping to partially conceal the results of her husband's latest temper tantrum, projecting an outward calm and presence of mind she did not feel inside.

"This tea doesn't taste right."

Christina's hand closed around the powder puff, squeezing it into a ball. Jim had assured her he wouldn't suspect a thing. He had assured her arsenic was tasteless! White-faced, she looked over her shoulder at Robert.

"What did you say?"

"Tea doesn't taste right. You forgot the sugar."

"I'll get you some," Christina said quickly, relieved. She started to rise.

Robert shook his head. "Forget it." Taking another swallow, he set the cup on the bedside table and got up to raise the window. "Stuffy in here," he mumbled and stood a moment gazing out at the night and the dark, uneven line of the Catarina Mountains to the north. "We're holding a cattlemen's meeting tomorrow at the Cosmopolitan Hotel," he told her. "It'll probably last all day. I doubt if I'll be in for supper so don't wait up for me."

Christina listened to his deep, toneless voice and cast a swift glance at the cup on the table. It was almost empty. Maybe that wasn't enough. How much arsenic did it take to kill a man? She didn't know, and it frightened her to think she might have to go through this all over again. She wasn't sure if she could do it.

"Why all the primping?" He was looking at her now, studying her curiously.

"Just passing the time," she said. "I'm not sleepy."

He moved behind her and ran his hand up her back and beneath her hair. Christina stiffened at his touch, feeling his palm hot against the nape of her neck, his thumb moving in slow little circles against her scalp at the hairline while his fingertips curled around almost to her throat.

"Come on to bed," he told her.

"I said I wasn't sleepy."

"Neither am I."

She raised her eyes, looking at him standing over her in the mirror.

"Come on to bed," he said again.

"Please, Robert. Not tonight."

His features hardened, the lips in the wide mouth narrowing into a thin, grim line, nostrils flaring a little. Christina felt the tips of his fingers dig into her throat. Expecting the worst, she braced herself, gripping the edge of the dresser with both hands.

He squeezed her throat until her pulse throbbed against his hand and the blood pounded in her temples, listened a moment to her labored breathing, and at last, let his hand fall to his side. He stepped away from her.

"Who are you saving it for, Christina?"

Lips parted, she touched her throat and stared at him without answering.

"Is it one of the hired hands?"

"What are you talking about?" she asked.

"You tell me." He sat down on the edge of the bed, and Christina watched in silence as he wiped the sudden sweat from his forehead and upper lip. "When I find out who it is," he said slowly, "I'll make you watch while I kill him, and then I'll kill you."

His last words didn't surprise her. He had made the threat

before, and she believed him. It was only a matter of time.

Pushing her chair back, Christina stood up and extinguished the two swinging bracket lamps on either side of the dresser mirror. She turned to her husband.

"You look sick," she said. Her voice was calm.

Glancing up, he caught her intent stare and frowned. "Do I?"

"Yes. I thought you might be bilious."

"I feel a little strange," Robert admitted. "Something I ate . . ." He lay back on the bed and gazed up at the ceiling, frowning slightly. "Stomach's queasy."

"Do you want anything?"

"Just a glass of water."

Christina left the bedroom, silently shut the door behind her, leaned against the frame and closed her eyes. It had started. The arsenic was taking effect. She didn't know whether to feel happy or sad. Her emotions were jumbled.

Pushing away from the wall, Christina gathered her gown up in front and hurried downstairs to the parlor. She felt her way to the table by the window, struck a match, and touched it to the lamp's wick. The clock on the fireplace mantel showed 7:45. Jim Mitchell should have been here over thirty minutes ago. What if he broke his promise and didn't come at all? She shuddered at the possibility.

Parting the lace curtains, she gazed out the window a moment and listened to the solemn tick-tock of the passing seconds. It was less than an hour's ride between the western-most boundary of the Tanque Verde Ranch and the town of Pennington several miles to the southwest, a little longer by team and wagon. She couldn't imagine what was keeping Jim.

A glass of water in hand, Christina went upstairs again, more slowly this time, stopping every few steps to listen for the pounding of hooves or a knock at the door, but there was nothing.

She opened the bedroom door and slipped inside. Robert was sitting up, hands on knees, head bowed. He looked up at her approach, and she was shocked by the pallor of his face. Sweat stood out in beads across his forehead.

"Something's wrong," he said. His voice was a hoarse croak. "It's bad. It hurts so bad."

Christina held the glass out to him, but he only shook his head and hugged his stomach as another spasm of pain racked his insides.

"I need a doctor," he gasped.

Christina sat next to him and brushed the damp hair from his forehead. His skin felt clammy.

"Poor man," she whispered. "I could have loved you so much."

Rocking back and forth slightly, Robert looked at her with tortured eyes. "What?"

She shook her head. "Never mind. It's too late now. Here . . . I've brought you your water."

"Too late?" He struck the glass from her hand and grasped her wrist. "What do you mean it's too late?"

"Robert, let me go."

He stared at her, teeth gritted against the pain, body trembling.

"Let go, Robert. Please . . ."

Doubling over, Robert retched violently, and his hold on her wrist slackened and fell away. He dropped to the floor on his hands and knees.

Gently massaging her bruised wrist, Christina remained seated at the foot of the bed and watched her husband's body heave and strain and quake, this man who had never been seriously ill in his whole life, and her mind was strangely distanced from the horrible reality. She glanced at the folded newspaper, thinking she should spread it on the floor so Robert wouldn't muss the carpet, but made no move to get up, just sat and watched.

Curled up in agony on his side while arsenic gnawed at his stomach and bowels, Robert Cates caught her eye, and his mouth twisted as he uttered the last words he would ever say to her.

"Crazy bitch."

Sad-faced, Christina clasped her hands in her lap and said nothing.

CHAPTER TWO

It was 3:30 in the morning when Christina heard the ringing of the bell pull in the front hallway.

She tiptoed to the door and stood with her ear to the crack and her right hand on the knob.

"Jim?"

"Yeah!"

She slid the bolt back and opened the door.

Grinning, Jim Mitchell pitched his cheroot over the veranda railing, stepped inside, and spread his arms. "Is it done?"

"It's done."

He gave her a hard, quick hug and slammed the door shut with his foot. Christina followed him into the lighted parlor.

Jim Mitchell was nicely dressed in a dark, Western-cut suit with a gold watch chain across the vest, a black string tie, and a gray Stetson that looked as if it had just been taken out of its box. His hair, his most prized possession, was blond and wavy, and he had confided to Christina once that if he ever went bald he'd shoot himself. Like Samson, his hair was his strength, he claimed.

Though Christina liked him well enough, she admitted he was a bit of a dandy. He was also the duly-elected sheriff of Hohokam County, Arizona Territory.

Jim twisted one end of his sand-colored mustache around his forefinger. "So where's the old man?"

"In the bedroom upstairs."

"Have any trouble?"

Christina threw him an indignant look. "No, considering I had to go through it alone."

"Ah, honey . . ."

"Not only that, but you lied to me."

Jim looked surprised. "How did I lie?"

"You told me it would be a quick, easy death," Christina said, her voice rising. "You told me he wouldn't have to suffer long. Jim, he suffered for hours!"

"Well, how the hell was I supposed to know? I've never seen arsenic used on anything but rats." He suddenly laughed. "Come to think of it, you just killed a two-legged rodent yourself."

"Why didn't you come early like you told me you would?"

"Got held up," he said absently, looking around at the richly furnished room, up at the crystal chandelier, then back to her, blue eyes glinting in the light. "I could have been here sooner, but I got to thinking, Why not make her wonder? Make her see how much she needs me." He stepped toward her. "Do you follow what I'm saying, Christina?"

She stared at him, not answering.

"Yeah, you get it," he said. "You're a smart girl." He turned his back on her. "Come on, let's get this over with."

He took the stairs two at a time, and Christina trailed behind, dreading the task at hand, dreading having to look upon the sallow face of her husband and remember those last torturous hours, the convulsions, the stench of vomit and diarrhea. She shook her head and tried not to think about it. After seven years of marriage to the likes of Robert Cates, she had learned how to shut down her emotions and close her mind to anything unpleasant, revealing nothing, feeling nothing. Until now, this had been her only defense.

"Jesus Christ. You got him laid out like he's in a funeral parlor. Hope to hell he ain't stiff yet."

Standing in the doorway, Christina frowned and watched Jim step over the body. She had washed her husband, dressed him in clean clothes, and stretched his body out straight upon the floor with his hands crossed over his chest.

"What should I have done?" she asked.

Kneeling, he glanced up at her. "You did all right. But remember, we don't want this to look suspicious. I'm glad I got here before the rigor mortis did." He grasped Robert Cates under the arms and dragged him toward the door. "Get dressed and bring me that bottle of poison. We'll get rid of it on the way."

"On the way to where?"

"Town. Or right outside town really." At the head of the stairs, he looked at her and winked before stooping and hefting Robert Cates' body over his shoulder. "The plan's the same. I just don't want to do it here. We'll dump the old man close to Mexican town instead, fix him up so he looks like he was robbed and bumped off. That way you won't have reporters and busy-bodies snooping around the house. How's that sound?"

"Will it still be in your jurisdiction so close to town?"

"Sure it will." Grunting, he started down the stairs, trailing his left hand along the banister to keep from stumbling beneath the dead weight of Robert's body. "I've got it all figured out. Don't worry."

"I should stay here then, shouldn't I?"

"No, I might need your help," he said. "We're in this together, remember?"

Christina shook her head. "I did my part already."

Half-turning, Jim looked up at her from the bottom of the stairway. "Honey, your part's just started. Now get some clothes on and hurry it up."

Pulling her nightgown over her head, Christina quickly changed into the same white blouse and indigo print skirt she had worn the previous day and pinned her hair up loosely in back. On her way out the bedroom door, she looked over her shoulder one last time and sighed. She vowed she'd never sleep in that room again.

Jim had already deposited Robert Cates in the back end of his buckboard and was covering the dead man with a heavy quilt when Christina stepped outside. The night was moonlit and cool, and a gentle breeze fanned her face, carrying with it sweet offerings from a few late-blooming desert poppies and lupines she had planted around the edge of the veranda. Crickets chirped undisturbed beneath the flowers.

Jim beckoned to her. "Let's go."

Gathering her skirts, Christina climbed unassisted onto the buckboard seat, and Jim threw the brake and flicked the lines.

"We'd better hurry," he said. "I want to get you back here before daylight."

Even so, he held the team to a slow walk until they had passed the cluster of adobes a quarter mile down the road where Robert's Mexican ranch hands lived with their families. The buckboard creaked and rattled only slightly, yet Christina held her breath, sure any minute she would see a light appear in one of the windows.

She turned to Jim. "This is too risky."

"I told you not to worry. I've got everything under control."

"Someone's liable to see us." She glanced back again at the flat-roofed houses barely visible now in the dusky distance. "On the way back, we'll have to take the long road around."

"Whatever you say, Mommy."

Christina shot him a look, irritated by his pert, breezy manner. He was taking this awfully light, as if there was nothing to worry about. She wished she could feel so sure.

Once he was certain they were out of danger of being heard, Jim urged the horses on faster and spoke openly to Christina of all they would do now that Robert was out of the way. She only half-listened.

A deep, dark sadness had settled over her like a black cloud. Contrary to her earlier expectations, she didn't feel free, and she realized she was as trapped now as she had ever been.

If only Robert had changed. Christina had clung to the possibility that he would and had tried to be a good wife to him. She had faced one serious obstacle. Robert wanted a family.

After six years of trying to have a baby, Christina finally conceived a year ago. Both she and Robert were overjoyed, and for a short while at least, things went smoothly.

It was during her second month of pregnancy that the nightmare began all over again, this time in deadly earnest.

Christina remembered it with dreadful clarity. They were living in town at the time, and tired of being cooped up in the house, she went shopping with a friend. Two hours later, she returned home to find Robert pacing the floor and boiling mad. He struck her across the face with the back of his hand and cursed her for daring to set foot out the door without his say-so. Frightened, Christina fled upstairs. He caught up with her near the top. She remembered begging him not to hurt her, to think of the baby growing inside her, but Robert's rage could not be assuaged. He punched her in the face, and when she fell to her knees, he kicked her down the stairway.

Christina lost the baby that day, and that same day she

ceased trying to be a good wife to Robert Cates.

Robert's rages grew more violent after that, and he swore he would kill her if she ever filed for divorce. She attempted to run away instead, buying tickets with money secretly earned selling eggs to a neighbor and taking the first train or stagecoach out of Pennington, not caring where it was going as long as it was away. Three times she attempted to leave him, and three times he caught up with her, dragged her home, and beat her mercilessly. There was no escaping his wrath. Or so she had thought.

Robert Cates wouldn't kill any more babies.

"He should never have introduced us," she said suddenly.

Jim looked at her. "Huh?"

"Robert should never have invited you over for dinner that day," she said. "He'd still be alive."

Jim grinned. "What would you do without me?"

"I don't know. Because of you, every time I close my eyes I'll see the look on his face when he realized what I did to him."

"Hey, now." Jim nudged her with his elbow. "Snap out of it. You wanted this."

"I wanted away from him," she said, looking at Jim now, searching his face in the dim light of the moon. "You could have helped me to run away, Jim."

"I could have," he admitted. "But where were you gonna run? You don't have any money. Hell, you don't even have any family."

Christina nodded sadly, thinking of her dear father who had died six years ago of a stroke. Jim was right about that much. She had no one.

"Anyway, I like it this way better," he continued. "This way, you'll think twice before you decide you want to run away from me, too."

"Why? What would you do?"

"I'd go after you and arrest you for premeditated murder."

"You couldn't prove it."

"Maybe not. Then again, you never know, do you?"

Christina hesitated, then shrugged and looked away. "I won't leave you, Jim."

"I know you won't."

The many lights twinkling in Pennington proved Jim Mitchell and Christina Cates were not the only owls out tonight. Sprawled across the bottom of the Santa Cruz Basin, the town appeared large and alive and inviting, and Christina wished she were there instead of out here in the darkness with a dead man on her conscience.

Jim took the cut-off from the main road and headed for the south part of town and the barrio. Christina didn't understand why they must leave the body so close to town. To her, it was a foolish and unnecessary risk. Jim brushed off her concerns and told her it was all part of the plan. He refused to explain, however, what that plan entailed.

They were out of the foothills and had already passed half a dozen scattered shacks and adobes on the outskirts of Pennington when Jim reined the team off the road. Christina braced herself against the bouncing and jiggling of the buckboard as they neared the dark line of trees bordering an arroyo. Jim stopped the team and set the brake.

Christina climbed down from the seat and felt the loose gravel grate beneath her boots as she walked with Jim to the back of the buckboard.

"We're not far from Regino Vega's place," he whispered, "so keep your eyes and ears peeled while I dump Bobby here in the bushes."

Flipping the blanket back, he took hold of Robert Cates'

arms and pulled him out of the buckboard. Christina looked around her uneasily, not wanting to watch as Jim dragged the body through the weeds, and heard the scuffing sound of Robert's heels trailing across the gravely soil. She followed at a distance and carefully picked her way through the mesquites and catclaw acacia growing along the wash. On the opposite bank, a lone saguaro appeared black against the skyline, standing watch over them with uplifted arms, a silent witness to their terrible deed.

A narrow, hard-packed trail twisted through the trees and brush. White caliche shone in the moonlight, making the trail easy to follow with the eye, and here Jim left the body of Robert Cates.

He looked over at Christina and grinned, teeth flashing in the shadow of his hat. "Now for the final touch," he whispered.

Slowly rubbing her hand up and down her right arm, Christina watched him kneel and turn Robert's pants pockets inside out. He rumpled and tore Robert's shirt open to make it appear as if someone had searched him for money and valuables.

Up the wash a little way, a dog's strident bark broke the stillness. Christina heard Jim curse. Still on his knees, he reached behind him, whipped something from beneath his suitcoat, and raised his arm. He drew a sharp breath. The knife in his hand flashed seconds before he drove it hilt-deep into Robert Cates' stomach.

"No!" Christina's cry came out as a half-sob. Shocked, she winced and squeezed her eyes shut.

Jim jerked the knife free and leaped to his feet. "What the hell are you squealin' about?" he hissed. "He's already dead!"

He grabbed her by the arm and dragged her along, running now, the dog still barking behind them. She felt mesquite thorns snag her skirt and scratch her face. Jim slowed to a walk as they neared the edge of the scrub and brush and glanced over his shoulder, listening. Faint with distance, a man's voice called out in an angry eruption of Spanish, ordering the dog to shut up.

Jim spoke softly to Christina. "Let's get out of here." He sounded shaken.

Trembling, she climbed back into the buckboard and pressed her fingers against throbbing temples. She would be glad when this night was over.

A twig snapped in the nearby brush just as Jim sat down and took up the lines. Eyes wide, Christina touched his hand.

"Did you hear that?"

"Hear what?"

"Someone's out there, Jim. I heard them."

He shook his head. "Relax. Who'd be wandering around here this time of night?" Even so, he sat perfectly still for almost a full minute, staring into the shadows. When nothing stirred, he slapped the reins. "No one's out there. You're just jumpy."

Christina slipped a hand beneath his arm and held on to him. "I hope you're right," she murmured.

The dust had settled, and the sounds of jingling harnesses and trace chains had faded into the night before the man kneeling in the brush pushed himself to his feet. R. J. Devens hawked and spat and wiped his mouth, grimacing at the foul taste on his tongue. He had spent all evening with a buddy who happened to have a corn-liquor still in his cow pasture. Not a drinking man ordinarily, R.J. was suffering the effects of a rare moment of overindulgence.

Riding home, he had nearly passed out and had fallen off his horse. Unable to climb back into the saddle, he left his mount tethered near the road and took a short snooze among the brittlebush. It was the noise of the team and buckboard that woke him. He had watched the proceedings in silent puzzlement.

Now, stirred by curiosity, R.J. walked toward the arroyo on unsteady legs. He struck the narrow little path and cautiously followed it until he spotted the sprawled figure of a man lying near the edge of the trail. He gazed down at the body and rasped a forefinger back and forth across the white stubble on his chin.

He had always suspected Sheriff Jim Mitchell wasn't as clean as he let on to be. His suspicions, it appeared, had been right.

CHAPTER THREE

Lane Devens had been following the trail of the four Apaches since daybreak. His reasons for doing so were simple enough: They were headed west and so was he, and he lacked anything better to do. It was a dangerous way of passing the time.

Though the morning was young, the wind was already picking up, occasionally throwing grit into Lane's face, and the haze across the horizon suggested the day would be a dirty one. Lane didn't care. He was glad to be on the move. Glad to be free. Three months in the Fort Bowie guardhouse had given him a new appreciation for the great outdoors.

The trail he followed was a fresh one, perhaps an hour old. Lane suspected the Indians were either stragglers left behind by Geronimo during his flight to Mexico last summer, or they were four of a small party of malcontents who had defected from Chato's band at San Carlos. Whatever the case, their presence would not be taken lightly by the settlers in this region between the Santa Cruz and San Pedro rivers. These people had lost patience with "wild injuns" and tended to shoot first and ask questions later.

That these were not reservation Apaches was almost a certainty. Lane had studied the sign the four Indians left behind at last night's camp and noticed that the droppings of both man and horse contained seeds and fibers of desert plants. While the Apaches on the San Carlos Reservation were almost entirely dependent upon government rations, these men were living off the land and traveling fast. Whether they were hunting trouble or not remained to be seen.

Lane Devens rode cautiously, eyes busy, searching, senses alert, and gloried in the feel of a good horse beneath him and the warmth of the sun cloaking his shoulders. He had been riding with his right knee touching the stock of his old Spencer carbine, and he drew it from the scabbard now and rested it across his lap. Reaching down, he slipped the rawhide thong from the hammer of his six-shooter.

What he was doing this blustery April morning was not new to him. For the past seven years, he had done little else. Employed by the United States Army at sixty dollars a month, Lane Devens had tracked Apaches and fought Apaches ever since he was nineteen years old. Though his dishonorable discharge of a week ago still gnawed at his pride, it hadn't severed the force of habit. At heart, he was still a scout.

A movement off to Lane's right caught his eye, and he reined in to scan the area. Blended perfectly into its dull surroundings, a coyote met his gaze, tucked its tail, and slunk back into the brush.

It had been almost a year since Lane had ridden the bajadas and foothills of the Catarinas. To many, it was simply more desert, but this was home for Lane, or very near it, and he took a moment to look around him at the low hills and rocky ridges. Saguaros stood straight and tall on the slopes, reaching for the sky, surrendering themselves to the will of the desert. Sometimes it rained. Sometimes it did not. Their patience was infinite.

This past winter had brought little rainfall, so spring growth was minimal. The few annuals that had bloomed were already tattered and faded; palo verdes and flowering brittlebush relieved their tired colors with splashes of green and sunny yellow, but these, too, would soon abandon leaves and blooms in the torrid heat. Even at its driest, however, the Sonoran Desert was lush and alive compared to the truly arid regions of the southwest and of Old Mexico. To Lane, it was a veritable flower garden.

The land through which the Apache trail now led him was owned by a man named Robert Cates. Cates laid claim to two ranches that Lane knew of—this, the Tanque Verde, and another much larger tract of land south of here in the shadow of the Santa Ritas. In the tradition of Pete Kitchen, John Slaughter, and other early Arizona cattlemen, Robert Cates had fought Apaches and Mexican *bandidos* for what was now a ranching empire and had, in the process, gained the grudging respect of both factions.

The four Apaches surely knew the risks they were taking by encroaching on Cates' territory, not to mention the close proximity of Pennington and Fort Lowe. Yet even as the thought crossed Lane's mind, he noticed the trail began to veer in a more northerly direction, into the very heart of the Tanque Verde.

Lane hesitated, not sure what course he wanted to take. Part of him, the curious part, wanted to follow the Apaches. The rest of him just wished for a bath—his first real one in three months—and a soft, clean bed. This was his third day out since his departure from Bowie, and it should be his last. If he continued on west, he could make Pennington by noon, eat a home-cooked meal, relax, visit with his mother . . .

And then, of course, there was Abbie Maginnis. Picturing her in his mind's eye, seeing her teasing smile and her clean white skin, he almost forgot the Apaches entirely.

But Lane's moment of indecision didn't last long. A rifle shot crashed in the distance, the sound rolling across the foothills, and he pointed the rangy buckskin north.

More shots followed the first, then silence, then another rifle shot, but Lane didn't hurry, not wanting to get caught in the middle of something he might never get out of. He followed the tracks and the sounds of gunfire, steadily climbing, leaving the largest saguaro behind him as he reached the cooler, higher slopes. He dismounted at the base of a hogback ridge.

Unbuckling the flap on his saddlebag, he took out four loading tubes for the Spencer and squinted up at the hogback. The best he could remember, there was a rough, rarely used wagon road on the opposite side of the ridge. The shooting had come from there. Lane left the buckskin and moved easily among the scrub oak and manzanita bushes. He climbed the steep ridge by way of a narrow, hard-packed ravine.

Nearing the top, he squatted down and listened a moment. There was nothing but the sound of wind. It whipped his hair about his neck and whistled through the desert scrub. Tightening the chin strap on his hat, he stuffed the loading tubes into his pants, slipped his arm through the Spencer's leather sling, and crawled to the crest of the ridge on hands and knees.

A buckboard and two matched sorrels were standing stockstill in their harnesses, staring uneasily at the half-naked Apache sprawled on his stomach practically under their noses.

Off to Lane's right and on the other side of the road, three mangy ponies were loose and grazing, and two hundred feet below him among the boulders at the bottom of the ridge stood the fourth pony. Lane saw the animal flinch and start to bolt as someone reached out to grab at the single rawhide rein attached to its lower lip. The pony drew up short, the rein extended taut between its lip and the now unseen hand of its owner.

Lane eased himself into a comfortable position, lying flat on his belly with the Spencer's short barrel pushed out in front of him, and chewed on a grass stem. His gaze moved over the scene below him. Nothing stirred but the wind and the horses.

Suddenly remembering the field glasses strapped around his neck, he looked through them at the buckboard, saw a blanket or quilt lying in the back, noticed something else, something wrong with one of the back wheels. The rim had slipped off the wheel's felloe. He could see it clearly now—the owner of the buckboard looking at that busted wheel, maybe cussing it at first, then scratching his head, not sure what to do next when he happened to glance up to see four mounted Apaches looking down on him from the top of the ridge. Lane pictured it in his mind, how the Apaches had probably yelled and whooped as they kicked their horses down the slope and closed in on their hapless victim.

But no, something must have gone wrong, he thought. The only victim down there is that dead Apache spread-eagle in the middle of the road. And all those gunshots. Somebody had put up a good fight.

There was an outcrop of rock and brush on the other side of the road, not far from the buckboard. That would be where the driver was hiding, possibly wounded. From his elevated position, Lane could see the crown of a hat showing above the boulders.

A flicker of movement directly below caught his eye. He set the field glasses aside. The Apaches were moving, getting into position. Lane speculated on what they would do. The one holding the pony would stay where he was, while the other two spread out, ghosting through the pile-up of rocks along the base of the ridge. They would flank the driver more than likely, cross the road while the buck in the middle covered them, then dive behind a boulder or drop into a ravine and open fire on the man hiding behind the outcrop.

Lane's right thumb eased the Spencer's hammer back while his finger rested lightly on the trigger. With the grass stem still dangling from his mouth, he pressed his cheek against the gunstock and waited.

Unaware of his audience, the Apache on the left exposed his back to Lane for a moment as he shifted his position. A moment was all Lane needed. He took quick aim and fired.

The Spencer bellowed, and Lane saw the Apache's back arch as he took a .56 caliber bullet square between the shoulders.

Before the smoke had even stopped roiling from the carbine's muzzle, another shot cracked, this time from behind the outcrop, and the Indian pony buckled and dropped as if it had been struck by lightning. Lane wondered idly what the purpose of that was. The horse hadn't done anything wrong. He guessed the man had an itchy finger.

Lane looked through the glasses at the Apache he had shot, checking if he was dead or just playing a convincing game of possum. No, he was dead.

Nothing much happened after that. The sun was climbing, and Lane was starting to get hot and bored and desperately wished for a cigarette. If something interesting didn't happen soon, he was leaving.

On sudden impulse, he cupped his hands around his mouth and hollered to the men below.

"Hey! Anybody down there got tobacco?"

His reply came in the form of a lead bullet. It spit gravel into his face, and he saw a puff of gunsmoke appear over the boulders on his far right. Having pinpointed the Indian's position, Lane opened fire, shooting as fast as he could lever rounds into the chamber and aiming at the broad face of rock directly in front of the Apache's hiding place. Ricocheting bullets whined and moaned, and to keep from being cut to pieces, the Apache rolled out into the open, making for another point of cover. The man behind the outcrop fired a shot at him, and the brave dropped to his stomach, scrambling out of sight into the brush.

Lane loaded a fresh magazine tube into the butt of his carbine and pulled the lever down and up. The wind had lulled to a bare stirring for the moment, and the metallic snap and click sounded sharply threatening in the stillness.

Two Apaches were dead, the third possibly wounded, maybe dying. The fourth Apache, Lane knew, would bide his time, waiting for the safety of nightfall with nothing but a dead pony and a swarm of blow flies to keep him company.

Lane called out to him in a jumbled mixture of Spanish, English, and Apache, his voice taunting.

"You should have remained on the reservation with your woman! Tonight, she will share your wickiup with another while your blood flows like a river during *tiempo de aguas!*"

The Apache answered him in flawless Spanish. "You speak in ignorance! My wife waits for me in the mountains." He paused, then added, "I know your voice from another time!"

Lane considered that. Did he know this man? Something in the way he spoke, in the fullness of his voice, struck a familiar chord. Lane's curiosity was piqued. Touching his tongue to his upper lip, he took a moment to gather more Spanish words and formed a reply.

"It is good that you remember me! Lay down your guns, and we will talk . . . face to face, as brothers."

"First, you tell your white-eye friend what we say!" the Apache shouted. "Prove to me your heart is still good, Lane Devens, and we will make talk as you wish!"

Lane listened closely to the man's voice, and something in his memory made a connection. The voice had a face now.

"Ojo Loco! Crazy Eye! It is you?"

It was, indeed, Crazy Eye, the bowlegged, squat-bodied little Indian with the wandering left eye. Lane remembered him well. A Mescalero Apache, Crazy Eye had married a Chiricahua woman and rode for a time with Geronimo until he was captured and herded onto a reservation. After General Crook adopted the policy of pitting the friendly Chiricahuas against the hostiles, Crazy Eye volunteered his services as a scout. Unable to beat the army, he joined it.

Three years ago, a drunken brave shot Lane in the knee while he was stationed at Fort Apache, and it was Crazy Eye who had eased his boredom during the nearly two months that he was laid up, teaching him Apache words, playing games of chance, telling stories. A bond had formed between the two men that bridged the differences in race and culture.

Lane asked after the health of his friend.

"I am well, but my comrades are not so lucky!"

"Are they all dead?"

"All but one! A foolish *ish-kay-nay,*" he added, returning for a moment to his native tongue.

A foolish boy, a boy who could shoot and kill as readily as a full grown man. Crazy Eye seemed to read Lane's thoughts. "I've spoken to the boy! He says he will save his bullets for better game!"

That was comforting. Lane pushed himself to his feet and felt a sudden gust of wind rock him back on his heels. He cautiously made his way down from the crest of the ridge. A little stiff, his right knee ached from that old gunshot wound, and he tried not to limp, not wanting to appear weak.

Halfway to the bottom, he paused and looked toward the outcrop of rock and brush across the road from him. The owner of the buckboard still waited there in silence, and Lane wondered what manner of man he was. Whoever he was, he had evidently given Crazy Eye and his *compadres* more than they had bargained on.

Gripping the Spencer in his right hand, Lane lifted it above his head and pumped it up and down a couple of times.

"Hey, you behind the rocks! You can come out now! Everybody's friends!"

CHAPTER FOUR

A blond-haired man in a dusty suit moved out into the open with both six-shooters drawn but pointed down. Behind him, surprisingly, was a woman. She drew up next to the man, one hand shading her eyes, the other holding her skirts bunched up in front so that Lane could see the tops of her black, high-heeled boots. They watched him descend the slope, neither of them saying a word.

"Stay where you are," Lane said.

The blond-haired man spoke then. "Damned Indians." He wiped his nose with the back of his hand. A gold star on his lapel winked brightly in the sunshine. "Thought they had us there for a minute."

Lane didn't reply. He was nearing the dead pony. "Crazy Eye?"

"I am here."

Alarmed, Lane whirled around as the man rose up behind him a scant ten feet from where he had just passed. It shook him a little when he realized what could have happened. Finding cover where there seemed to be none, Crazy Eye had abandoned his former hiding place for another higher up the slope. Even from his perch atop the ridge, Lane hadn't seen the Apache slithering through the grass and weeds like a brown-skinned snake. He was glad this Apache was friendly.

Crazy Eye strode toward Lane and gave him a lazy salute, mocking the soldiers at Fort Bowie. "You have grown careless," he said and grasped Lane's forearm in greeting.

Lane gestured to the two dead Apaches. "I'm not alone."

Crazy Eye nodded, then scowled, watching the Apache boy sidle toward them. He was perhaps fourteen or fifteen, a skinny youngster with knobby knees and bushy black hair. Lane noted that his face and torso were streaked ceremoniously with dried antelope blood, and a dirty rag was tied around his arm where a bullet had nicked him. He gave Lane a sour look.

Crazy Eye spoke to him in Apache, a short sharp bark, and the boy bowed his head in shame. His eyes slanted toward the man and woman standing together on the other side of the road.

Crazy Eye turned to Lane. "We saw the white-eye wagon and thought the man and his squaw might have goods to trade . . . cornmeal, flour, sugar. I have some blue-soldier dollars. We came in peace. Our guns were not drawn."

"What happened then?" Lane asked.

"They had no goods. I wanted to leave, but that one—" he motioned with his rifle to the Apache lying in the road, "—said we should take their horses. He started to cut them loose, and the yellow-haired man shot him."

"I'm sorry for your loss," Lane said.

Crazy Eye made a face, as if something smelled badly, and his left eye rolled. "They were of Chato's band and no friends of mine. They were like dogs. We traveled together only." He turned a stern eye on the boy. "This one, my nephew, calls himself a warrior, but he moves like one who is blind. I keep poor company, no?"

The boy understood a little Spanish, enough to catch the general drift of the conversation, and his face turned a deep red. Despite the harsh words, Lane sensed Crazy Eye's affection for his nephew and was glad he hadn't been seriously hurt. To save the boy from further shame, Lane changed the subject.

"Why did you leave the army?"

The lines in Crazy Eye's face seemed to deepen. "Our *nant'*á is dead."

There was no need for him to say more. Saddened at the mention of his commander's death, Lane gazed down at the scuffed toes of his boots. Captain Emmet Crawford had been a good and honest man and highly respected by his company of scouts. He was killed by Mexican irregulars last January in the heart of the Sierra Madre, less than a month following Lane's court-martial. Lane was sure his three-month imprisonment and dishonorable discharge would never have been carried out if the captain had had a say in the affair.

The truth was, Lane would have been booted out of the army long ago had it not been for the likes of Crawford and General George Crook. During his first three years of service, he was promoted twice to the rank of sergeant but was demoted each time due to a propensity for fighting and disobeying orders. He was a good scout, however, and both officers chose to ignore his occasional bouts of unruliness. But even they had their limitations. With the resignation of one and the death of the other, Lane was almost glad to leave the army behind him.

Crazy Eye agreed. "This new general," he said, "General Miles. I do not trust him. His heart is black toward all my people—the good as well as the bad. There are rumors that he plans to send many of the *Ndé* to a place called Florida. I fear the good *Ndé* will be forced to live there also."

Not doubting his words, Lane nodded, then glanced up to see the blond-haired man crossing the road. He squinted at the sheriff's badge pinned to the lapel of the man's suitcoat.

A cocky look in his eyes, the sheriff drew up about four feet from Lane, tipped his head to the side, and rested his hands on the grips of his holstered revolvers.

"Tell Chief Jackass him and his little knock-kneed pal there are under arrest."

Crazy Eye gave the lawman a sidelong glance and turned back to Lane. "What does he say?"

"He says you are a man to be respected and feared."

The Apache nodded. "Tell him he fought well for a white-eye."

Lane addressed the sheriff. "He says for me to tell you if you don't back off he's gonna cut a hole in your belly, pull your guts out, and wrap 'em around your neck."

The sheriff gave Lane a suspicious look, as if he didn't quite swallow that, but backed up a few steps to be on the safe side.

Crazy Eye beckoned to the boy and bade his friend farewell.

"I can help you load your dead on one of the ponies," Lane offered.

The Apache tugged his breechclout higher on his hips and waved a hand. He must hurry. His family was waiting for him in the mountains to the north, and these two who were dead meant nothing to him.

"Perhaps we shall meet again during better times and share a smoke," he said and smiled.

Lane nodded. "I would enjoy that."

Crazy Eye and his nephew took their leave, swinging astride their ponies and heading north over the scrubby hills.

Lane watched them go, rolled his tongue around inside his mouth, glanced at the sheriff, then turned his back on him and walked over to where the dead Apache lay in the road. He flipped him over with his foot and squatted down to look at him.

The sheriff joined him. "Another one of your friends?"

"Not him," Lane said and rose. He watched the woman walk toward them, a tall, nice-looking woman with long, windblown hair that shone like copper in the sunshine. "This is one of the bucks that was in on the killing of that Indian agent last month," he said, his eyes still on the woman. "They cut off the agent's head, played a game of catch with it and ran for the hills."

The woman stared back at him, expressionless, not reacting the way he expected her to, not cringing or squealing, "Oh, my, how dreadful!" He admired her for it.

The sheriff held out his hand. "Name's Jim Mitchell. Sheriff Jim Mitchell." They shook hands, and he gestured carelessly to the woman. "Christina Cates."

"Nice to meet you, ma'am," Lane murmured and tipped his hat. He introduced himself and saw Mitchell's too-handsome face split in a wide grin.

"Devens. Hell, I know you! Read about you in the newspaper." He looked at the woman and jerked his thumb at Lane. "He's the fella who broke that lieutenant's nose and dunked his head in the water trough."

Embarrassed, Lane didn't say anything. He could feel Christina Cates' dark eyes on him, adding to his discomfort. He flicked a blade of grass from his shirt, as if it mattered, brushing dirt and grass from a shirt that hadn't seen a washboard in months, beard on his face, black hair hanging down past his collar, sticking to the sweat on his neck.

Careful to stay downwind of the woman, Lane walked to the back of the buckboard and kicked at the hub on the busted wheel. "You could drive some wedges between the rim and felly. It might get you to where you're going if it ain't too far and you drive slow."

"Thank you for helping us, Mr. Devens." Christina Cates

stepped carefully around the Apache's body, averting her eyes. "I'm not sure what we would have done," she added. Her voice was low-pitched for a woman's and surprisingly calm, considering what she had just experienced.

"You must be Robert Cates' daughter."

"No," she said, "I'm his wife."

That surprised him. While Cates would surely have to be sixty some-odd years old, this woman, his wife, appeared to be in her mid-twenties, closer to Lane's age. Though she was pretty, there was a haunted expression in her eyes, as if she had seen something she shouldn't have. Her face was scratched and bruised. Lane could guess who had been beating on her. Robert Cates was a hard man.

"I worked for your husband several years ago," Lane told her. "Breaking horses."

She didn't appear impressed.

Sheriff Mitchell reached beneath the buckboard seat and dragged out a box of tools. "That Indian you were talking to—friend of yours?"

"Yeah, we used to work together," Lane replied. He dipped his fingers into his shirt pocket for tobacco and papers before he remembered he didn't have any. "You wouldn't happen to have the makings, would you?"

Straightening up, the sheriff drew a slim cigar from inside his suit coat and handed it to him. He watched Lane pass the cheroot beneath his nose, smelling it, then clamp it between his teeth and rustle for a match.

"I guess you realize I'm gonna have to send a posse after him."

Lane lit his cheroot. "I'd rather you didn't."

"I don't have much choice. When the people of this county voted me into office, I took an oath to uphold the law. Your friend broke it."

"That's awful righteous of you," Lane said calmly, "but not very smart. He'll be hiding his trail now and watching his back. He'll be ready for you."

"Like any other outlaw," the sheriff replied. He stroked his handlebar mustache. "I've seen my share and know what to expect."

Leaning against the wheel, Lane hooked a heel on one of the spokes and drew deeply on his cheroot. "If you think an Apache is like some ordinary owl-hoot, then you don't know your hind end from a hole in the ground, Sheriff."

Jim Mitchell sent him a flinty-eyed stare, hands resting on his gun grips, trying to look offended but not very successfully. Lane decided the man didn't take much of anything seriously, except for perhaps his appearance, and he found himself not liking him. Even while Mitchell spoke of upholding the law, there was that same cocky smirk on his face, and his words sounded rehearsed. He was probably shallow and insincere.

Lane wondered what the sheriff and Robert Cates' wife were doing out here together, miles from the main road. Pushing away from the wheel, he glanced inside the buckboard and noticed the patchwork quilt, too good a quilt to be lying in the back of a dusty buckboard without good reason. He had seen his mother piece quilts when he was a boy and knew the time and work that went into it.

"Somebody been sick?" he asked suddenly.

Mitchell hesitated, glancing at the woman before answering. "No, why?"

Lane nodded toward the quilt. "I thought you might've had to haul somebody to the doctor."

When Mitchell didn't say anything, Christina Cates frowned at him and spoke in her quiet, clear voice.

"You must be wondering what we're doing out here."

"It crossed my mind."

"My husband didn't come home last night," she said. "I was worried about him, so I went to town to look for him. The sheriff was kind enough to drive me home."

Mitchell nodded. "It's like I told her. Robert's probably at the house right now, pacing the floor and worried sick about her." He paused, head bowed, brow furrowed slightly, thoughtfully biting his lower lip. "The truth is, Devens, Robert's a mighty jealous man. I hoped to get Mrs. Cates home without anyone seeing us. If word gets back to him she was with me, he's liable to take things the wrong way." He suddenly grinned. "I have been known to turn a few ladies' heads."

Lane's eyes glazed over.

"Anyway, you can look at the bruises on Mrs. Cates' face and see she doesn't need any more trouble," Mitchell continued. "I thought you and me might make a deal."

"What sort of a deal?"

"You forget about seeing me and Mrs. Cates together, and I won't send a posse after your injun buddy."

Standing hip-shot in the sun, feeling the wind in his face, Lane took one last drag on his cheroot, dropped it in the road, and ground it into the dirt with his heel. He lifted his carbine, laid it across his shoulder. The sleeves of his faded calico shirt had been ripped out at the seams, and the muscles in his arms rolled smoothly beneath dark skin.

"I don't take bribes, Sheriff."

Mitchell grinned, shaking his head. "Why, this isn't a bribe. It's a deal, a bargain. You know . . ."

"I know what it is," Lane replied, his voice mild. He studied Sheriff Jim Mitchell through narrowed eyes, thinking Robert Cates would probably have every right in the world to be angry at finding his young wife alone with this joker.

"If you ride after Crazy Eye," he said finally, "you'd better find somebody who knows Apaches and let him lead the way. Else you might not make it back."

Smiling, he glanced at Christina Cates, touched a finger to his hat brim, and turned to leave, picking his way through the gnarled oaks and the brush and the hot, sun-baked rocks.

CHAPTER FIVE

"Sorry half-breed-looking son of a bitch."

Christina listened to Jim Mitchell complain and cuss and watched him pace around the parlor, stomping a path into the maroon-colored carpet.

"Who in the devil does he think he is anyway?"

She patted the cushion next to her on the sofa. "Come sit down, Jim. It doesn't matter."

"Doesn't matter?" Shaking his head in disgust, he drummed the fingers of his left hand on the piano top and glared out the window. "Nosy bastard."

Christina sighed, feeling the weariness settling deep into her muscles, feeling the grit on her face and between her teeth, the sting of mesquite thorn scratches. Sweaty dirt lined the palms of her hands. She leaned her head back to rest against the sofa and closed her eyes.

"I don't think he'll tell anyone about us," she said. "I don't think he really cared one way or another."

Jim grunted.

"He just didn't like you pushing him," she said.

"How'd I push him? Tell me that. I thought I was being damned reasonable!"

His raised voice made Christina's head hurt. "I told him Robert didn't come home last night, that I went to town to look for him, and that you drove me home," she said quietly. "If you had left it at that, I'm sure he wouldn't have given it a second thought."

Jim didn't say anything.

Eyes still closed, Christina thought about Lane Devens, seeing the rangy, black-haired man coming down off the ridge, speaking to the two Apaches as if they were good friends.

She knew why Jim was so angry. It had little to do with her husband's murder and everything to do with Lane Devens. Jim appeared second best against Devens, and he couldn't stand it.

"I'll take care of him," Jim said suddenly.

Christina's eyes opened, and she looked at him, a little V-shaped frown etched into her forehead. "Jim, no."

"Nothing like that," he assured her and grinned, his usual cheery mood reasserting itself. "I'm gonna keep close tabs on Devens. If he so much as looks cross-eyed at somebody, he's going straight to jail. And if he's the hothead I think he is, it won't take long."

Though she thought Jim was overreacting, Christina nodded in agreement, not voicing her true opinion. Arguing with Jim Mitchell was rarely worthwhile.

He swaggered across the room and leaned over her, resting one hand on the back of the sofa, the other on the arm.

"Tired?"

"Terribly."

"So am I." He leaned closer and kissed her on the lips, drew back, and smiled. "I'm glad he's dead, Christina. We'll be married soon."

"But not too soon."

He shrugged.

"We don't want to appear too eager," she said.

"Whatever. Just don't forget our bargain. You promised you'd marry me if I helped you." He gently touched the bruise on her cheek. "The old man's dead and gone."

"The old man," Christina said. "I never thought of him that way. He was so strong, so powerful, and people respected him for it." She shook her head, regret filling her eyes. "He was a good man in some ways. It's too bad he never brought any of that goodness home to me."

Jim Mitchell squeezed her hand, kissed her again, and straightened up, pushing his hat back. "I'd better go. Got a lot of work to do. I'll stop by and tell the police chief we've got a pillar of the community missing, spread the word. We'll see what happens."

Christina rose and walked him to the door. "When do you think they'll find him?" she asked, her voice almost a whisper.

"Soon. Especially if I order a search. One of my deputies will probably run across his body. Or somebody'll smell him."

"Oh, my God . . ."

He laughed, almost as if he enjoyed her misery. His moods kept shifting—one minute so sweet, the next cruel. She never knew what to expect.

"In the meantime," he said, "I'll find a way to keep an eye on Devens, and you stick to your same story." He pressed a hand to his heart and made his voice sound like a woman's: "Bobby didn't come home last night. Whatever shall I do?"

He fluttered his eyelashes at her, causing her to smile even when she didn't want to.

Once Jim had left, Christina retired again to the sofa but was soon on her feet, discovering relaxation impossible in a house that oozed with unpleasant memories. She roamed silently from parlor to kitchen to hallway and stopped before the massive door opening into Robert's study. It was one room she'd never ventured into without her husband's invitation, a masculine room of heavy, somber furnishings and paintings depicting bloody scenes of war and buffalo hunts. She touched the knob, feeling the cool brass beneath her fingertips but could not bring herself to open the door. To do so would violate her husband's rules, and though he was dead, her fear of him lived on.

It hadn't always been so. When Robert Cates first began to call on her, a naïve girl of seventeen, she had felt safe in his presence, even perhaps a little flattered that a man of his power and wealth would take interest in a shopkeeper's daughter. Having only recently settled in Pennington from Illinois following the death of her mother, Christina was instantly attracted to Robert Cates, thinking he was all that personified the men of the West, fearless, strong, and competent. Her father, too, had admired him, and when Robert eventually asked for her hand in marriage, John McClure gave them his blessings. A gentle, kind man who had never struck anyone in anger, he could not be blamed for failing to perceive that Robert Cates might harm his beloved only child, and not wanting to upset him, Christina never complained.

Raising her left hand, she gazed a moment at the wide band of gold encircling her finger. She remembered the day Robert had slipped the wedding band upon her finger, vividly recalled his smile and her own joy at having married such a generous and successful gentleman. They had traveled by train to San Francisco for their honeymoon. Life had seemed wonderful and exciting then.

Yet Robert's abusive behavior had begun long before their marriage. Uncompromising and strict, often times overbearingly so, he had taken control of Christina's life by degrees, at first suggesting that she behave a certain way . . . later demanding it. His control began so subtly Christina was not even aware of its progression until five months into their marriage when he struck her for the first time. Her shock had been greater than her pain, and life had slowly spiralled downward from that point on.

Recalling the day Robert Cates stole her happiness, Christina pried the gold band from her finger and on sudden impulse, flung open the great, forbidden door of her husband's study and hurled the ring across the room. It struck the far wall with a resounding plunk.

It was late afternoon when Lane Devens rode through town. Pennington, or Penny Town as the locals fondly called it, hadn't changed much in the months that he'd been away. With its population nearing nine thousand, it was difficult to believe that this thriving little city had started out as a walled-in Mexican presidio back before Arizona was even a territory of the United States. Its survival and growth through years of Apache raids, droughts, floods, and drastic political upheavals was an unspoken testament to the courage and strength of those first generations of pioneers.

The arrival of the railroad in 1880 brought an abrupt end to the settlement's isolation. From its new name to its rapidly growing white population, Pennington was becoming more and more Anglicized. Frame buildings were being erected in the central business district and in white residential areas, and the ancestors of the old presidio's first inhabitants—the Mexicans, the Papagoes, and the Apache Mansos—were being pushed south of the crumbling adobe walls that still marked the fortress's boundaries.

The barrio remained Mexican in appearance, consisting mostly of flat-roofed adobes with chili peppers drying in bunches from the *ramadas* and tiny gardens of *carrizo, yerba buena,* and *manzanilla* gracing front- and backyards. All of this was surrounded by desert and distant, hazy-blue mountains.

The most pleasing sight to Lane's eyes, however, was the newly refurbished Cosmopolitan Hotel, touting all the luxuries of the hotels back East, namely indoor plumbing and gas lighting. It was a high-classed place and too expensive for Lane, but he liked to think that someday he'd be able to afford at least a short stay in the Cosmopolitan. What the hell? Stranger things had happened.

Lane rode along Penny Street, turned up busy Main, and continued north, past the court plaza and the old presidial grounds, and out of town by way of the Yuma road.

As Pennington's population grew, so did its demand for fresh produce, and the floodplain farms between the Santa Cruz River and town supplied much of what was needed. Lane's stepfather, R. J. Devens, owned one hundred ten acres of floodplain farmland where he raised winter wheat and barley and ran a few head of cows in the mesquite bosques this side of the river. Most years he barely broke even.

Lane cut west through the cultivated fields along Sisters' Road and presently came in sight of his parents' little weathered-gray shanty. His attention, however, was not on the house but on the fields themselves. All the crops he had seen north of Sisters' Road were suffering from lack of rain, his stepfather's included, and the *acequias,* or irrigation canals, were dry.

Unlike most southwestern rivers, the Santa Cruz flowed from south to north, and as far as irrigation water was concerned, the small downstream farmers were at the mercy of the large landholders to the south of them. It was a dispute that had been going on for the past four or five years with no happy ending in sight, at least not for small farmers like R. J. Devens.

Lane rode into the hard-packed yard. The Devens' home was painfully modest and plain, and he felt a stab of guilt when he remembered how he had promised his mother several years ago that he would plant some trees around the house. She had also wanted a picket fence built for the front yard. He never got around to doing any of it.

Lane dismounted and led the buckskin gelding up to the house, walking slowly, too tired by this time to bother with hiding his limp. He glanced toward the stable and toolshed out back. There was no sign of R.J., and Lane hoped he wasn't home. The less they had to do with each other, the better.

Tethering his horse in the shade on the east side of the house, he went inside.

Before his eyes had adjusted to the dim light, Lane knew something was wrong. The minute he stepped through the door, he stumbled over a pair of dirty trousers. Ann Devens was a meticulous housekeeper. He looked around him at the combination kitchen-living room. Dirty clothes on the floor, food-crusted dishes piled high on the table and cabinet, dusty furniture. Lane's stomach tightened with anxiety.

"R.J.? Is that you?"

His mother's voice left him weak with relief. He moved toward the bedroom door and peered inside to see Ann sitting up in bed, dressed in her old, blue nightgown, her Bible lying open across her lap.

"It's just me, Mama."

Her thin face lit up, and she opened her arms wide. Lane sat on the edge of the bed and hugged her, appalled by her frailness.

She kissed him on the cheek. "My goodness! I'm so glad you're finally home!" she exclaimed. "You've been in my thoughts so much lately." Ann searched his eyes, his face, soaking in every detail, and there was a touch of sadness in her voice when she said, "You're the spitting image of your father, Lane."

This last wasn't entirely true. The strong Indian features Lane had inherited from his father were softened somewhat by those of his white mother. His cheekbones were high but not too high; his nose crooking a shade off center, was narrow and only slightly aquiline. Lane's eyes, his most striking feature, were smoke-gray in color and contrasted oddly against the tawny cast of his skin. Though hardened by a rough, sometimes uncertain life, laugh lines framed his mouth, indicating a sense of humor lurked very near the surface and broke through quite frequently.

At the mention of his Navajo father, Niyol, Lane glanced down at the ketoh thonged to his left wrist. It was a broad band of leather decorated with silver and turquoise and worn to protect a warrior's wrist from the slap of his bowstring. This one had belonged to Niyol. Ann had given it to Lane when he turned eighteen to remind him of a father he could not remember, and he wore it more for her than anything, sometimes cleaning the silver with yucca soap and water to keep it shiny.

She grasped his hand. "I've been so worried about you."

"I'm worried about you right now," he said. "How long have you been sick?"

"A little over a week. But I've been feeling better these last two days, and I know having you here will help."

"Is it your heart again?"

Ann nodded and sighed. "I'm afraid it's got the flutters. It was so bad a week ago I could hardly catch my breath." She smoothed her graying hair away from her forehead. "I must look a mess, and the house is filthy. Just because you're poor doesn't mean you have to be dirty."

Lane studied her face, pale and drawn, and wished there

was something he could do for her. Her poor health always left him feeling helpless.

She noticed him looking at her and raised a hand to her face, a familiar gesture, covering the tattoo on her chin with her fingers. Lane grinned and gently brushed her hand away.

"Don't hide it," he said.

She smiled, and the five thin, black lines on her chin spread like a tiny fan.

The tattoo was of Mojave Indian origin. Lane remembered his mother telling him how the Mojave medicine man had pricked her skin with a sharp stick until it bled, forming a pattern, then had filled the open wounds with a dye he had prepared. It was by this mark that the Mojaves could identify their captives should they escape or be stolen by another tribe.

Ann Devens was taken captive by the Mojaves nearly thirty years ago. Shortly after they were married, she and R.J. and eight other families had decided to try their luck in the California gold fields and were traveling over the Old Government Road to Los Angeles when their wagon train was attacked by the Mojaves. Several people were killed, and Ann and another young woman were abducted.

She spent two miserable years with the Mojaves as a slave and then changed hands, traded to an Apache for a horse and blanket. The Apache lost her a year later to the Navajoes while betting on pony races.

Though Ann Devens spoke freely of her captivity among the Navajoes, she rarely mentioned those three years with the Mojaves and Apaches. When Lane asked too many questions, she'd grow snappish, and her lips would press together in a hard line.

By the time Ann was sent to live with the Navajoes, she was certain that R.J. had not survived the Mojave raid and gave up all hope of ever being reunited with her own people.

Though at war with the Americans, the Navajoes treated her well, and a young man called Niyol took a particular interest in her welfare.

A warrior under Navajo chief Manuelito, Niyol was killed by Kit Carson's New Mexico Volunteers when Lane was three years old. Shortly before Manuelito's surrender in 1866, Ann and several Navajo women and children, all of them sick and half-starved, were captured by soldiers. Ann was finally reunited with her husband at Fort Wingate.

The tattoo on Ann Devens's face was the mark of her captivity, just as Lane was a product of it.

Reaching out to him, Ann pressed a roughened palm against his cheek and shook her head. "You wouldn't listen to me, would you? You had to find it out the hard way."

"Find out what?"

"I told you over and over it was a mistake to work for the army," she said. "I warned you it would come to no good end."

"I guess you heard what happened."

"Of course, I did. I've been worried sick about you. I practically begged R.J. to take me to Fort Bowie to see you, but you know how he is. Work, work, work."

Lane had an idea it wasn't just work that kept R.J. from taking her to visit him during his confinement at Bowie.

"They say you hit one of the officers, that you deserved your punishment," Ann said, a worried frown deepening the blueness of her eyes. She brushed a hand across her face. "I'd like to hear your side of the story for a change."

Lane shrugged, head bowed. "Not much to tell," he said. "I guess most of what you heard is probably true." He looked up at her. "It's not like this was the first time I ever lost my temper."

"What happened?"

Lane gazed out the window at a cloudless sky tinged brown with dust, and drew a deep breath. "Last November, we crossed into Mexico in hot pursuit of Geronimo's band," he said. "The advance guard captured some of his people, mostly women and kids and a handful of old men, and Lieutenant Mallory and a few of us who'd been in the field a long time without a break were ordered to escort them back to Fort Bowie.

"By the time we got back to the post, I'd had about all I could stand of Mallory's high-nosed attitude. None of the scouts liked him. At Bowie, Mallory declared the Apaches we'd caught prisoners of war and ordered them to be kept under guard in the quartermaster corral."

Lane paused, idly twirling his black, flat-brimmed hat by its chin strap, eyes focused internally, seeing the Apache women and children being herded into the muddy corral like cattle.

"Mallory wouldn't allow them to have any food or water. They didn't have any shelter, no blankets. Some of the people were sick." He glanced at Ann. "I told Mallory if he didn't do something we were gonna have a bunch of dead Apaches on our hands. I think that's what he wanted. He threatened to throw me in there with 'em if I didn't mind my own business, and that's when I busted his nose."

Ann sighed and lay her head back to rest against the pillow. She gazed up at the ceiling. "I'll never forget how the soldiers took Niyol's scalp and paraded it around like it was a prize trophy. Savages can be found as easily on one side as on the other." She rolled her head to the side to look at him. "At least now you're out of the army and not chasing those horrible Apaches around. The army was using you anyway. You were expendable."

Lane frowned. "I don't know about that. The pay was all

right, better than what I'd have got riding herd or working in the mines."

"There are other jobs besides those," Ann said, and her usually gentle voice was mildly scolding. "Lane, don't sell yourself short because you have Indian blood in you. You can do anything you want."

"Yeah, well, Indians aren't looked on very highly right now, Ma."

He decided not to tell her about the telegram he had received at Bowie, directly following his release. It had been sent by Regino Vega, a friend of his who lived a mile or two south of Penny Town, and indicated that there was a job waiting for him if he was interested. What that job might be, Lane couldn't guess, but Regino had advised him to keep his mouth shut about it.

"You look tired," Ann said. "Why do you never take the train? It would be easier on you, not to mention safer."

Ashamed of his phobia, Lane glanced over at her, smiled sheepishly, and shrugged. "They're too loud," he said, and restless, he rose and made a slow turn around the bedroom, hands thrust into the back pockets of his Levis. "Is there something I can get you? Maybe fix you something to eat?"

She shook her head. "I'm fine. R.J. came in from the field to check on me not long ago."

"Is he taking good care of you?"

"Oh, yes. He's doing his best."

Lane made a face. "I've tasted his cooking. If he's the one who's fixing your meals, I'd say his best ain't good enough."

"Isn't good enough."

"Huh?"

"Isn't," Ann replied. "Don't say ain't, honey." She smiled up at him. "There is one thing you can do for me."

"What's that?"

"Talk to R.J. when he comes in from work. Find out what's bothering him."

"Why? What's he been up to?"

Ann frowned. "R.J. went over to the Kimball place yesterday evening and didn't come in until early this morning, something he rarely does. He's been acting strangely ever since." She paused, gazing out the window. "He's jumpy and quiet, not himself at all. Something's bothering him."

"Probably constipated," Lane mumbled.

"Be nice." Ann tried to sound stern but smiled in spite of herself. "You don't think it's anything serious?"

"I doubt it. He took too many nips of Kimball's corn juice is all." Lane picked up his hat and settled it back on his head. "I'll leave you alone now, Mama, and let you get some rest."

"But you barely got here!" Ann protested. "And you haven't even seen R.J. yet."

Lane didn't say anything. He had supposed that to be the main reason for leaving in the first place.

CHAPTER SIX

Lane's dislike for his stepfather began the day he first set eyes on him, and the feeling was mutual.

Shortly after Ann returned to her husband following her captivity, R.J. bundled Lane up and hustled him off to the Franciscan Mission School for Indians in California. Lane had been only six years old then, but he knew how to hold a grudge. When Ann's unhappiness at being separated from her son finally forced R.J. to bring him home again seven years later, Lane's sullen animosity toward his stepfather was still very much intact.

Not even the strict, fault-finding missionaries at the school could deny the fact that this mixed-blood boy was a mighty good hater.

So was the man, but he said nothing of it as he leaned over to kiss his mother good-bye.

Before leaving, Lane stepped inside the tiny kitchen pantry to see if there was anything he needed to pick up in town and felt a sudden flash of anger. The shelves were almost bare. He looked into the vegetable bin and saw it was empty. No wonder Ann was sick, living on nothing but salt pork and biscuits. It appeared to Lane that R.J. and Ann were feeling the pinch. Either that, or R.J. simply didn't want to shop for groceries. Lane suspected the former. He had tried to send them a little money through the years, but R.J. always returned it with a note saying he didn't accept charity.

Looking around him one more time at the messy house, Lane decided he'd hire someone to come out and cook and clean until Ann got back on her feet again. It would pretty much wipe him out financially if the job Regino Vega had lined up for him didn't work out, but it might at least give Ann some comfort and peace of mind. R.J., of course, wouldn't like it.

But R.J. can go to hell, he thought.

Knowing he wasn't in the proper frame of mind to confront his stepfather today, Lane hoped to get away without seeing him. So naturally the first thing he did was bump into him on the way out the door.

Surprised, R.J. backed up a step. "Oh," he said, "it's you."

R. J. Devens always looked the same—weather-beaten, potbellied, and unsmiling with a seemingly permanent growth of course white stubble on his face that reminded Lane of cactus spines.

"Figured you were still at Bowie," R.J. said. "When did you get in?"

"About an hour ago."

"You and Ann have a good visit?"

"Yeah." Lane paused, knowing he should leave it there, but decided to have his say and be done with it. "You're killing her, R.J."

"What?"

"You're killing her. You've got her living in a pigsty and eatin' slop. How's that gonna help her get well?"

R.J. jutted his lower jaw out like a bulldog's and hooked his thumbs beneath red suspenders. "I can't exactly afford clam chowder and pastries." He gave Lane a critical look. "If anything would make her sick, it's seeing you walking around looking like a dirty, long-haired Indian."

Lane hid his anger behind a smile. "You can't stand it,

can you?" he asked softly.

The insult was subtle but effective. R.J.'s lips pressed together in a grim line, and he suddenly looked very old and tired. It wasn't the first time Lane had thrown his parentage into his stepfather's face, knowing full well that the fact Ann had found love with another man, particularly an Indian, would always be a sore spot for him.

R.J. combed his fingers through the horseshoe of thin, gray hair encircling the bald top of his head. "You're too big for me to lay into with a switch anymore," he said, "and I ain't in the mood to stand here and argue with you." Clapping his old straw hat back on, he drew himself up a little straighter but was still a full head shorter than Lane. "If you're staying the night, spare me your smart-alecky remarks."

"You can relax. I'm leaving."

"It'd please Ann if you stayed," R.J. said, trying hard to be civil.

"I'll be back tomorrow." Lane reached into his pants pocket and drew out a roll of greenbacks. Lips moving silently, he counted out half a month's pay and held it toward R.J. "Do me a favor and buy Mama some decent food, anything she wants. You know what's needed better than I do."

R.J.'s eyes flicked from the greenbacks to Lane's face, and he scowled. "I don't want your money."

"This isn't for you. It's for Ann."

"I said I don't want it," R.J. repeated, growing more annoyed. "We don't need it."

Lane stared at him in disbelief. "You hardheaded old buzzard," he said, his voice barely above a whisper. "You'd let her starve to death before you'd accept any help from me, wouldn't you?"

"You damned right I would."

That was too much.

Face tensed, eyes stormy, Lane grasped R.J. by the front of his shirt, lifted him up on his tiptoes, and backed him hard against the wall. Shocked, R.J. started to protest, and Lane crammed the wad of bills into his open mouth.

"This," he said, "is for Ann."

His temper burned out almost as quickly as it had flared up, and he backed away from R.J., brushing his forearm across his mouth, aware of the rapid pounding of his heart. Never in his life had he laid a hand on his stepfather until today. He turned and strode toward his horse.

Red-faced, R.J. spit the greenbacks into his open palm and followed him around to the side of the house.

"You wait a minute," he demanded. "I got something to say to you."

One foot in the stirrup, Lane glanced over his shoulder at him.

"Maybe you think you can push me around like I'm nothing," R.J. said bitterly. "You and everybody else. But there's coming a time when nobody pushes me around. You wait and see, blame it. I'm gonna be rich one of these days."

Lane gave a short laugh. "Robbing whose bank?"

"You won't think it's so funny pretty soon," R.J. replied. "I'll be sixty years old in another couple of months. I've lived honest and worked hard all my life, and you see where it's got me. Well, the poor man's fixing to get his ice in the summer for a change."

"Hold on a minute. What are you talking about?"

Seeing that he had snared Lane's attention, R.J. savored the moment and put on an air of secrecy. "Wouldn't you love to know."

Lane guessed he would but didn't tell him so, wondering if this was for real or just a lot of hot air. R.J. might say anything to offset the shame of feeling like a charity case.

Shaking his head, Lane turned his back on him and swung into the saddle. He rode away with the same sense of pity he usually felt for his stepfather after an argument, and he hated himself for it.

Lane checked into the Russ Hotel that evening following a long, hot soak in the bathhouse behind Tully's Barbershop, ate a quick supper in the hotel, and dragged himself upstairs to his room. Despite a lumpy mattress and a squeaky bedstead, he slept soundly for the better part of two hours until a knock at the door snapped him awake.

Reaching in the dark for his gunbelt hanging on the bedpost, Lane slipped his revolver from its holster and stared at the light shining through the crack beneath his door. He could see two moving shadows of someone's feet.

His visitor knocked once more, three quick raps, and called to him in a hushed voice: "Lane? You awake?" There was a pause, then: "Put your gun away, *amigo,* and open the door. It's me. Regino."

Relaxing, Lane yawned, lit the lamp, and rolling out of bed, he staggered across the room in his underwear and unlocked the door.

Regino Vega opened the door a crack and peered in at him. "Get some clothes on and let's go."

"Where to?"

"You'll see. Is your horse in the stables next door?"

Lane nodded.

"The big buckskin, right? *Bueno.* I'll saddle him for you while you get dressed."

Standing with a hand on his hip, Lane rubbed the back of his neck with the other and looked at his friend through squinted eyes. "What time is it?"

"Half past ten." Regino flashed him a smile. "Long time no see, eh, Lane? You hurry now. I haven't got all night."

He left, and Lane splashed cold water on his face from the wash basin, got dressed, and stepped out into the hall. He descended the stairs two at a time. Crossing the empty lobby, he glanced toward the clerk and saw him slumped in a chair behind the counter, slack-jawed and sound asleep. Lane envied him the rest.

Regino was waiting for him outside the hotel with their horses. He looked the same to Lane, perhaps a little more serious than he remembered, but still thin-faced and slim-bodied, like a boy with a wispy, black mustache.

Seeing Lane, he shoved away from one of the support posts below the hotel balcony and swung astride his horse. "You take a long time, man. I thought maybe you decided to go back to sleep."

"What's this all about?"

"You got my telegram?"

"Yeah."

"That's what this is about."

His explanation didn't tell Lane much, but he didn't press him further.

Pennington's many saloons, gambling dens, and dancehalls were teeming with life and light and music while the Saturday night crowds blew off the steam of another work week. Lane felt a slight queasiness in his stomach as he and Regino walked their horses down the gas-lit street. It had been a long time since he'd been in the midst of so many people and so much noise all at once. Lane felt the buckskin's body quiver beneath him and knew he was uneasy, too. It was going to take them both a while to adjust to city life again.

Regino cuffed his broad-brimmed hat off his forehead and glanced sideways at Lane. "I wasn't sure if you'd come back to Penny Town or not."

"I got no place else to go," Lane replied. "How'd you know where to find me?"

Regino shrugged. "I checked every hotel and rooming house in town tonight, looking for you." He gave Lane a sly smile. "I even went by Abbie Maginnis's place, but she said she hadn't seen you in almost a year. You shouldn't keep a woman like that waiting, Lane."

He chose to ignore that. "I would've stopped by your house tomorrow. What's the big hurry?"

"Time is short," Regino said simply.

Horses lined the hitch rail in front of the Congress House Saloon, and Lane and Regino had difficulty finding a place to tether their own mounts.

Standing close beside the buckskin, Lane looped his gunbelt over the saddlehorn and snugged the barrel of his Colt down the back of his Levis, hiding the weapon beneath his soft, leather vest. Pennington's gentry no longer tolerated gun-toters, but Lane was reluctant to enter the saloon unarmed.

Gas street lamps and light flooding from the wide-open double doors of the Congress House Saloon illuminated the boardwalk. Lane ducked under the hitching rail and stood with Regino beneath the overhang, listening to the piano music and watching the passersby. His tongue sticking out the corner of his mouth, Regino leaned halfway inside the saloon, looked around the crowded room, and turned back to Lane.

"He isn't here yet."

"Who?"

"Mariano Diego. He wanted to meet with us here. He has a job to offer you. A good one, I think."

Lane was surprised. Mariano Diego was one of the wealthiest men in the county.

"What sort of job?" he asked.

"Be patient. You'll find out soon enough."

Neither Lane nor Regino made a move to enter the saloon. Most of the Congress House's patrons consisted of officers from the fort and wealthy ranchers and businessmen who expected saddle tramps to congregate elsewhere. Standing near the door with his thumbs tucked into his pants pockets, Lane could look inside the saloon and see men in suits and ties standing at the bar, smoking long Cuban cigars and drinking and bobbing their heads in serious conversation, talking business no doubt. Or talking about one of the fine-looking whores working over in the Red Light District, Lane thought wryly. The only thing setting these men apart from the people Lane associated with was the healthy jingle in their pockets.

Ill at ease, Lane drew a rosary of shiny black beads from his vest, and gathering the string into his palm, he stroked the small crucifix between his thumb and forefinger, feeling the familiar designs engraved into the silver. It was a nervous habit, something he'd done for so long that he ceased to be aware of it. Sister Julia at the Franciscan Mission School had given the rosary to him when he was a boy, and while he no longer used it for prayer, he kept the beads close at hand to remember this kind woman. Oddly enough, it still gave him a small measure of comfort.

Leaning relaxed against the wall, Regino watched him fidget and laughed. "If I didn't know better, my friend, I'd say you were counting prayers like a good Catholic should," he remarked.

Lane glanced over at him, realized what he was doing, and stuffed the rosary back into his pocket. "What's taking Diego so long?"

"Don't worry. He'll come."

"Let's go inside and wait."

Regino's eyebrows raised. "Without an invitation? One of those *ricos* in there would have us thrown out, no?"

"I guess our money's as good as theirs."

"But not so plentiful," Regino said and shrugged. "All right. The dust is bad out here."

They stepped inside the saloon and into a blue haze of tobacco smoke, hanging mammoth lamps, mirrors, and tapestried walls. The largest part of the crowd had gradually trickled into the adjoining game room to watch the high-stakes poker games in progress and to play roulette, so Lane and Regino had no trouble finding a place at the mahogany bar. Lane looked at the array of glasses and bottles arranged along the back bar, noticed an ice box and snack bar standing across the open end, and glanced at Regino. This was quite a contrast compared to the cantinas down in the south part of town with their dirt floors and barefoot *señoritas*.

A bartender in white shirt and apron drew up in front of them, looked them over with obvious distaste, and asked for their order.

"Two beers," Lane said.

"I'm afraid I'll have to ask you boys to pay up front."

Propping a booted foot on the brass rail, Lane studied the bartender a moment, trying to decide if the request was meant as an insult, and decided it probably was. He slid a silver dollar across the top of the bar and put on a nice, friendly smile.

"Make sure those mugs are clean ones," he said and leaned forward, lowering his voice in a confidential manner. "Last time I was in here, there were roaches all over the place."

"Now you listen here . . ."

"Hey, don't mind him," Regino cut in. "It was a joke." He

gave Lane's side a sharp gouge with his elbow as the bartender left to get their drinks. "You're asking for trouble."

Lane started to say something, then froze, eyes riveted on the back bar mirror. "What the hell's he doing here?" he muttered.

"Who?"

Lane gazed at the image in the mirror, the stocky man with the heavy-boned face standing by the door, lieutenant's stripes on his sleeves, kepi tucked under one arm. Lane slowly turned and looked at the man in person. Their eyes met, and the lieutenant scowled.

"Kirk Mallory," Lane whispered.

"Maybe we'd better go."

"No." Lane faced the bar again, his body tensed. "What's he doing here?"

"He was transferred to Fort Lowe last month," Regino said. "You didn't know?"

Out of the corner of his eye, Lane saw Mallory draw up beside him and plop his kepi down on the bar.

"Two fingers of bourbon, Harry," Mallory said and jerked his head to the side, gesturing to Lane. "Since when did you start serving redskins?"

Harry, the bartender, set two mugs of beer on the counter, made a face, and reached for a shot glass.

"There is a saying," Mallory continued as Lane picked up his mug, "that goes like this: Indian takes drink, drink takes Indian, all chase squaw. Since there aren't any women in here, I'd wager a guess that this Indian won't hang around long."

Listening to his words, Lane took a swallow of beer, set his mug down, and dug into his pocket for papers and a sack of tobacco. "Speaking of Indians," he said quietly, "how many more women and children have you slaughtered lately?"

"Too damned few."

Regino placed his hand on Lane's shoulder. "Let's leave. There's no point in this."

Ignoring him, Lane rested an elbow on the bar and needled, "Tell me something else, Lieutenant . . ." He paused to touch his tongue to the brown cigarette paper, cool gray eyes lifting to meet Mallory's. "How's the nose?"

Mallory's face stiffened.

"Lane." Regino's hand tightened on his shoulder, and he grasped him by the arm with the other hand and drew him aside. "Don't start anything," he said, "or you'll wind up in the *calabozo*."

"He's the one who started this," Lane replied, never taking his eyes off Mallory.

While the game room was loud with men's voices and laughter, the noise in the saloon itself had hushed and all eyes were on the three men at the bar. Lane yanked free of Regino's grasp and held the lieutenant's belligerent gaze a few more dragging seconds, reassured by the presence of his own six-gun pressing against the small of his back, aware of his fists clenched tight and ready. Knife, gun, or fists, it would be a pleasure.

Scowling, Mallory twisted his fat, gold Academy ring round and round on his finger. He was the first to look away. He tossed down his drink and slammed the glass hard against the bar. His face flushed a little as the bourbon burned down his throat.

"I asked you a question, Mallory."

The bartender spoke to Regino. "Get your friend out of here, or I will."

"I'm surprised you allowed a whodunit mutt in here in the first place," the lieutenant remarked.

Lane calmly picked up his beer. "Why, Kirk, I couldn't agree with you more," he said, and when Mallory looked at him in surprise, he splashed the mug of beer into the cavalryman's face.

Not giving Mallory time to recover his wits, Lane moved in and followed up with a solid, well-aimed punch to the man's mouth. Blood streamed from Mallory's mangled lips as he stumbled backwards. Cursing, he caught hold of the bar to steady himself, shook his head like a mad bull, and charged.

Anticipating the move, a man grasped Mallory from behind, hooking an arm around his blue-veined neck, and Regino Vega stepped in front of Lane to block his path while another man pinned his straining arms behind his back. Together, they barely managed to avoid a fight.

"All right, that's it!" The bartender crashed his fist against the bar and jabbed a forefinger in Lane's direction. "You! Out!"

"Wait a minute."

The request was mildly spoken, yet authoritative, and was heard and heeded by everyone in the room. Nostrils flaring slightly, Lane looked away from Lieutenant Mallory's bloody, beer-soaked visage and saw a distinguished gentleman in a gray suit break through the crowd, followed closely by three leather-clad vaqueros. He appeared to be in his mid to late fifties, a proud man who carried himself with a straight-backed military erectness. His commanding features were accentuated by thick salt-and-pepper hair and a neatly trimmed mustache and goatee to match. Lane recognized Mariano Diego.

Don Mariano nodded to Regino in silent greeting and gestured at Lane with his gold-handled walking stick.

"This man stays," he said. "He will join us in a game of chance."

CHAPTER SEVEN

Lane knew he hadn't seen the last of Lieutenant Kirk Mallory. Not only had he rearranged the man's face again, but he had publicly humiliated him a second time, as well. At least now he no longer had the United States Army to answer to. Sooner or later, this dispute between himself and Mallory would have to be settled.

Just in case it was sooner, Lane kept a sharp eye on the lieutenant as he followed Mariano Diego into one of the Congress House's private back rooms where high stakes poker games were often played. He chose a seat where his back was to the wall and where he had a clear view of the door. Regino pulled up a chair next to him. Dr. Ben Udall, a squat, pot-gutted old man with a heavy, unkempt soup-strainer that more than compensated for the hair missing on his head, flopped down in the chair on Lane's left, while Mariano Diego sat across from him.

One of Diego's bodyguards brought in a bottle of whiskey and glasses for all and then left, silently shutting the door behind him. Lane had no doubt that the three bodyguards would remain within the saloon, sober and watchful, and though he had seen no weapons showing, likely well armed. Don Mariano Diego held strong opinions on various controversial issues, opinions not always popular with many of Pennington's citizens, and he had taken the precautions he deemed necessary.

Diego poured a measure of whiskey into each of the four men's glasses and set the bottle aside, heavy eyebrows plunged low, lean face grave with thoughtfulness. Lane shifted uneasily in his chair. Doubtful that he had been called here for a game of poker, he couldn't imagine what Diego and Udall wanted of him. Though he had heard of both men practically his whole life, he knew little about them, excepting what he had read in the newspapers.

Mariano Diego was one of the few Mexicans elected to various political seats during recent years. While his freighting company had been badly crippled with the coming of the iron rails, he still shipped supplies to outlying communities and owned several southern Arizona stagelines and a cattle and sheep operation. The best Lane could remember, Don Mariano was now representing Pennington's Mexican community as city councilman.

Doc Udall was the county coroner and had been practicing medicine in Pennington for as long as Lane could remember. He had recently opened a second office in the barrio.

Udall filled his pipe and glancing at Lane, gave him a friendly smile. "I hear this isn't the first time you've ruined the lieutenant's good looks."

Massaging his knuckles, Lane shrugged. "He asked for it."

"Both times," Regino added.

Diego rested his elbows on the table and laced his fingers together. He peered over his hands at Lane. "Your conduct tonight and also in the past makes me wonder if perhaps I've made a mistake," he said grimly. "The job I have to offer will require a degree of subtlety and self-restraint, not to mention patience. You don't seem to possess any of the above."

Lane leaned forward. "Let's get some things straight here. First of all, whatever this job is, I never asked for it. Second, I ain't gonna pretend I'm deaf and can't hear insults from a lowlife like Kirk Mallory."

Udall smiled. "He has a point there, Mari."

Mariano Diego sighed and spread his hands in an air of resignation. "It seems I have little choice but to trust that what Regino says about you is true."

Puzzled, Lane cast a sidelong glance at his friend.

"I told him that, though you're a *pistolero,* you are an honest one and very tough and capable," Regino explained and grinned. "Don't disappoint me, *amigo.*"

"I understand you have good relations with the Spanish-speaking people in this area," Diego said.

"Pretty good, I guess. Why?"

"Because these are the people I'm hiring you to help, the small farmers and ranchers, especially those along the Río Santa Cruz."

Udall spoke clumsily around the stem of his pipe which jutted from one corner of his mouth. "They're not all Mexicans, Mari," he reminded him. "Many are white, like Mr. Devens' stepfather, for instance."

Diego scowled. His fierce, unblinking stare gave his face a mask-like appearance.

"I have no sympathy for the Anglos," he said. "They've taken over our town, they're destroying the traditions of my people, destroying the land and the river with their dams and canals." His unblinking glare passed from Udall to Lane, and his tone grew bitter. "Before the Gadsden Purchase, when southern Arizona was still part of Sonora, all of this—" he swept his left arm in a wide arc, "—all of this land south of the Gila belonged to us. From mountain to mountain, from river to river, the land was owned by Mexicans. Then the *extranjeros,* the outsiders, arrived and the small Mexican *ranchos* were finished."

Udall smiled. "You're living in the past," he chided. "We're a progressive society now."

"Progress!" Diego's scowl deepened. "My father and grandfather told me stories of true progress—how men worked in harmony toward a common good. All for one and one for all. That, my friend, is the only true progress. Now all we have are *gringo* thieves like George Nimitz, traitors like Estevan Carrillo."

"Which brings us back to the reason why we're here tonight," Udall said. "Nimitz and Carrillo."

Lane took off his hat and dropped it on the floor beside his chair. "You wouldn't be talking about the water rights war that's been going on the past few years, would you?"

"Only in part," Diego answered. "As you may know, the primary aggressors in this war, as you call it, are these two men."

Lane nodded. He had heard R.J. cuss Nimitz and Carrillo enough in the past to know that much. Both were county supervisors, speculators, and business partners who owned land south of Sisters' Road. They had appointed themselves as water commissioners and had instructed the *zanjero,* or water overseer, not to allow any water to the downstream farmers north of Sisters' Road unless there happened to be a surplus—a rare event in this part of the country. In addition, Carrillo had recently leased much of his land to Chinese farmers who turned the old traditional farming system into a neighbors-be-damned production for profit.

Mariano Diego sipped his drink and continued. "Nimitz and Carrillo now want more than the water. They want the land itself."

"And they're getting it by hook or by crook," Udall added.

Diego nodded in agreement and explained the situation to Lane.

In the past two years, several families owning choice bits of farm- and rangeland had been run off their property in ways both legal and otherwise. More familiar with the Homestead and Desert Land Acts than many of the farmers and ranchers, George Nimitz and Estevan Carrillo began their land-grabbing campaign by first filing claims on acreage occupied without title. Though it was an unscrupulous measure, they acted within the bounds of the law, and pioneering families who had settled here when the only law was the law of the gun wound up losing everything they owned.

Sheriff Jim Mitchell had also proved to be instrumental in booting these people off their land. It was a common practice for local newspapers to publish lists identifying individuals who were delinquent in paying their property taxes. According to Mariano Diego, however, Mitchell failed to make public the list of Mexicans who owed taxes to the county. As a result, some of the locals lost their property when it was either auctioned off or sold outright to Nimitz and Carrillo by the sheriff's department for a piddling sum of money.

"Most of our county officials are corrupt," Diego concluded.

"Why do Nimitz and Carrillo want so much land?" Lane asked.

"Cattle?"

Diego shook his head. "They've formed a company called Arizona Land and Development. The company advertises, sells, and leases mining claims, timber tracts, irrigated agricultural land, and grazing acreages," he explained. "Considering they're acquiring the land for practically nothing, there are huge profits to be made."

Lane shrugged, not too surprised by what he had heard so far. "Sounds like the same old story," he said and smiled a little, absently gazing at the burning tip of his cigarette. "No offense, but the rich have always stomped on the poor."

"Not always, Mr. Devens. I for one have never lost touch with the real world. With your help, I hope to bring Nimitz, Carrillo, and Jim Mitchell to justice."

Lane didn't doubt the man's sincerity, but there was still something he didn't understand. "Why do you need me?" he asked. "Seems like the first thing you need to do is rally the voters and kick the thugs out of office. That'd be a step in the right direction."

Regino grinned. "He makes it sound so easy."

"Bribery and intimidation are what hold these men in office," Diego said, "and I think Mitchell's deputies may have tampered with the ballots in the '84 election, as well, but could never prove it."

"You forgot to tell him about the latest atrocity," Udall said.

Diego nodded. "Last month, Regino's brother-in-law, Ruben Peña, had some trouble of his own. One morning, the sheriff and two of his deputies showed up at his home and ordered him and his family outside. The deputies searched Mr. Peña's house and barn. They found a saddle in the corral reported to have been stolen the day before from a rancher, and Peña was arrested for its theft."

"So?"

"My brother-in-law's not a thief," Regino pointed out.

"The night before he was arrested, Ruben's son saw a man sneaking around the barn, but when he called out to him, the man ran for his horse and rode away. We think he may have planted the stolen saddle in Ruben's corral."

"Any idea who this man was?" Lane asked.

"It was dark, but my nephew told me he looked like one of Mitchell's deputies, the one with the red hair."

"Del Hardy," Udall said.

Regino nodded. "The whole family chipped in to pay Ruben's bail. When he was freed, he took his wife and kids and went to Mexico. All for a stolen saddle." Regino sloshed more whiskey into his glass and looked at Lane. "I think Mitchell must have threatened to kill him if he didn't leave. Guess who got his land." He knocked back his drink, passed the back of his hand across his mouth, and answered his own query. "Arizona Land and Development."

"What concerns me most are the night raids we've had this past year," Udall said. "Edward Stevens, Sam Coleman, and Ezra Hughes and his family all bought land from the company. These same three were burned out of their homes a few months ago by a group of horsemen wearing gunnysacks over their heads. They lost everything. Houses and barns were burned to the ground, crops were trampled, livestock either killed or stampeded. We're not sure who's behind it all."

Lane listened intently. This was getting interesting.

"Maybe Nimitz and Carrillo are running these people off their property so they can buy it back cheap and sell it again," Regino speculated. "Make double the profit on the same piece of land."

"Well, they did buy out Hughes and Coleman," Udall said, "but anyone could be responsible for the raids. There are Mexicans around here who are mad enough to vent their anger on anyone. Especially whites."

Diego disagreed. "Like Regino, I believe it is the work of Nimitz and Carrillo. They would steal from their own mothers."

"If all this is true," Lane said slowly, "then why hasn't something been done long before now?"

"One of the county supervisors, Robert Cates, has contacted everyone from the district attorney and the deputy U. S. marshal here in Pennington to the Arizona Rangers, and they've refused to touch this case," Diego answered. "If our suspicions are false, or if they are unable to get an indictment, it could mean the end of their careers as law enforcement officers. As you know, the sheriff holds a very powerful position here."

"What about the territorial legislators?" Lane ventured.

"Any luck there?"

"None. They're either bought off or reluctant to oppose the actions of wealthy men like Nimitz and Carrillo. They fear it would be political suicide."

"So where do I come in?"

Mariano Diego laid it out for him in simple, straightforward instructions. "Your job will be to gain Jim Mitchell's confidence and uncover solid evidence that will expose him, George Nimitz, Estevan Carrillo, and whoever else may be involved. We must have witnesses, credible witnesses who are willing to talk, in order to make a case that will result in grand jury indictments."

He leaned toward Lane, his face set and grim. "The means by which these men have acquired land has ranged from legal to questionable to outright thievery. I fear the worst is yet to come. They must be stopped."

Remembering his encounter with Jim Mitchell this morning, Lane almost laughed. Gaining the sheriff's confidence might take some doing. He should have let the Apaches finish him off.

"I'm not sure why you chose me," he said after a moment. "I'm not a detective."

"Robert Cates speaks highly of you," Udall answered.

"And you are known and trusted by the Mexican community," Diego added. "That is very helpful. Furthermore, you have no dependents."

"Dependents?"

"A wife and children. Make no mistake, you will be

putting yourself in a dangerous position."

Accustomed to danger after his years with the army, Lane merely nodded and said, "How much will this job pay?"

"Three thousand up front and three thousand more once it is completed."

Lane whistled in surprise. "Those are fighting wages," he said softly, looking from Diego to Udall. "What gives?"

The two men exchanged glances.

"This isn't blood money, Mr. Devens," Diego replied. "Yet considering the men you are up against, you may at some point find it necessary to fight fire with fire. Do it only as a last resort."

Not interested in hiring on as anyone's paid assassin, Lane was pleased with his answer.

"Who all knows about this?"

"The four of us and Robert Cates," Diego said. "Cates has confronted Carrillo and Nimitz many times, making it known to them that he's well aware of their crimes, but the rest of us are not so foolish." He lifted a hand, indicating Dr. Udall and Regino Vega. "For the safety of ourselves and our families, we wish to remain behind the scenes. You'll tell no one of the subject of this meeting."

Lane understood their caution. Frowning slightly, he considered Mariano Diego's offer. The challenge of it intrigued him. And the money was also worth considering.

He rubbed out his cigarette in the ashtray. "Before we call this a deal, I have one request," he said and fixed Diego with a hard, impersonal stare. "I call the shots. I'll do this in my own time and in my own way, and the minute you or Cates or the doc here start giving orders is the minute I quit. Savvy?"

The bluntness of his words didn't set well with Diego. Evidently unused to being spoken to in such a manner, his face drew taut with anger. Doc Udall, on the other hand, appeared mildly amused, while Regino squirmed uncomfortably in his chair and downed more whiskey.

Udall cast a sidelong glance at Diego and pulled his pipe from his mouth. "Sounds fine to me. Mari?"

"Very well then. But if your actions get you into trouble, don't expect me to bail you out of it," Diego cautioned. "This will be the last time you and I will meet face to face. If you have something of importance to tell me, you'll go through Regino." He reached inside his suit coat, drew out an envelope, and passed it across the table to Lane. It was fat with greenbacks. "Here are three thousand dollars. After your . . . ordeal at Fort Bowie, you might want to take a day or two to recuperate before you begin your investigation."

Lane accepted the money and shook hands with Diego and the doctor. The bargain was sealed. He wondered if, after a good night's sleep and a clear head, he would regret taking the job.

Probably so.

CHAPTER EIGHT

Jim Mitchell's office was located on the ground floor of the Hohokam County Courthouse, and from his desk by the window he could see the twenty-foot brick wall of the jail yard and a couple of dozen prisoners milling about in the morning sunshine.

Tomorrow they would be sweating under that same sun, clearing drainage ditches and repairing roads for Nugent & Sons' Consolidated Mines, but today was Sunday and a day of rest. Another few minutes of stretching their legs, and the prisoners would be herded back into their cells to await the morrow.

Jim got up and leaned out the open window. "Good morning, boys!" Grinning, he waved cheerfully.

The prisoners, most of them Mexicans, responded to his greeting with hateful stares. A cowboy arrested two weeks ago for practicing his artistic skills with a running-iron on somebody else's cows stood looking at him with his hands on his hips, shaking his head and spitting in disgust. Jim reflected that this prisoner hadn't been convicted yet, hadn't even talked to a lawyer, but that didn't keep him out of the work detail.

The more prisoners there were to hire out to the mining companies, the more money went into Jim Mitchell's pocket.

"You fellas take it easy now, you hear! Got a long, fun-filled week planned for you!" Enjoying himself, Jim waved again, still grinning so hard his face hurt, and slammed the window down. Stupid jailbirds.

"Hey, Jim."

He turned to see his red-haired, bucktoothed deputy, Del Hardy, amble into the office and drop into a chair. "Any word on Cates?"

"None so far," Jim said and turned back toward the window to watch the prisoners file up the steps to the jail. "I rode out to the ranch to talk to his wife. She says he went to town day before yesterday to deposit some money in the bank."

"Maybe he was robbed on the way," Del suggested.

Jim felt a smile start. "Could be."

"If that's the case, don't you figger he's dead?"

"Sounds pretty logical, don't it?"

Del got up and shut the office door. When he looked back at Jim, his round, freckly face was alight with eagerness. "Man, Jim, if it's true, this is our lucky day!"

"What makes you say that?" Jim asked.

"Think about it! He's been a monkey on our backs ever since you took office."

Without looking at him, Jim sat behind his desk and lit a cheroot. Inhaling deeply, he leaned back in his chair and met the deputy's gaze. He gave him a conspiratory smile.

Del laughed. "You've already give that some thought, I bet."

"Great minds think alike."

"I'll say. If he's really dead, who do you reckon will take his place on the board?"

"Carrillo and Nimitz'll put their heads together and appoint a new supervisor who's blind, deaf, and dumb."

Or at least he hoped so. He couldn't stomach another Robert Cates breathing down the back of his neck. Jim distrusted honest men. He didn't understand the mind-set of anyone who couldn't be bribed.

George Nimitz and Estevan Carrillo, on the other hand, were both crooked, and while Jim didn't like them either, he at least knew what to expect from them.

"Are you gonna organize a search party to look for Cates?" Del asked.

"First thing in the morning," Jim said. "Gotta keep the voters happy."

"You bet. Say, I checked on Devens for you."

Jim's face lit up with interest. He leaned forward and rested his arms on his desk. "What'd you find out?"

"He checked into the Russ Hotel late yesterday evening," Del said.

"How many days did he pay for?"

"The clerk said just one, but that don't mean much."

Jim nodded.

"Last night, I asked around a little about Devens," Del continued. "He's got family here. R. J. Devens is his stepdaddy. He's one of those poor clods lives north of Sisters' Road."

"His wife was kidnapped by Indians, wasn't she?"

"Yeah. Ann Devens. Lane's part Navajo."

"Thought he looked it," Jim commented. "Go on."

"Well, from what I gathered last night, this Devens fella is your typical half-breed. It's said he's a bad hombre. Got a nose for trouble."

"He ever been in trouble with the law?"

Del nodded. "Devens shot and killed a man when he was eighteen or so in some cantina down in the south part of town. The man called him a dirty injun and badmouthed his ma, and Devens shot him twice through the brisket."

"Was he tried?"

"No, it turned out this fella he killed went for his gun first, so the law wound up letting Devens go since it was self-defense." Del propped his feet on Jim's desk. "He's rumored to be one of the best Indian fighters in the territory but was court-martialed by the army for slugging an officer."

"Anything else?"

Del shrugged and gave him a bucktoothed grin. "Supposedly there's none slicker with a six-gun."

"Rumor or fact?"

"Fact." Del studied him curiously. "What's this all about, Jim? Why are you interested in him?"

"Personal reasons," Jim replied. "I want to keep a close eye on him."

"Him and a hunnerd other hell-raisers."

Jim shook his head. "This one's different. Have you ever met somebody you hated so much you almost admired him?"

Del was puzzled.

"I guess you haven't. Well, it's hard to put into words." Jim frowned and nibbled at his lower lip. "You say he's supposed to be good with a gun?"

"Real good."

"And presently unemployed," Jim mused.

"Hey, wait a minute. You ain't thinking about hiring him, are you?"

"He'd make a damned fine deputy."

Dell mulled it over, thoughtfully chewing on his fingernail. "The Mexicans and tame Indians in this county are always bellyaching because all the peace officers are white," Jim said. "Well, Devens is only half-white."

"Yeah, but if you tell him about our little on the side business ventures, he might not go for it, Jim."

"If he's a killer he can't have too many morals," Jim reasoned, "but you're right. We may have to keep him in the dark for a time."

Del still looked doubtful. "Charlie won't like it," he said, referring to Charlie Reed, Jim's undersheriff. "You know how he hates Indians."

"And Mexicans, and darkies, and anybody else who ain't white. Charlie's too . . ."

Jim stopped, hearing hurried footsteps in the hallway outside his office and glanced up as the door swung open. A wild-eyed man burst into the office and yanked off his sombrero.

"*Señor* Sheriff, something terrible happen! There is a dead man! It look like *Señor* Cates!"

CHAPTER NINE

By the time Jim and Del reached the arroyo where Robert Cates had been found, the body had already been dragged out into the open, and several parked wagons, buggies, and tethered saddle mounts lined the road. A group of men was standing on the upwind side of the body, murmuring and shaking their heads. They looked expectantly at Jim as he swung out of the saddle and tied his horse.

Aware of their attention, Jim walked over to the body, grimaced, chewed his lip, and let his gaze slowly follow the scuff marks leading to the edge of the mesquite bosque where Cates had recently been dragged.

"Who moved the body?" he demanded.

The men looked around at one another, stuffing their hands into their trouser pockets, trying to appear perplexed and innocent all at once. No one cared to take the blame.

"Well, that's a hell of a note," Jim remarked. "First time I've known of a dead man dragging himself out of the bushes. I guess he made all these footprints, too, eh? Wanted to be sure and cover up the tracks of his killer so he'd get off scot-free."

One of the men spoke up. "Sorry, Sheriff. Guess we got kinda excited."

"I guess you did. Del, go get my reata and rope off this area. There might be some sign of the killer still left."

Jim covered his nose and mouth with his white kerchief

and squatted down to look at Cates, pretending to be deeply concerned. An important man had been murdered, after all. A man who had been elected to the county board of supervisors four terms in a row and was worth over three hundred thousand dollars in livestock and property deserved respect. A fly crawled out of the wealthy county supervisor's left nostril and rubbed its back legs together. The fly didn't care who the man was.

Jim felt himself start to gag and quickly rose. Scanning the crowd, he singled out the man who had come to his office and beckoned to him.

"Were you the one who first found him?"

"*Sí*. My goats was stray into the mesquites, and when I go to chase them out, what you think I find? *Señor* Cates." He crossed himself and crumpled the brim of his sombrero with unsteady hands. "Could it be that he was kill? Who would want to kill him?"

"Is this about the way Cates looked when you found him?"

"How you mean?"

"Were his pockets turned inside out?"

"I think so. Yes, they were."

"Be sure now."

"They were."

Nodding, Jim dug a pencil and notepad from his vest pocket and wrote down the information, plus the Mexican's name and place of residence. The morning was hot and still, and the scratching sound of Jim's pencil sounded loud in his ears. He felt a dribble of sweat trickle down the length of his nose and hang suspended from the tip a moment before it splashed onto his paper and soaked in.

One of the onlookers shuffled his feet. "What do you make of this, Jim?"

"He was robbed and murdered. Knife job, looks like."

A murmur of voices swept through the crowd of men.

"If he was stabbed, you can bet it was a Mexican did it," somebody said. "And right here close to the *barrio* to boot."

Jose Rodriguez, the man who had found Cates, shook his head. "You are mistake. *Señor* Cates was a friend to my people. Why would we want him dead?"

"He's right," Del agreed. "Cates stood up for the Mexican farmers."

Jim shrugged and tucked his pencil and pad back into his pocket. "I'm not ruling anyone out right now."

"Somebody'll have to break the news to Mrs. Cates," another man said quietly.

His comrade nodded in agreement. "Cates treated her pretty rough, I hear."

"Maybe, but that weren't nobody's business but theirs."

Only half-listening to their idle chat, Jim instructed Rodriguez to show him where he had found Robert Cates' body and followed the man into the mesquites along the wash. Rodriguez pointed out the spot on the caliche trail.

Jim looked around at the myriad of tracks, both human and goat, and glanced at Del Hardy. "If the killer left any clear footprints behind, they're gone now."

"This is gonna be a hard one to solve, Jim."

"Could be."

Jim walked off a short distance, slipping his left hand beneath his suitcoat. His fingers closed on the knife tucked inside his waistband. He glanced around to make sure no one was watching and swiftly lifted the knife, unwound the blood-stained rag he had wrapped around the blade the night of the murder, and dropped the knife into the weeds. Grimacing, he crammed the stiffened rag back into his pocket and wiped his hands on his pant legs. His fingers felt dirty now, and he couldn't rid his mind of the memory of plunging the knife into Robert Cates' cold corpse. He felt queasy.

Drawing a deep breath to clear his head, Jim walked slowly back toward Del. "See anything?"

Del shook his head. "All the tracks are fresh," he said, "and you know Cates has been dead for more than twenty-four hours."

"Uh-huh." Jim glanced at Rodriguez. "I don't guess you noticed any footprints when you stumbled across the body, did you?"

"No, I see the body only, and then I come to you."

Inwardly pleased, Jim nodded and started to turn away.

"There's one thing," Rodriguez said suddenly, and he waited for Jim to look at him and held out a small bit of cloth. "I found this on a mesquite thorn as I was walking down the trail . . . before I found *Señor* Cates. I pick it up. Why?" He shrugged. "I don't know. I had forget it was in my hand until now."

Jim took the cloth, a swatch of frayed indigo print fabric, and examined it briefly. The memory of the knife blade glinting in the moonlight, the barking dog, Christina Cates' anguished cry all flashed through his mind, and Jim remembered how he and Christina had raced through the brush in panic. This must have been torn from Christina's skirt. "Will that help?" Rodriguez asked hopefully.

Jim gave him a tight smile. "Sure, Jose. Every little bit helps."

"Hey, Jim! Jim! Look at this!" Del ran up to him, stumbling through the brush in his haste to show Jim his discovery.

"Well, well, well, what do we have here?"

"Derned if I didn't find the murder weapon!" Del exclaimed.

Jim took the knife from him, turned it over in his hands and inspected the weapon as if he'd never seen it before. It was an old knife but sharp, and the blade was smeared with dried blood. The initials RV were scratched into the handle.

"Where'd you find it, Del?"

"About five, six feet from where Cates was laying."

Jim held the knife up for everyone to see. "Anybody recognize this?" he asked and walked around, showing it to the men. "Eli? You recognize this? Jack, how about you? Help me out here."

One of the men took the knife, looked it over, and nodded. "That's Regino Vega's knife, Sheriff."

Jim eyed him curiously. "How do you know?"

"Seen him ear-mark calves with this same knife during spring roundup. That wasn't more'n a month ago." The cowhand paused to spit and roll his quid around inside his mouth. "Me and him was both workin' for the Circle K outfit."

"Would any more of the Circle K boys recognize Vega's knife?"

"Hell, yeah. He must've ear-marked a couple hunnerd calf brutes with it. Vega's a good, fast cutter."

Jim glanced at Cates' body. "Obviously."

"*¡Qué, va!* This cannot be!" Rodriguez stared at him in open-mouthed dismay. "Regino would never do a thing like this! I know him. He is a good man!"

Del grinned and jerked a thumb at Rodriguez. "Good thing I found the knife 'fore he did."

Jim brushed past the Mexican, ducked under the rope Del had strung up, and headed for his horse. "Somebody load Cates up and haul him to Doc Udall's office. I want to make damn sure that's a stab wound in his gut."

"What are you figuring on doing, Sheriff?"

Jim mounted up and looked back at the cluster of men.

"Fixin' to pay Mr. Vega a visit," he said, giving them a cocky grin. "What else?"

Regino Vega lived just outside town and a quarter mile up the road from where the body of Robert Cates had been discovered. Jim and Del met the undersheriff, Charlie Reed, on the way, and Jim explained what had happened.

Charlie Reed's pale, ice-cube eyes bore into him. "You do it?"

"Do what?"

"Kill him."

Jim was shocked. "You think I killed him? I've never killed anybody in my whole life . . . except an Apache or two. Hey, I killed an Apache just a coupla days ago. Did I tell you boys about that?"

"You talk too much," Charlie grumbled.

Del looked interested. "You saw an Apache?"

"What makes you think I killed Cates?" Jim asked, ignoring Del and giving Charlie a sidelong look. "Hell, I was as surprised as anybody."

Not one for explaining, Charlie merely grunted, and Jim knew he didn't care one way or another. Charlie Reed didn't care about much of anything.

Regino Vega lived with his wife, two children, and his mother-in-law in an adobe house surrounded by flat, treeless desert. The house looked as if it had been newly plastered and whitewashed, everything neat and clean and shining white. Not your typical mud hut, Jim thought. He hated adobe houses, thinking of them as being little more than spider and scorpion traps.

Out back, there were a vegetable garden, a chicken coop, and a small mesquite-pole corral with two horses and a mule dozing in the heat. Looking around, Jim spotted Vega's wife spreading clothes out to dry on a couple of bushes growing on the south side of the house.

"What's the plan?" Del asked.

"Just act natural and let me do the talking."

"It's gonna be hard to act natural," Del said. "Look behind us."

Jim glanced over his shoulder and saw that his party of oglers had followed him and were quietly watching from the safety of the road. No matter. Jim appreciated an audience.

As the three men neared the house, a yellow-haired mutt ran out to meet them with bristles raised. Jim figured it was the same dog that had barked at him and Christina that night, and he fought off the urge to shoot it between the eyes.

They dismounted in front of the brush ramada shading the front doorstep, and Jim flipped out his pocket watch. Straight up twelve. Vega should be home.

Sure enough, Regino Vega opened the door and stepped outside. "Howdy!" Jim said pleasantly.

Vega nodded, looking from one man to the other, already suspicious of them. Jim heard the wagon bearing Robert Cates' body rattle past but didn't look back.

"Mind if we talk?"

Vega glanced at his wife as she drew up beside him with a few dry clothes draped over her left arm and said something to her in Spanish. She glanced uneasily at Jim and hurried inside. Vega turned back to Jim. "We can talk."

"Good, good." Jim smiled and ducked his head as he moved beneath the shady ramada. "It's really nothing important," he said and showed Vega the knife. "Del Hardy found this. One of the Circle K hands recognized it, said it might be yours."

"You know it's mine," Vega said slowly, uncertainly. "I left it in your . . ."

"It's yours, you say?"

Vega frowned. “Yes.”

Jim nodded at Charlie Reed and stepped back out of the way as the big man brushed past him and drew a pair of handcuffs from his pocket. Vega took one look at the cuffs and bolted for the door.

“Get him!”

Charlie and Del both rushed forward and lunged at Vega before he could make it inside and wrestled him to the ground. Women screamed, children squealed, and bent on protecting its master, the yellow dog darted in and out of the ramada, growling at the two deputies with curled lips and nipping at them from behind.

Standing off to the side, Jim calmly drew his revolver and leveled it at the dog. He shot the animal twice, once as it was about to latch onto Del Hardy’s leg and again as it was twitching spasmodically in the dust.

Jim walked over to where Regino Vega lay struggling on the ground and watched Charlie press his knee into the man’s back while Del cuffed his hands together.

“Sorry ’bout the dog, Paco.”

Vega turned hate-filled eyes up to look at him. “I haven’t done anything wrong. Why are you doing this?”

“You killed Robert Cates.”

Shocked, Vega stopped struggling. “What are you talking about? Cates is dead?”

“Yeah,” Jim said. He emptied the spent shells from his gun and thumbed in fresh ones. “Don’t act so surprised, Paco. You know what this is about. You murdered him.”

Vega’s wife appeared in the doorway, holding a frightened child in her arms and sobbing. *“¡Por favor, Sheriff, deténgase! Usted no tiene razón. ¡Regino está inocente!”*

Not understanding what she was saying, Jim swept off his hat. “And a lovely day to you, too, ma’am!”

CHAPTER TEN

Christina Cates stared straight ahead as the fast-stepping bay drew her carriage down Penny Street, seemingly oblivious of the heat and the powdery dust and the stares she drew from pedestrians and passersby. The buggy's leather top was up, protecting her from the merciless sun, and a black veil shrouded her face from the public. There had been a time when she had enjoyed the attention and admiration showered upon her by the people of Pennington, but not any more. Now all she wished for were peace of mind and anonymity.

When the courthouse came into view, she touched her driver's sleeve with a black-gloved hand. "Park on the west side, Joaquín."

"Sí, señora."

He turned up Court Street, expertly steering horse and buggy through the heavier traffic, pulled over to the side, and drew to a halt beneath the lacy shade of a small cottonwood tree near the west entrance of the courthouse. Joaquín jumped down, hurried around to the other side of the buggy, and waited for Christina to remove the linen lap robe from around her voluminous skirts before holding his hand out to her. He helped her climb down from the buggy seat, and his face creased in a kind smile.

"I'll walk you to the door."

She nodded and took his arm, and together, they strolled up the stone path. Christina gazed up at the two-story courthouse with its fancy cupola and high-pitched roofs and wondered if she'd have any trouble finding Jim Mitchell's office. This would mark the first time she'd ever set foot inside the Hohokam County Courthouse.

Well-tended peach trees and shrubs were growing around the building, and nearing the steps to the entrance, Christina could hear winged insects buzzing and humming in the still, arid heat. Behind her, a water wagon rattled past, sprinkling the street in a futile effort to settle the dust.

"Would you like for me to go inside with you?" Joaquín asked.

Christina glanced up at him. Hard-working and dependable, Joaquín Mendoza was the strawboss of the Tanque Verde Ranch and had more important things to be doing than playing escort to her. She suddenly remembered something he had mentioned on the way to town.

"You told me you wanted to stop by the church to say a prayer for Mr. Vega and his family."

He nodded.

"Why don't you do that now while I talk to the sheriff. And Joaquín? Say a prayer for Robert, too, won't you?"

"Of course, *señora*. And one for you also. You've been in my prayers very much these past two days." He turned to go. "I won't be long."

Christina watched the bent, bow-legged little *vaquero* walk away, drew a deep breath, and opened the door. Inside, the courthouse was cool, and she found herself in a dimly lit hall. Waiting a few seconds for her eyes to adjust, Christina listened to the dry rattle of papers coming from the office next to her. Men's voices echoed somewhere down the hall, and her high heels clicked against the shiny tiles as she walked slowly forward, reading the names on the office doors. Past the district attorney's office and almost to the stairway leading to the second story, she found a door to her left slightly ajar, and peering inside, saw Jim bent over his desk, writing. He was alone.

Hearing her step, he looked up from his work. "Christina? That you?"

Tall and graceful in a black satin dress, Christina stepped inside and quietly shut the door behind her. Jim met her halfway across the room.

"I didn't recognize you with this on," he said and lifted the black veil from her face and folded it back over her head. Before she could respond, he kissed her on the mouth, drew back, and smiled. "Damn, Christina, you know what you remind me of? A black widow."

"Very funny."

"You're the last person I expected to see here today. Everything all right?"

"No."

Frowning, he sat on the edge of his desk. "What's the matter now?"

"How could you do it, Jim?"

"Do what?"

"Frame an innocent man for Robert's murder."

"Oh . . . that." He shrugged and reached into his vest pocket for a cheroot. "It just sort of happened. A long story."

Christina walked slowly around the office, glancing out the window at the empty jailyard, looking at Jim's cluttered desk and his file cabinet with the drawers vomiting crumpled papers. There were three chairs and a small round table in one corner, the table top scarred where Jim's deputies had propped their feet and carved initials. She stopped in front of the gun cabinet and gazed at the rifles and shotguns stored safely behind locked glass doors.

"I like stories," she said finally.

"Well, let's see. Where should I start?"

"Tell me about Regino Vega's knife."

"Remember that dog that yapped its head off at us that night?" Jim asked abruptly. "It's dead. I shot it yesterday."

Christina stared at him with troubled eyes, not understanding his purpose in telling her this.

"I never did like dogs," Jim continued.

Christina took a tentative step toward him. A frown wrinkled her forehead. "What does that have to do with the knife?"

"The dog's the reason I left Vega's knife behind," Jim told her, almost impatiently, as if this was a logical explanation. "When it started barking at us that night, I sort of panicked, dropped the knife, and ran like hell. You remember."

"I thought I saw you put it in your pocket. And how did you get Vega's knife in the first place?"

"He left it in my office one day last week." Jim clamped the smoking cheroot between his teeth and dug into his pants pocket. He held up a small jackknife for her to see. "This is the only knife I own, so I used Vega's. Satisfied?" He flicked the blade out and proceeded to trim his fingernails.

Christina was far from satisfied. Joaquín Mendoza had told her how, after Vega was arrested, Jim and his deputies returned to the man's house with a search warrant and found Robert's pocket watch and wallet. Jim, she was certain, had taken these items from her without her knowledge and planted them in Vega's home.

Just like he planted the knife next to Robert's body, Christina thought. That he could sit there on the edge of his desk, relaxed, smoking a cigar and manicuring his fingernails, and spin tales without batting an eye caused her to wonder how many more lies he had told her lately. And why would he wish to frame Regino Vega for murder? What did he have against the man?

Yet even as the shadow of doubt and suspicion crossed Christina's mind, fear that Jim would turn against her eclipsed all else. She didn't question his explanation. Not yet.

"Don't worry about Vega," Jim said. "He'll get off on some legal blunder or other, most likely."

"What if he doesn't and gets the death penalty? Are you going to hang him, Jim?"

Twisting half around, Jim laid his cheroot in the ashtray on his desk, stood up, and drew Christina into his arms. "If that's what it takes," he said and bent his head, pressing his mouth to her right ear. "I'd hang this whole town if I thought it'd help you."

Christina rested her head against his chest, soothed by his gentle touch, if not by his words, when suddenly she felt his arms stiffen, and he pushed her away. Christina looked up at him in surprise, then followed his gaze to the door.

"Hope I ain't disturbin' nothing."

A man Christina had never seen before was standing in the doorway, looking at them with a funny little smile on his face and rasping a forefinger back and forth across the white stubbles on his chin. He shut the door and took off his old crumpled straw hat.

"You ever hear of knocking?" Jim demanded.

"Well, seeing as how I'm a taxpayer," the man said, "I figure this here office is as much mine as yours."

"Mrs. Cates and me were having a private discussion."

"I noticed that," the man replied.

Feeling her knees grow weak, Christina turned to Jim. "I'd better go."

"No, ma'am, you'd might as well stay here," the man said, and his tone of voice changed, now serious and tense. "What

I have to say concerns both of you."

Christina and Jim exchanged glances.

"Who are you and what's your business?" Jim asked.

"My name's R. J. Devens."

Jim's eyebrows raised. "Devens, eh?" He sat down and cocked his feet on the desk top. "What can I do for you, Mr. Devens?"

"It's what Mrs. Cates can do really," Devens said. "By the way, ma'am, I'm sorry 'bout your husband. Not surprised, but sorry."

Christina stared at him in silence.

"Why weren't you surprised?" Jim asked.

"Because I saw it happen."

Edging away from Devens, Christina sat down in one of the straight-backed chairs before her quaking legs gave out beneath her.

Jim fixed the man with an intense stare. "Saw what happen, Mr. Devens?"

"I saw Cates being dragged into the brush." Devens hitched up his trousers, settled his hat back on his head, and tucked both thumbs beneath red suspenders. "I was riding home from a friend's house the night it happened," he said, his gaze traveling aimlessly around the office, occasionally touching either Jim or Christina. "Saw a man and a woman dragging a body into the mesquite trees along that wash that runs by Regino Vega's place."

"A man . . . and a woman?" Jim glanced at Christina, then back to Devens and smiled, shaking his head in disbelief. "I never gave Vega's wife a thought," he said coolly. "Do you think she might have helped her husband kill and rob Mr. Cates?"

"No, I don't think so, Sheriff. It wasn't Vega or his wife, either one. The man was taller than Vega." Devens eyed Jim closely. "Why, Sheriff, I believe he was about your height. And the woman . . ." He paused, shaking his head. "If I didn't know better, I would've swore it was Mrs. Cates here. Now don't that beat all?" He looked at her and shrugged, as if he didn't know what to make of it.

Christina gripped her pocketbook with white-knuckled fingers. The office grew deathly still, then Jim's feet came off the desk and hit the floor with a loud double clunk that made Christina jump. He leaned forward in his chair, his face stiff.

"Exactly what are you trying to say, Devens?"

"I think we all know." He sucked on his teeth a moment, looking from Jim to Christina. "Give me what I want and this'll stay our secret."

"What do you want?" Jim asked.

"One hundred thousand dollars," Devens replied. "I want it in cash, and I want it by next week." His surly gaze settled on Christina. "At twelve-thirty next Tuesday, I'll be waiting for you in front of the Hudson and Company Bank. You know where it is?"

Christina swallowed hard and nodded.

"You be there with the money. If you ain't there, I'm going straight to the deputy U.S. marshal."

"You're a damned fool if you really think you can get away with this," Jim said.

Devens turned to look at him. "I'll be sleeping with a double-barreled shotgun, Sheriff, so unless you want a hole blowed in your belly, you'd best keep your distance."

Jim chewed his lower lip, regarding the older man with mocking eyes. "We'll see about that," he said. "Now get out of my office."

When Devens started backing for the door, Jim stood up. "Hold on. Tell me one thing. Does Lane know about this?"

"Lane?" Devens gave him a suspicious look. "Why do you ask?"

"Look here, old man, does he or doesn't he?"

"This ain't none of Lane's business," Devens growled and opened the door. "Next Tuesday at twelve-thirty, Mrs. Cates. You be there."

Christina watched him leave, stunned, her body rocking slightly and causing the uneven legs of her chair to thump against the floor. She couldn't believe this was happening. Would the nightmare ever end?

"I'll have to wait until after Robert's will is read before I can withdraw the money," she said, her voice quiet, toneless.

"Uh-uh." Jim shook his head. "You're not paying Devens a dime."

"But if I don't he'll . . ."

"He won't do a thing," Jim cut in. "No out-at-the-pants sodbuster is gonna get away with blackmailing us."

Christina got up and stood next to him by the window. "What will you do?"

"Something. I need to think."

"Maybe I should just give him the money."

"Forget it." He grinned at her, already in high spirits again, and as always, it amazed Christina how quickly his moods could change. He winked at her and tapped his temple with a forefinger. "An idea's already forming."

"What is it?"

"You leave that to me." He rested his hands on her shoulders, looking deep into her eyes. "You gotta learn to trust me more, Christina. We'll be tying the knot pretty soon."

"Exactly how soon are you talking about?"

Jim's face lit with eagerness. "How soon? How does tomorrow sound?"

"Jim . . ."

"All right, next week."

Christina frowned.

"Next month?"

"We're being blackmailed, yet you stand here and make jokes." She gave him a sober look. "Sometimes I wonder if it's me you want or Robert's money."

"Now that's a hell of a thing to say!"

"Well, really. You're in such a hurry. What am I supposed to think?"

He favored her with a cocky smile. "Let me lock the door, and I'll show you what I want right here and now."

"Not until we're married," Christina said firmly, and she stepped away from him. "You promised me you'd wait, and I plan to hold you to it. As for getting married, I'll let you know when the time is right."

He spread his hands, still smiling a little. "Fine, but don't take too long, Christina. I can't wait forever."

She paused with her hand on the doorknob and looked over her shoulder at him. "If you truly love me, Jim, you'll wait until I'm ready."

With that, she arranged the black veil over her face again and slipped out the door.

CHAPTER ELEVEN

Abbie Maginnis lived on the corner of Belknap and Penny streets, midway between Rosel's Restaurant where she waited tables and the Congress Street School where her eleven-year-old son, Seth, learned the three R's. It was a modest middle-class neighborhood that was just far enough away from the Southern Pacific line to keep the windows from rattling each time a train chugged through the eastern fringes of town.

Not in any great hurry, Lane Devens left his horse in the livery stable and walked from the Russ Hotel to the restaurant, only to find Abbie not there. She hadn't shown up for work that morning, one of the waitresses said, and Rosel, the big brawny Swedish woman who ran the place, was furious.

A little in awe of the muscle-bound Rosel, Lane didn't tarry long. He walked east along Penny Street to Abbie's house and idly watched as buggies and wagons passed by him, many of them heading either to or from the depot.

Lane waved a fly from his face and ran his palm down the back of his neck, still getting used to the feel of a haircut. He was wearing a new shirt, flame red in color, and though his once black pants were faded to a soft gray with wear, they, too, were clean and pressed, and his boots were polished. Straight and tall, he moved with long-legged ease. Anyone who had seen him when he first rode into town two days before would not have recognized him as the same man today.

There was a dusty runabout drawn by two skinny rental

horses parked in front of Abbie's house. Lane glanced at it as he opened the gate, surprised that she might already have company. He hadn't given that possibility a thought.

He stopped at the door and raised a hand, about to knock, when he heard a man's voice and Abbie's light, pleasant laughter. He hesitated, not sure what to do. He had expected her guest to be of the feminine variety, not male, and the realization that there might be another man in her life hit him like an eight pound sledge and knocked the breath out of him.

He leaned against the door facing a moment, listening to their voices and laughter. Perhaps it was a casual acquaintance, someone she had met at the restaurant, the same place she and Lane had met three years ago. Or maybe it was her brother. Did Abbie have a brother? He didn't think so.

Without knocking and without further pause, Lane pushed away from the facing, opened the door, and stepped inside.

His entrance was met by astonished silence. Abbie was lounging on the sofa staring up at him with wide eyes and across from her, her friend twisted around to look past the back of his chair at him.

Ignoring Abbie, Lane walked slowly toward the stranger, looking him over and sizing him up with swift and brutal scrutiny. The man held a black derby in his left hand—the sorriest excuse for a hat Lane had ever seen—and was tapping it rather nervously against the arm of his chair. He had clean, trim fingernails and soft hands, an untanned face, and wore a flashy but cheap suit. Lane pegged him for a gambler . . . but not a very good one.

The gambler cast a reassuring look at Abbie and affected an air of superiority. "Pardon me, sir, but I don't believe you were invited. In fact," he added, "I don't recall hearing you knock."

"That's because I didn't," Lane replied.

He reached down, pried the glass of wine from the man's hand, and held it up to the light. He tasted it, barely touching his lips and tongue to the brim, and made a face. Cheap wine. Stepping to the side, he deliberately poured the contents of the glass into Abbie's potted geranium.

"Now you hold on a minute! I have a mind to . . ."

Lane turned to look at him. "You have a mind to what?"

The gambler was suddenly confused.

Lane planted both hands on the arms of the man's chair and leaned toward him, a faint smile curving one corner of his mouth.

"Don't you have something you need to be doing?"

"What? Oh. You mean . . . Yes, I see what you mean."

Lane straightened, and the gambler rose, put on his derby, and glanced at his pocket watch. "Beg your pardon, Abbie. I just remembered I have an appointment, and it appears I'll be late if I don't hurry." Keeping a wary eye on Lane, he tipped his hat to Abbie and backed toward the door. "I thank you for the invitation but perhaps another time would be more convenient for both of us."

Smiling in amusement, Abbie nodded and watched him leave, then tilted her head up to look at Lane. "You haven't changed a bit, have you?"

Lane dropped into the armchair the gambler had vacated and stretched his game leg out in front of him. He watched the curtains in the window next to him swell with a slight breeze.

"If that wine kills my geranium, I'm gonna kill you," Abbie threatened as she set her glass on the coffee table.

"Who's the tinhorn?"

"A fella I met a few days ago. I invited him over to help me celebrate."

"Celebrate what?"

"My birthday."

"Really? How old are you?"

She wagged a finger at him. "That's not polite."

Lane studied her momentarily, this woman whom he neither understood nor fully trusted but still loved and wanted. She looked exactly the way he had pictured her over and over in his mind, with her honey-blonde hair swept up high and her dress cut low, and her laughing hazel eyes artfully lined in black so that they appeared almost slanted, like a cat's.

She would be in her middle thirties he knew, but the fact that she was older than he didn't bother him. What bothered him was the knowledge that she had been entertaining a tinhorn gambler. And no telling who else, he thought.

"Is that why you skipped work?" he asked. "Because it's your birthday?"

"You bet, it is. Who wants to work when they should be having fun?"

Lane picked at a worn spot in the tapestry on the seat of his chair. "Looks like you could find better company than some two-bit cardsharp."

"Are you jealous, Lane?"

He glanced up at her, frowning. "Did I say that? I don't care what you do."

"You're jealous!" Abbie threw her head back and laughed, giving the bottom of his foot a playful kick. "What did you think me and Jesse were gonna do? Roll naked together on the floor?"

"Like I said, I don't give a damn what you do."

"Well, we weren't," she assured him and wrinkled her nose. "He's not my type." Still smiling, she picked up her glass and took a sip of wine, never taking her eyes off him. "You're so funny when you're mad."

"I'm not mad."

She shrugged. "When did you get in?"

"Late Saturday."

"Why didn't you come see me?"

"I was tired."

"In case you've forgotten, I have a bed."

He settled back in his chair, feeling the tension inside him start to ease a little. "I didn't forget, but I had some things to take care of. It was easier to check into a hotel."

"What'd you do yesterday?"

"Went to Mass, had Sunday dinner with the folks . . ."

"You went to church with your parents?"

"No, alone. They're not Catholic. Why?"

She studied him curiously. "Just wondered. I can't picture you going to church without somebody dragging you by the ear."

"I bet the padre thought the same thing. I had about two years' worth of sins to confess."

Abbie laughed. "Well, lover, if you plan to stay with me, you're gonna have a lot more."

He didn't doubt that this was true.

"You look good, Lane."

"So do you."

"Why'd you stop writing me?"

"Didn't have time."

"Seth'll be tickled to see you."

Lane smiled. "Where is he anyway?"

"School, learning something useful, I hope. He'll be out for summer vacation pretty soon. You'll have to take him hunting or fishing or whatever it is you men like to do."

Lane nodded.

"He won't be in for another hour or so," Abbie said. "That gives us some time alone."

Listening to her words and their implied meaning, Lane let his gaze wander around the tiny livingroom, looking at anything and everything but Abbie Maginnis, at the pictures on the wall, the rag rugs on the floor, the two armchairs and matching sofa with cigarette burns in the upholstery. There was a big, well-thumbed book of poetry by Percy Bysshe Shelley on the coffee table. The room had a cozy, lived-in feel about it that Lane liked. He noticed a pair of boy's trousers draped over the back of one of the chairs with a tear in the knee, waiting to be patched.

"Lane . . ."

When he looked at her, Abbie rose and moved toward him, lifted her skirts slightly, and sat in his lap. Her hands reached for his shirt, unbuttoning it, fingers working downward, fumbling at his belt buckle. Lane didn't touch her. He gazed out the window instead, trying to remain detached, trying to decide whether or not this was what he really wanted. He was still irritated. He knew she had been with other men in his absence, and it hurt his pride to think that she might want anyone but him, especially after she had promised to wait for him.

Yet while his mind remained undecided, the rest of him did not. He breathed in the scent of her. She smelled faintly of lavender powder and perspiration and wine. He passed his right arm around her waist and pulled her closer, responding the way she expected him to.

"You act nervous," she said. "Loosen up some."

"I can't help it. I'm out of practice."

Her muffled laugh was hot against his neck. "Aren't there any women at Fort Bowie?"

Lane hesitated, wishing he hadn't revealed so much of

himself to her. He was annoyed with his obvious lack of experience and tried to pass it off with a joke.

"Yeah, but you're the only one that bathes regular."

CHAPTER TWELVE

Lane was teetering on the border of wakefulness, aware only of the sparrows chirping outside the bedroom window and the cool sheets and the boneless feeling of his body. It occurred to him that he hadn't felt this relaxed in ages. How many nights in the past year had he slept on the hard ground with one eye open and his finger on the trigger, alert and skittish of every sound? Peaceful sleep was a rare and wonderful thing. Lane felt as if his body would melt clean through the mattress to the floor.

Though no longer dozing, he kept his eyes closed and turned over onto his side, smelling the lingering remains of Abbie's perfume on his pillow. He stretched an arm out to where her body should have been before he remembered she had already left for work. That made him think about Mariano Diego and the job he had accepted from him and suddenly his peace of mind was gone.

He was still uncertain as to how he should accomplish this. He needed proof, and he needed talkative witnesses, preferably someone who'd be willing to spill his guts to save his neck. One of Mitchell's deputies perhaps? That would be something worth looking into. Lane wondered, *If Jim Mitchell was up to his eyeballs in Carrillo and Nimitz's land-grabbing scheme, what exactly was he getting out of it? Pay offs? Political backing?* That was something else he needed to think about.

Estevan Carrillo and George Nimitz were unapproachable. So for now at least, Mitchell seemed to be Lane's only key to gaining entrance into this corrupt little ring of politicians and businessmen, and he didn't know how to get friendly with someone he didn't like.

Just grit your teeth and bear it, he thought. And stop worrying. Abbie was always scolding him, *Stop being so damned serious!*

Lane had debated the night before whether or not to tell her about his meeting with Diego and Udall and had decided it would be wisest to leave her in the dark. If Abbie kept secrets the way she kept promises, this one would be broken and forgotten in about half an hour. And he wasn't fooling himself into believing that she ever gave him more than a fleeting thought anyway. So long as he paid the monthly rent, she'd be satisfied and not ask too many questions.

Lane heard a whisper of sound, the bedroom door opening, tentative footsteps approaching his bed, and he opened his eyes to see Abbie's son tiptoeing toward him.

"Morning, Seth."

Seth smiled shyly. "Good morning."

"What you got there?"

"Coffee." Seth held up the cup for him to see. "Ma said you might want some."

"Sounds good."

Raising up on one elbow, Lane took the cup from the boy's hand, cooled it a little with his breath, and took a drink. He thought Seth must have stumped his toe while adding the sugar but didn't let on.

"You make this?"

"Yes, sir."

"Good coffee."

Seth beamed with pleasure. "Thanks." He sat on the edge

of the bed. "Ma said you're gonna take me hunting this weekend."

"She did, did she?"

Seth nodded.

"But I'm the last to know about it, right?"

"Huh?"

Lane grinned. "Nothing. What do you want to hunt?"

"It don't matter."

"Antelope?"

"That sounds fine."

"Can you shoot?"

"No."

"Well, at least you're honest." Lane studied the boy, a nice-looking kid, quiet, shy, eager to please. His blond hair was wet and slicked down flat against his head, though Lane knew by the time it dried he'd have a rooster tail sticking up in back. "You have school today?" he asked.

Seth didn't say anything.

Lane forced down another gulp of syrupy coffee and glanced out the window. The sun was breaking over the horizon, brightening the bedroom with its warm, yellow glow.

"I sure would like to stay home from school," the boy said finally, wistfully.

Lane looked at him, started to say something, but heard a knock at the front door and saw a chance to dodge Seth's not-so-subtle hint.

"Go see who that is while I get dressed."

Seth jumped up and ran out the door.

Left alone, Lane threw the sheet off, sat up, and reached for his clothes, yawning. That was when he noticed the pair of leather gloves lying together on the floor at the edge of the bed. He picked them up. They were the large-cuffed, tight-fitting gauntlets favored by soldiers in the cavalry. Lane gazed down at them with a strange feeling in his chest, the muscles in his jaws ticcing. A deep weariness that was not physical crept through him and settled in his mind.

The gauntlets were not his, of course, and were much too large to be Seth's. Someone had left them here. Someone . . .

Why did he put up with this? He didn't know exactly. Abbie Maginnis was like an addiction. No matter how much she hurt him, he always came back for more. He needed her, or thought he did, the only woman he had ever held, kissed, loved. Lane heard Seth say something in the next room and a man's voice answering him, the voice growing louder as he stepped inside the house. Maybe it was Abbie's new lover, come to fetch his gloves. Not wanting to think about it any more, Lane tossed them back under the bed and out of his sight.

Seth stuck his head in the bedroom door and spoke to him in a loud whisper. "It's the sheriff!"

"Mitchell?"

Seth nodded. "He wants to talk to you."

"What d'you know about that?" Lane said softly. "Tell him I'll be out in a minute. And don't look so worried. I'm not in trouble."

Relieved, the boy smiled at him and disappeared.

Pulling on his pants, Lane wondered what Jim Mitchell wanted and how he had known where to find him. It irritated him a little. A private man, he preferred not to have everyone in town knowing more about his business than even he did, yet the fact remained that this might be the very opportunity he'd been hoping for.

He wasn't sure what he should do. Lick Mitchell's boots clean, or act natural? Lane shrugged. Be yourself, he decided. If you were an actor, you'd be over at Reid's Opera House spouting Shakespeare. Whatever happens, happens.

He lifted his gunbelt from the bedpost, slung it around his hips, and buckling it on, padded out of the room in his socks.

Jim Mitchell was standing in the middle of the living room, looking around and rocking slowly to and fro on his heels when Lane walked in. On seeing him, he pulled the cheroot from his mouth and nodded.

"Good morning, Devens. Didn't mean to roust you out of bed."

"I was awake. What brings you here, Sheriff? I figured you'd still be out chasing Apaches."

Mitchell appeared mildly abashed. "I thought you and me might have a little talk."

"Look, if this is about the other day . . ."

"No, no, no." Mitchell grinned. "That's all forgotten. This is business."

"What sort of business?"

"How about a cup of coffee first?"

Lane nodded, then glanced at the boy, who was watching him with wide eyes. "Seth, you'd better rattle your hocks out of here, hadn't you? If you're late for school, your mama's liable to kill us both."

"All right." Seth reluctantly gathered his books and lunch bucket. "Will I see you this evening?"

"I'll be here," Lane assured him and watched him leave.

"Good kid," Mitchell remarked.

"Yeah."

The sheriff followed him into the kitchen and sat down.

"Is he your boy?"

"Seth?" Surprised, Lane turned from the stove to look at him and almost spilled his coffee. "No, he's not mine."

"I guess not. Hell, he's what? Eleven, twelve years old? Too old to be your kid, I reckon." Mitchell accepted the cup of coffee Lane offered him. "I stopped by Rosel's on the way over here," he said. "Saw Mrs. Maginnis. She's built for comfort, I'll tell you. I noticed she didn't give me a second glance this morning." He grinned and gave Lane a knowing wink. "Too tired maybe."

Lane eyed him over the top of his coffee cup. "Mitchell, you're right on the verge of overstaying your welcome. I'll give you two more minutes."

Mitchell chuckled, shaking his head. "That's what I like about you. Right to the point."

"Get to it."

"I will, but first a little warning: There's an ordinance that makes it illegal to carry a firearm inside the city limits." He looked at Lane leaning against the kitchen counter and gestured to the gun on his hip. "The city fathers are real particular about that sort of thing."

"You here to arrest me, Sheriff?"

"That's the police chief's job, not mine. I'm surprised he hasn't already brought you in."

"He's welcome to try," Lane said. "Seems to me like the man who abides by this law is at the mercy of those who don't."

"If I told you there was a way to carry a weapon legally and out in the open, would you be interested?"

Not sure what Mitchell was getting at, Lane merely shrugged.

"Let me swear you in as my deputy," Mitchell said, "and you can prance naked down Main Street with a cannon under each arm."

Lane laughed.

"I'm serious," Mitchell said, but his face spread in a broad grin, and he stroked his mustache, apparently much pleased at having broken through Lane's wall of ice. "None of my deputies have gone so far as that, but you're welcome to."

Still smiling, Lane rolled a cigarette and lit up. "That'd be something, wouldn't it?"

"Are you interested?"

"In being your deputy? I don't know," Lane said. He smoked in silence a moment, mulling it over, and sat across from Mitchell. The sheriff's proposal came as a surprise. He was making this easier than Lane dreamed possible, but he cautioned himself not to jump too quick.

"Why me?" he asked finally.

"Why not? You've got what it takes to be a good deputy, and I need some help."

"This must be election year," Lane remarked. "How do you know I'm qualified?"

Mitchell smiled and sipped his coffee. "I know your whole life history, Devens. Hell, I know everything that goes on in this whole county. How'd you think I knew you were staying here with Abbie Maginnis?"

Lane didn't like the sound of that. How, indeed?

"So what do you say? Do you want the job, or not?"

"You haven't mentioned how much it pays."

"Seventy-five a month," Mitchell answered. "Plus fines . . . and maybe some other benefits, as well," he added slyly, "but we'll talk about that later."

"Give me a day to think about it."

Mitchell nodded, ran his fingers through his hair, and put on his hat. "That sounds fair enough."

The two men rose and shook hands, and Lane walked the sheriff to the door.

"By the way," Mitchell said, "didn't you say you used to work for Robert Cates?"

Lane nodded. "Several years ago, yeah."

"I guess you heard he was murdered."

"What?"

"You didn't know?" Mitchell took out his pocket knife and cut a red rose from Abbie's bush growing near the front door. Smelling it, he looked over at Lane. "Man, where've you been? Hidin' under a rock? It's all over town."

"When was he killed?"

Mitchell shrugged. "We found his body day before yesterday, but he'd been dead a little while."

"Do you know who did it?"

"Regino Vega. I arrested him the same day."

Stunned, Lane stared at him a moment, then shook his head. "Not Gino. You've got the wrong man."

"Why do you say that?"

"I've known Gino Vega practically my whole life," Lane said. "He didn't kill Cates."

Mitchell carefully tucked the rose into the buttonhole on the lapel of his suit coat and stepped in front of one of the windows to study his reflection. Satisfied, he looked at Lane and smiled. "If Vega didn't do it, then tell me one thing. How'd his bloodstained knife get to the murder scene? Sprout legs and walk?"

CHAPTER THIRTEEN

In open defiance of City Ordinance Number 44, Sections 11 and 15, a mob of angry Mexicans armed with everything from rifles and shotguns to pitchforks and rocks was gathered in front of the courthouse's west entrance, shouting insults at the sheriff and anyone else who poked his head out the door. Watching them from across the street, Lane was amazed that Regino Vega had so many loyal friends.

He had arrived a little after eight o'clock, in time to see the work detail shuffle down the street in their chains and dirty, white uniforms. He had searched each prisoner's face, looking for Regino. His friend hadn't been among them. For security purposes, Regino was being kept under lock and key inside his cell, no visitors allowed.

That Regino had been framed for murder was a cinch, and Lane had a pretty good idea who was behind it. But why? Mariano Diego had assured him that the only man to openly accuse the sheriff and county supervisors of wrongdoing was Robert Cates. Now Cates was dead. Was it simply coincidence that Regino had been chosen to take the fall, or did Nimitz and Carrillo suspect that he also knew more than he was supposed to and decide to eliminate two problems with one stroke?

Trying to think how to get inside to see Regino, Lane leaned against the adobe wall bordering the opposite side of Court Street and watched the show.

The chief of police and five or six of his fellow men in blue had blocked off the streets surrounding the courthouse and were trying to keep matters under control. Mitchell and his deputies, however, were keeping a low profile. Lane didn't blame them.

A man's white, mustached face appeared in one of the second story windows, possibly Mitchell, and someone down below yelled and threw an empty whiskey bottle. The bottle barely missed hitting the window, struck the side of the building instead, and shattered. Fragments of glass tinkled against the stone walk, and gusty whoops of delight swept the crowd. Early morning drinkers slugged down their tequila and mescal and followed suit, hurling empty bottles at the courthouse. A well-aimed rock crashed through the same window at which Sheriff Mitchell had been standing only moments ago.

Lane figured it would be just a matter of time before bullets started flying, as well, and taking a long drag on his cigarette, he pushed away from the wall and sauntered up the street and out of the line of fire. The police chief, obviously fearing the same, was making a few arrests, slapping handcuffs on anyone who appeared to be drunk on something other than anger and hauling them off to the city jail. Lane saw two of Jim Mitchell's deputies hurrying toward the mob with their guns drawn.

Crossing the narrow street where it intersected with that of Ott, Lane vaulted the picket fence surrounding the courthouse, cut across to the corner of the jail yard, and slipped out of sight just as a brief exchange of gunfire exploded behind him.

While the rioters kept the law busy on the west side, Lane circled around to the east. He hugged the side of the building, trailing the fingers of his right hand along the wall and ducking low whenever he passed by a window. He tried the east door and wasn't surprised to find it locked.

In a quandary, he gazed at the door a moment, then glanced up the street when he heard the dull roar of running horses. The sound grew louder, and a loosely bunched group of horsemen presently swung into view. They were dressed in blue with yellow stripes up the sides of their pants legs and a red and white guidon waved in the wind and dust. It was with something of a shock that Lane realized why they were here. Matters must be worse than he had thought if the army was getting involved.

He watched as Troop A split up at the intersection of Ott and North Church streets and recognized Lieutenant Kirk Mallory. Their gazes met a split-second before Mallory's detachment thundered past, and in that fleeting instant, Lane saw the same bloodthirsty look in the lieutenant's eyes he had seen from time to time while under his command. Whomever had sent word to Fort Lowe for assistance evidently hadn't counted on the likes of Kirk Mallory. He tended to stir up more trouble than he settled.

As if to punctuate Lane's thoughts, another burst of gunfire erupted on the west side of the courthouse. Taking advantage of the disturbance, Lane drew his .45 from his waistband, shouted a warning to anyone who might be standing in the hallway on the other side of the door, and emptied four rounds into the area surrounding the keyhole plate and lock. The wood cracked and splintered, and after three tries, he managed to kick the door open. It banged hard against the wall, and he stepped inside.

A woman's pale, frightened face appeared in the doorway of the treasurer's office, and Lane tipped his hat and favored her with a lopsided grin.

"Better prop that busted door shut," he said. "This old

courthouse don't need no more hot air than it's already got."

Not impressed by his attempt at humor, she gave him a strange look and quickly retreated back into the safety of the office.

Lane walked down the hall, reloading his gun as he went, and paused near the stairway. He could hear voices above him on the second floor, and outside there were muffled sounds of shouting men and popping guns. Aware of the jingle of his spurs, he unbuckled them before continuing down the hall and turning the corner, quietly making his way toward the back of the courthouse, past the water closet and the guards' cramped cubicle to the jail.

There were two blocks of cells on the jail's ground floor, a dozen cells in all, each one measuring five feet by twelve—sixty square feet of stone and iron. Jailed here briefly when he was eighteen, Lane noticed no improvements, still just as dark, gloomy, and malodorous as ever. It was also empty.

Thinking Regino must be in one of the cells on the second floor, Lane left the jail and walked to the end of the corridor where there was a flight of stairs. He had his foot on the first step when a man's voice echoed up and down the narrow passageway.

"Hey, fella, you're not supposed to be in here." A greasy-haired man with watery, bloodshot eyes stood looking at him, frowning slightly. "How'd you get in here?"

Lane smiled, shrugged, and played dumb. "The door."

"The doors are all locked. I checked 'em myself."

"Better check again," Lane said. "The east door's wide open."

The jailer drew closer, squinting at him in the dim light. Lane returned the scrutiny. He had half a mind to tap him on the noggin with the butt of his revolver but decided against it when he didn't see any cell keys hanging from his belt.

"Look here, fella," the jailer said, "I don't know who you are, but you're gonna have to leave. I got orders to keep everybody out."

"Even the sheriff's deputies?"

"Huh?"

Lane laughed softly. "Hell, man, I'm sorry. Jim must not have told you. I'm Lane Devens, the new deputy. He swore me in this morning." Lane thrust out his hand and pumped the jailer's clammy one with overzealous alacrity. "Pleased to meet you, Mister . . ."

"Waller. Floyd Waller."

"Mr. Waller. Say, you'd better see about that east door. We sure wouldn't want any of that crazy mob outside to get in here."

Raising his hand in a parting farewell, Lane turned and headed up the stairs. At the top, he lingered a moment to make sure Waller wasn't entertaining any thoughts of following him and wondered if there were more jailers on duty. The next one might not be so easy to bluff.

When Waller didn't show, Lane walked down the long corridor to the jail entrance. The jail upstairs was an exact duplicate of the one below, with a cellblock on either side of the room and a wide passageway in between. Lane cast a swift glance inside and spotted Regino Vega sitting alone on his pallet in one of the cells nearest the door.

Seeing Lane, he jumped to his feet and met him at the bars. "*Por Díos,* it's good to see a friendly face! How did you get in?"

"The question is, how did you?"

Regino shook his head, the anger and humiliation showing plainly on his face. Unshaven, dirty, disgusted, he hadn't been sleeping well, and he looked it.

"They set me up," he said, spitting the words. "I didn't kill Cates."

"Who did? Mitchell?"

"Listen, I got a story to tell you." Regino rested his forearms on one of the crossbars. "Do you have any smokes?"

Lane handed him a book of brown cigarette papers, several matches, and a small muslin sack of Bull Durham tobacco. "Keep it," he said. "Now what happened?"

"You're right about Jim Mitchell. He killed Cates. I'm sure of it," Regino said. "Two weeks ago, there was a big *fandango* here in town. Much dancing, much more drinking. Some of us were arrested for shooting off our guns." He paused to light his cigarette and gazed past Lane at the square of pale-blue freedom showing through a barred window in the opposite cellblock. "There wasn't room for all of us in the city lock-up, so the police chief left me and a couple others in here to dry out. I said some things I shouldn't have to one of the deputies . . . What's his name?" He snapped his fingers, trying to remember. "Charlie Reed. I told this Reed *hombre* how he was the one ought to be in jail. Him and the sheriff and Arizona Land and Development. That's why they framed me."

Lane frowned. "They know you're wise to their crooked business dealings."

"I think so." Regino sighed, shaking his head. "When they let me go, I asked Mitchell where was my knife, and he told me he couldn't find it. The sneaky *cabrón* already had this all planned out."

"Well, I'll say one thing. He's a damned accomplished liar. He almost had me believing you were guilty."

Regino gave him a sharp look. "You've talked to Mitchell?"

"This morning. He stopped by the house, told me you killed Robert Cates."

"You shouldn't let on that we're friends," Regino said, and he suddenly looked worried. "In fact, you shouldn't be here now. You'll blow your cover."

"Forget that." Lane kicked at the bars. "Give me a day or two, and I'll break you out of here."

Regino's face brightened momentarily. The idea was tempting.

"I'll get Luz and the kids on a southbound stage to Mexico, and you can join them later," Lane said.

"But this is our home," Regino protested. "Not Mexico."

Lane thought a minute. "Do you remember Crazy Eye?" he asked finally.

"The Apache who speaks better Spanish than I do?" Regino smiled halfheartedly. "How could I forget him?"

"He's holed up with his family in the Catarinas. You could stay there for a while."

Regino suddenly made a decision. "I won't run, Lane. And I won't allow you to bust me out. You have a job to do."

"If you stay here, they'll hang you."

"Then so be it." Regino pressed his face against the bars. "You wouldn't be able to break me out anyway. They keep a close watch over me. This is the longest they've left me unguarded since I've been here." He suddenly smiled. "Because of my *amigos* outside the courthouse, I guess. Did you know Jim Mitchell won't even let me share a cell with the other prisoners? At night when they come in from work, the deputies lock me up in a little room by myself so I can't talk to nobody."

Lane glanced over his shoulder, listened for footsteps, and turned back to Regino. "Mitchell offered me a job as deputy this morning."

Regino's brows lifted. "Really?"

"Yeah. I guess I'll take it, maybe try to keep an eye on you, make sure they don't lynch you before the trial."

"You do that."

"I could give you my gun."

"No," Regino said, his voice firm. "If I had to shoot somebody, I really would be in a mess. Just go talk to Doc Udall. He'll know what to do. You have . . ."

Lane lifted a hand, silencing him, his head canted a little to the side, listening. The sound of boots clumping on the back stairway reached his ears, and he swiftly moved away from Regino's cell to the jail entrance. He could hear men's voices in the corridor outside.

Trying to think how to handle this, he glanced at Regino. "Pretend your sick," he whispered.

"Wha . . ."

"Lay down. Pretend you're sick."

It was an odd request, but Regino dropped to the floor without further delay and curled up on his hard, narrow pallet, hugging his stomach. Lane watched him and was satisfied.

The first man to enter the jail was Mitchell's undersheriff, a hulking man with a bullish neck and a florid, square face topped by straight, pale yellow hair. This would be Charlie Reed. He was followed by the jailer, Floyd Waller. Both had their guns drawn.

Reed threw a look at Regino, then swung back around to face Lane. "Who are you?" he demanded.

"No time for that," Lane said. "You'd better get a doctor in here to take a look at your prisoner. He's pretty bad off."

"What happened?" Waller asked.

"I don't know. That's just how I found him."

Reed tapped on the bars with his gun. "Hey, Mex! Look at me! What's the matter?"

Regino moaned.

Floyd Waller shook his head, genuinely concerned. "I told the sheriff yesterday they was feeding the prisoners spoiled meat. I bet that's why he's ailing."

"He'll get over it," Reed snapped.

"Well . . ." Waller holstered his gun and took a few uncertain, shuffling steps toward the door. "I'd better fetch Doc Udall. Just to be safe."

Reed waved him out the door and jabbed a thick finger at Lane. "You come with me."

Lane eyed him coolly. "Where to?"

"Mitchell's office."

Nodding, Lane preceded Charlie Reed out of the jail, and the two men walked along the corridor and down the stairs. Taciturn, unfriendly, Reed didn't say a word and neither did Lane. The sheriff could talk enough for them both.

Sure enough, the first thing they heard on reaching the main hallway was Mitchell's angry voice. The office door was open, and Reed ushered Lane inside.

"I want you to find out who the son of a bitch was that called in the damned cavalry!" Mitchell stormed. He was talking to the deputy, Del Hardy. "One man dead, four wounded! That's what happens when the army pokes its nose into civilian affairs!"

Hardy shrugged. "I figgered you'd be glad to see 'em, Jim."

"Not when it makes me look bad."

"Well, at least they got them hotheads under control. I knew derned well it was gonna come to this sooner or later. Didn't I tell you . . ."

He stopped, following Mitchell's gaze to the door.

"Come on in, Devens," Mitchell said. His mood seemed to lighten unexpectedly. "Have a seat. Make yourself comfortable."

"Found him upstairs with Vega," Reed said.

The sheriff's eyes narrowed. He watched Lane sit down and start to buckle on his spurs. "You two have a nice chat?"

Lane shook his head. "He was sick. Too sick to talk."

"Sick?" The sheriff looked at Reed, and when the big man nodded, he turned back to Lane. "Don't waste any pity on Regino Vega. He's nothing but a cold-blooded killer, not to mention a thief."

Lane stretched his legs out in front of him, relaxed, and met the sheriff's curious gaze. "You really believe that?"

"Don't you? Given the evidence against him?"

Lane shrugged. "I'll wait until after his trial to decide."

"Innocent until proven guilty, eh? All right." Jim Mitchell laughed, as if he hadn't a worry in the world. "You didn't come here to talk about Vega, I bet."

Lane smiled and nodded at Charlie Reed. "Actually, it was his idea I come see you. But I guess while I'm here, I might as well accept that job you offered me this morning."

"What job?" Reed asked, scowling now, staring at Lane balefully.

Mitchell ignored him. He reached inside a drawer and flipped something across his desk to Lane. It was a shiny, nickel-plated badge. Engraved into it were the words: DEPUTY SHERIFF, HOHOKAM COUNTY.

"Welcome to the club, Devens." Mitchell leaned back in his chair and clasped his hands behind his head, still grinning. "You can buy the county a brand new door with your first paycheck."

CHAPTER FOURTEEN

Lane's first day on the job was an educational one. Working closely with Jim Mitchell and knowing his dirty little secrets at the same time, he saw his earlier impression of the man crumble. What took its place was difficult to put a label on.

Mitchell's kaleidoscopic personality kept everyone he worked with in a constant state of confusion and left Lane completely nonplussed. It soon became apparent to Lane that the sheriff's character changed with the elements. He simply whisked along in whichever direction the wind was blowing and never stood on principle since he didn't appear to have any.

The one thing Lane was a hundred percent sure of was that behind Jim Mitchell's dandified facade was a dirty rat.

Twenty minutes following the sheriff's vociferous indignation over the army's involvement in this morning's uprising, he was joking and laughing his head off about the whole ordeal. Del Hardy later investigated the matter and reported that it was none other than George Nimitz who had called in the troops. Mitchell at first seemed surprised, then bored, and ended up bawling Hardy out for wasting his time with trivialities when the hapless deputy had simply been following orders.

Today, important work to Jim Mitchell was not restoring the peace, but rather it was arguing with city officials as to whom had custody over the Mexicans arrested during the riot. Given the fact that it was county property that had been damaged, Jim insisted the prisoners belonged to him. Childishly, he ranted about it until he finally got his way, and Lane helped escort seventeen men to the county jail.

Why Mitchell wanted the prisoners so badly, Lane couldn't guess. Was it to make him look good in the eyes of the public, or was there more to it than that? Through the leasing program, the county was making money off the prisoners, but unless Mitchell was profiting personally from it, Lane couldn't see why he'd go to so much trouble to get these seventeen men transferred. The jail was already overcrowded as it was.

One of the prisoners, a short, swarthy man with sad eyes and a fresh cut on his forehead, staggered a little as he was being ushered into a cell, and Lane caught him by the arm.

"Hey, fella, you all right? *¿Qué, tienes?*"

The Mexican looked up at him and touched a hand to his forehead, as if he just now noticed he was bleeding. *"No tengo nada,"* he said hoarsely, passing it off. "I'm fine." His melancholy gaze settled on the badge pinned to Lane's vest. "Is it true you've sided against us?"

"No." Lane glanced over his shoulder to make sure Hardy and Reed weren't watching and spoke quietly in Spanish. "Tell your friends not to worry. Tell them Mitchell will pay for what he has done to you and Regino."

"Devens, this ain't no social gathering." Charlie Reed pushed Lane aside with the back of his hand and shoved the Mexican roughly into his cell, sending him sprawling to the floor. "No talking to the prisoners," he grumbled and slammed the door shut.

"Next time I see you knock down some man who's twice your age and half your size," Lane said, "I'll kick your ass clean out of this county."

His voice was soft, matter-of-fact, his face void of expression. Surprised, Reed turned to look at him.

"What?"

"You heard me."

Reed's eyes half-closed, a pair of azure slots in a red face. At the prospect of a fight, the prisoners' voices dropped to hushed whispers as bets were placed. Charlie Reed's gaze flicked down to the holstered six-gun snugged low on Lane's right thigh.

"You're a touchy bastard, ain't you, Devens?"

"I don't like bullies," Lane replied. "You've been warned."

Del Hardy stepped between them. "Come on, Charlie. Like it or not, he's one of us now, and Jim don't like us fightin' amongst ourselves, you know."

"He'll never be one of us," Reed muttered, and turning his back on them, he lumbered out of the jail.

Lane caught the double meaning of his remark and knew he was right. He could never fit in. Even if he wanted to.

Lane and Del left the jail together and walked down the corridor, Del hurrying to keep up with Lane's long strides. Rather short with broad shoulders and a wide butt, the deputy had the makings of a fat man, but Mitchell generally kept him on his toes, so he didn't sit still long enough to gain weight. He was twenty-two years old, barely old enough to vote for his boss, and wore his badge in the same self-conscious manner that he wore his gun. Though not overly bright, he likely would have made a good lawman under the right circumstances, but Lane had a feeling he was already too soiled by the sheriff to ever come clean again.

"Don't mind Charlie," Hardy said suddenly. "He's got a chip on his shoulder, is all."

"I sort of gathered that."

"Jim's already warned him not to brace you, not with guns anyway. Heck, you'd nail poor Charlie 'fore he could even clear leather."

Lane glanced sideways at the redhead, left eyebrow cocked up slightly. "What makes you think that?"

Hardy gave him a dopey smile. "Just a hunch," he said and changed the subject. "Jim must think you're something special. He's got other deputies, you know, over in Wilmot, Rillito, and Tubac, but it's the ones he keeps with him here in Penny Town that's his favorites. The pay's better, too."

"Since you're one of his favorites, I guess he confides in you a lot, huh?"

"Derned right he does."

"Then you must know why he wanted responsibility of those seventeen prisoners so bad," Lane presumed.

"Sure. The county leases 'em out to the mining companies. The more prisoners there are, the more money we get."

"We?" Lane glanced at Hardy, smiling slyly, and winked. "Meaning the county or Jim Mitchell?"

Hardy returned his grin. "You got a suspicious mind."

"Not really," Lane replied. "All I'm saying is that in a tough job like this, I figure a man deserves a little something extra if he can get it."

Brow furrowed in thought, Del chewed his fingernails and didn't reply. They walked down the hall in silence, and Lane had almost decided he'd read the young deputy wrong when Del Hardy suddenly nudged him and drew him aside. He glanced up and down the hall before turning back to Lane.

"What makes you think Jim's pocketing the lease money?"

Lane shrugged and flicked the ash from his cigarette, the picture of nonchalance. "It's what I would do," he said simply.

"Well, you're not slow, I'll give you that," Hardy marveled. "You hit the nail square on the head."

Lane nodded. "Figured as much. Mitchell's got brains. How does he get around the county board?"

"Oh, that's easy," Hardy said. "We—Jim, Charlie, and me, that is—have done some favors for a couple of the supervisors. One way they pay us back is to give Jim forty percent of the lease money."

"Mitchell give you and Reed a pretty good cut of that?" Lane asked.

"Pretty good," Hardy admitted. "Jim'll let you in on it, too, fairly soon, I reckon. Until then, you better keep mum about what I just told you. Jim might not like it."

"No problem," Lane said with a smile.

Del Hardy's revelation didn't surprise him. What did surprise Lane was the ease with which he had extracted the information from him. Hardy, much like his boss, had a bad case of diarrhea of the mouth, and Lane couldn't have been happier.

When the work detail returned late that afternoon, Lane waited for the guards to leave and discreetly questioned some of the prisoners. It quickly became apparent that conditions here were even worse than he had suspected.

Through the leasing system, an inmate was required to work off his fine at sixty cents a day. Once the fine was paid or the sentence served, he was free to go. Many of the prisoners Lane spoke with had, however, been on the chain gang for weeks, even months, without the vaguest notion as to why they had even been arrested in the first place. Most of these same prisoners hadn't even talked to a lawyer.

Lane now understood why the majority of the inmates were either Mexican or Indian. It had little to do with their inability to afford their fines and a great deal to do with their unfamiliarity with the Sixth Amendment. Speaking little or no English, they had no way of knowing their rights or that there was even due process of law, and the county was making money off their ignorance.

Calculation with pencil and paper gave Lane a rough idea of how much these men were worth to Jim Mitchell. There were fifty-one prisoners housed in the county jail at the present time. Working for the mining companies at sixty cents a day per man, they would bring in close to eight hundred dollars in a month, with a little over three hundred of that going into the sheriff's pocket. That, of course, wasn't counting Mitchell's regular salary and whatever else Estevan Carrillo and George Nimitz were shelling out to him on the sly.

For a man accustomed to making between thirty and sixty dollars a month, these numbers were staggering, and the injustice of it even more so.

That same evening, Lane and Del Hardy left the courthouse to make a final round of the town before heading home. The streets were almost too quiet, and Lane wondered how long it would last. The killing of the Mexican rioter this morning by one of the soldiers and the arrests made by both the police and sheriff's deputies had put only a temporary lid on a pot of hot tempers. Until Sheriff Mitchell and Arizona Land and Development stopped stoking the fire, the pot would continue to boil over.

Troop A was still patrolling the town, armed and vigilant, and adding to the unease of the citizens. Martial law was a bitter pill for most people, and the fact that George Nimitz had called on both the territorial governor and Fort Lowe's commanding officer for assistance was, in Lane's viewpoint at least, one more example of the man's power and influence. He and Estevan Carrillo were like little gods, the supreme rulers of Hohokam County.

Lane and Del sat their horses on a narrow side street called Maiden Lane, not far from the Red Light District, and decided to call it a day.

"Not much need for us with the soldiers here," Hardy commented. He looked across at Lane and grinned. "Me and Charlie figured we'd meet at Big Fay's and catch up a couple of them painted girls, have us a little fun. You want to come?"

"If you're going to Fay's, you're liable to catch something besides a girl," Lane said.

"Aw, heck. They ain't any worse than Ab . . ." Hardy hesitated, catching the sudden glint in Lane's eye, and wisely decided not to finish that sentence. Gathering the reins into his right hand, he walked his horse up the street. "See you tomorrow, Devens."

Anxious to go home, Lane stopped by Rosel's and found the restaurant empty except for Abbie and another waitress. They were preparing to close up for the night. Seth Maginnis, absorbed in a dime novel and a piece of apple cobbler, was sitting at a table by the window, and Lane was about to tell him to unlock the door when Abbie stepped outside for a breath of fresh air. It had been a long day, and her face looked tired even in the poor light of the street lamp. Standing downwind of her, Lane could smell fried chicken and coffee.

She saw him and brushed the damp, stray wisps of hair from her forehead. "It's about time you showed up. I was beginning to wonder." Standing on her tiptoes, she wrapped her arms around his neck, and her lips made a smacking sound against his. "How was your day, lover? Or should I call you deputy?"

Lane managed to disentangle himself from her and tried to ignore the stares they drew from the few people on the street. Kissing was all right behind closed doors, but being with Abbie in public made him uncomfortable. It revealed a softer, more vulnerable side of him that he preferred to keep tucked out of sight.

She laughed, not the least bit bothered. "I couldn't believe it when I heard the news," she said. "You told me one time you'd never wear a badge."

"How'd you find out?"

"Are you kidding? Everybody's talking about you. You and this morning's ruckus at the courthouse. That reminds me—Dr. Udall dropped by about an hour ago and told me he needed to talk to you."

"Did he say what about?"

"Uh-uh, but since you don't look sick I assume you can wait until tomorrow to find out, can't you?"

"Better not," Lane said. "Will you be all right, walking home alone?"

Abbie rolled her eyes. "How do you think I walk home when you're not around?"

"I don't know." Lane regarded her curiously, wishing he could see past the blasé look in her eyes and know what she was thinking. His anger over the gloves he had found in her bedroom had dulled somewhat since this morning, but the hurt was still sharp as ever. "You don't always go home by yourself, Abbie," he said after a moment.

"Well, of course not. I have Seth." She winked at him and turned away, skirts rustling with the swing of her hips. At the door, she paused to look back at him. "Hurry home, Deputy."

Lane watched her go inside, listened to the tinkling of the bells on the restaurant door, and slowly walked back to his horse. He wondered how he could feel so sure of himself around men like Jim Mitchell, Charlie Reed, and Mariano Diego, yet fall to pieces around a little five-foot-two woman like Abbie Maginnis. It just didn't make sense.

CHAPTER FIFTEEN

Doc Udall was sitting with his back to the roll-top desk, enjoying his pipe and going over his latest coroner's report, when a knock on the office door suddenly jolted him out of his meditation. Sighing, he peered over steel frame spectacles at the door.

"Come in!"

Hat pushed off his forehead, Lane Devens stepped inside, glanced swiftly around the room, and closed the door. He paused, hand still resting on the knob, and looked across at Doc.

"Abbie said you wanted to see me."

Doc nodded and waved him in, motioning him toward the only other armchair in the office besides his own. "Have a seat, Lane. I've been waiting for you." He opened a drawer of the roll-top and took out a full bottle of whiskey and two shot glasses. "Care for a drink?"

Lane hesitated a moment, then nodded and sat down.

"I didn't know if you'd come tonight or not," Doc said, pouring their drinks. "I hope no one followed you."

"I doubt it. Mitchell's playing poker on Congress Street, and Del Hardy and Charlie Reed were looking forward to some horizontal refreshments."

Doc smiled at the choice of words.

"I left my horse up the alley a ways, though, just in case," Lane added and sipped his whiskey.

"You can never be too careful," Doc agreed.

He studied the young man guardedly, pleased with his and Mariano Diego's decision to hire him. Complicated and stubborn he might be, but that deputy's badge more than made up for the bad points. It was starting to look as if Lane Devens would be worth the six thousand dollars, after all.

Suddenly remembering that Lane's mother was one of his patients, Doc inquired about her health.

"I saw R.J. in town yesterday," Lane replied. "He told me Ma's up and around."

"Good, good. She'll be getting her strength back soon, I'm sure," Doc said. "Just so long as she doesn't overdo it." He leaned back in his chair, crossed his legs, and pulled on his pipe. "I've always admired your mother. She's never lost her pride."

"Why should she?"

Doc cast a quick look at him and frowned, wishing now he hadn't said anything. He warned himself to choose his words carefully.

"Unfair though it is, there's always been a stigma attached to women whose pasts are similar to that of your mother's." He paused, hoping his discomfort wasn't too obvious. "Ann doesn't seem to have let that stand in her way."

Eyes lowered, Lane took another sip of whiskey, and when he spoke, his voice was mild. "You didn't call me here to talk about my mother."

"No. No, you're right. I didn't." Doc picked up the coroner's report he had been reading earlier, and his face grew more serious. "Mariano Diego and I are very pleased with the progress you've made so far, my boy, but I'm afraid we have a new riddle to solve."

"Like who killed Robert Cates?"

"Precisely." He tucked the report inside its folder and tossed it into Lane's lap. "I examined Robert's body. Those are my findings."

He watched Lane's face as he scanned the report, saw his eyebrows raise in surprise, and smiled to himself. It was an understandable reaction.

Lane glanced up at him. "Is this the truth?"

Doc nodded.

"Holy Mary."

Turning the page, Lane returned his attention to the report, and Doc felt a sense of relief. His examination of Cates and later conclusion as to the cause of death were sure to bring him grief before this situation was over, and he didn't care to face it alone.

Doc was of the opinion that Robert Cates had, in a sense, been murdered twice. While Sheriff Mitchell seemed positive that it was the stab wound that had killed Cates, an external examination of the body had revealed several inconsistencies. Doc had found traces of dried vomit behind Cates' left ear and in his hairline, a smear of bloody feces on his right buttock, and oddly, his boots were on the wrong feet.

It was the stab wound itself, however, that gave Doc the best indication that Robert Cates had already been dead when someone knifed him. Once his heart stopped pumping, gravity drew the blood to the underside of his body where it stagnated and clotted within the blood vessels. This explained why there was little blood around the stab wound. Cates' blood had already ceased to flow.

Thinking this, Doc stroked his thick, white mustache and blew his breath out in a heavy gust. His inquest into Robert Cates' death had been one of the least pleasant tasks of his career, not only because the man happened to be a friend, but because of the decomposing state of the body. The reek of human mortality seemed to have settled in his mustache.

"I may have to shave it off," he mumbled and sadly twisted the ends into sharp points.

Lane looked up from the report. "Huh?"

"Oh, nothing." He sighed again and drained his glass. "So what do you think?"

"I think you've got a lot of guts, Doc."

"A lot of guts and no brains. Have another drink."

Lane lifted a hand, shaking his head. "I've had enough." He regarded Doc with new respect. "Who all's read this?"

"I had my secretary write out several copies. I delivered one to the district attorney this afternoon, and reporters from both the *Arizona Star* and *Las Fronteras* newspapers have interviewed me today, so the cat's definitely out of the bag." He poured himself a second shot of whiskey and returned the bottle to its drawer. "I gave a copy to our esteemed sheriff, but he was too busy yakking to look at it."

"You really think Cates was poisoned?"

"All the facts point to that conclusion. Robert's stomach was badly inflamed. Not only that, but I believe he was murdered in his own home. There were carpet fibers on his shirt, the same color as the carpet in his house, and Robert wouldn't roll around on the floor or put his boots on the opposite feet. Somebody poisoned him and then tried to make it look like he was stabbed and robbed."

Lane idly stroked his jaw with a forefinger. "Mitchell, Nimitz, and Carrillo had reason to want Cates dead."

"That's true," Doc agreed. "I just hope Christina didn't have anything to do with this."

"Who?"

"Christina Cates."

Lane stared at him for almost a full minute, obviously surprised, then reflective, and it was his soft, amused laughter that finally broke the silence.

"I'll be damned."

Doc frowned. "What's so funny?"

Lane leaned toward him, elbows resting on his knees, and told him about his first meeting with Jim Mitchell and Christina Cates that blustery Saturday morning in the foothills of the Catarinas. As Doc listened attentively, regret filled his eyes.

"Poor, sweet Christina," he lamented.

"Sweet, my ass!" Lane burst out. "She's probably part of the reason why Gino Vega's stuck in jail."

Doc slowly nodded his head. Lane might very well be right. Hadn't he feared that something like this would happen? Many times Robert Cates had called on him to tend his wife's cracked ribs, broken fingers, broken arms, her many cuts and bruises. Doc had heard all the excuses. He remembered the time a year ago when Christina supposedly fell down the stairs and lost her baby. According to Robert, the poor woman could trip over a pencil mark.

Doc felt the pain of his own guilt. As the Cates' friend and physician, he knew he should have confronted Robert, tried to reason with him, help him, help his wife. Instead, he had placed a bandage on the unhealthy situation and pushed it out of his mind. The wound, meanwhile, had continued to fester.

Now it appeared Christina was caught up in something as equally unpleasant as her marriage had been. Why else would she have been with Mitchell that morning? A glib-tongued ladies' man, the sheriff had probably wormed his way into her life with the intent of gaining her trust and cooperation. Doc wanted to believe that it was Mitchell's idea to kill Robert Cates and not Christina's.

"If you're so fond of Cates' wife, maybe you should have a talk with her," Lane suggested.

His depression deepening, Doc's round, stooped shoulders lifted and fell. "I wish there were some way of keeping her out of this. She's been hurt enough."

"She should've thought of that beforehand."

Doc studied Lane from beneath gathered brows. He was an unsympathetic cuss. Yet if Christina had, indeed, aided Mitchell in the murder of her husband, shouldn't she be punished? Doc didn't know, but an innocent man waited 'neath the shadow of the gallows while the real killer remained free.

"This district attorney," Lane said. "Is he honest?"

"He's George Nimitz's brother-in-law."

Lane swore.

"I know, but it's not entirely hopeless. Except for the knife Mitchell found at the murder scene, all the evidence so far is in Regino's favor. If the prosecution doesn't drop the charges, I have a feeling Judge Finnerty will dismiss the case himself."

"Gino needs a lawyer."

Doc smiled. "As of today, he has one. I wired an attorney in Globe the day Regino was arrested. He arrived here today on the noon train and has already had a lengthy conversation with both Regino and myself. He knows everything."

"You told him about me?" Lane asked, frowning.

"I had to. I felt he should have a clear picture."

Lane rose and paced a restless circle around the tiny office, moving with an animal-like grace, spurs softly chinging with each step. He paused in front of the dusty bookcase, his back to Doc, and absently scanned the titles before turning to look at him.

"What happens when this attorney of yours spills the beans?"

"He won't," Doc promised. "I guarantee it. Ned Owens is a good man. He's as outraged by this whole mess as we are."

Lane was dubious. "So was Regino, and you see what happened. He got to drinking, got a loose tongue, and now his tail's in a crack. Ours will be, too, if Owens opens his mouth before we're ready."

"I assure you, he won't," Doc insisted. "You're going to have to trust him, Lane. Together, we'll bring Arizona Land and Development to justice."

"As much justice as money can buy," Lane murmured.

Doc loosened his necktie and rested his head against the back of his chair, watching Lane stare out the window at nothing. "For such a young man," he said, "you're very cynical."

"You would be, too, if you were Jim Mitchell's deputy."

Doc chuckled. "Probably so. How was your first day on the job? Did you find out anything of importance?"

"Yeah." Lane glanced over his shoulder at him. "I know how the supervisors are paying Mitchell off."

Doc's eyes lit up with interest.

Dragging a hand down his face, Lane sat across from Doc again and gave him a concise rundown of his conversations with several of the prisoners and with Del Hardy. Doc found it difficult to believe that this had been going on under his very nose all the time. Lane drew a folded piece of paper from his vest pocket showing the actual dollar figures and summed it up for him with characteristic candor.

"Nimitz and Carrillo get their land, Mitchell gets his three-hundred-dollar monthly payoff, and the poor man gets to dig ditches," he concluded.

Doc shook his head, studying Lane's penciled calculations. "This is absurd."

"You're damned right it is."

"Do you think you can keep pumping Hardy for information without his getting suspicious?"

Lane nodded.

"Good." Doc took off his spectacles and rubbed his eyes. "He may end up being the stool pigeon we've needed all along. Be sure and write down the names of the prisoners you talked to today. I think Ned Owens will be interested in what they have to say when this finally goes to court."

Lane pointed to the paper in Doc's hand. "Look on the back."

Flipping the paper over, Doc saw a list of names and smiled. No wonder Robert Cates had spoken highly of Devens. When he did a job, he did it right. What was more, he could read, write, and figure. Doc was suddenly struck by the realization that Lane Devens would make a perfect replacement for Jim Mitchell as sheriff, but the possibility of that happening was almost nil. The Indian blood in his veins would surely destroy any chance he might have of gaining popularity with the voters.

When Lane put on his hat and stood up to leave, Doc rose also and walked him to the door.

"I'll tell Mariano about our visit," he said, clapping Lane on the shoulder. "I guess with Regino in jail, you'll have to check in with me from now on."

"He'd better not be in jail for long."

"His hearing's set for sometime next week. Ned will see to it that he gets a fair shake, Lane. In the meantime, you watch yourself. Don't take any unnecessary chances."

Lane looked at him and grinned. "You're the one taking the chances," he said and opened the door. "Watch your back, old man."

He slipped into the night and was gone.

Still standing by the door, Doc drew a deep breath and stuffed his hands into his trouser pockets. Old man. He snorted in disdain.

CHAPTER SIXTEEN

They called it the Hole. Small, dark, and bare with no windows or any other necessary creature comforts, the Hole was Regino Vega's new home, and he had visitors tonight.

There was hardly room for them all—Charlie Reed, Del Hardy, and Vega—so Jim stood in the doorway with the jailer and watched. Blinking in the sudden light, Vega shaded his eyes with his hand and pushed himself to his feet as Charlie hung the lantern on a nail.

"Open those sleepy eyes, Paco," Jim sang out.

Suffering from hay fever, Floyd Waller, the jailer, sneezed several times and blew his nose with a bubbly roar. Jim glanced over at him.

"You can go now, Floyd."

Waller wiped his nose and watering eyes with a soggy handkerchief. "This prisoner's been sick, Sheriff."

"Not too sick to talk to that shyster, Ned Owens, for over an hour."

Waller shrugged. "The half-breed fella you hired today said it might be a good idee for Doc Udall to have another look at him in the morning."

"Udall's the one who's gonna need a doctor," Del piped up. Jim shot the young deputy a warning look. "Del, did Devens go home?"

"Yep. Home to that whore of his," he answered. "That was about two hours ago."

Waller sneezed again and shook his head. “Devens didn’t go straight home. He stopped by here maybe twenty-five, thirty minutes before you all did.”

Del was shocked. “He did?”

“What’d he want?” Jim asked sharply.

“He checked on Vega.”

“They say anything?”

Waller shrugged again. “Just howdy do, how you doin’, see you tomorrow. I watched ’em the whole time.”

Jim turned his attention to Vega. “That right, Paco?”

Vega glared at him. “My name isn’t Paco.” His gaze shifted from Jim to the two deputies and back again. “What do you want?”

“We want answers, Paco.”

“I already told you I don’t know nothing.”

Without warning, Charlie stepped forward and sank a fist into Vega’s stomach.

“ ‘Thou shalt not bear false witness,’ ” Jim quoted cheerfully. “It’s bad for the soul, worse for the body.”

Vega groaned in pain, clutched his stomach with both hands, and doubled over.

“Floyd,” Jim said, “do me a favor and keep watch outside until we’re done here. I’m expecting the supervisors any minute now, but no one else. Understood?”

“Sure thing, Sheriff.”

Jim watched the jailer shuffle down the darkened hall and turned back to see Charlie eyeing him with cold disapproval.

“I don’t trust him,” he grumbled.

“Who? Waller?”

“Devens.”

Jim grinned. “Hell, Charlie, you don’t trust nobody.”

Still standing in the open doorway, he idly puffed on his cheroot and struck a pose, resting both hands on the shiny grips of his holstered six-guns, gray Stetson cocked to one side of his head. He'd practiced this particular stance before a mirror many times.

"Well, well, well, Paco," he said at last, speaking easily around the cheroot clamped between his teeth. "What d'you say we get down to brass tacks, eh?"

Vega stood with his back to the wall, a wary eye on the two deputies, and didn't reply.

"Who sent for the lawyer, Paco? One of your *amigos* down in Mex town?"

"I didn't ask."

Neither moving his feet, nor blinking an eye, Charlie slammed a massive right fist squarely into Vega's lower jaw. The back of his head bounced against the wall. Pushing himself forward, Vega balled up a fist as if to strike back, but Del stepped in and rapped him a solid blow across the knuckles with an ax handle. Vega retreated against the wall, tenderly rubbing his sore jaw.

"I'm telling you the truth," he said. "I don't know who sent for Ned Owens."

Charlie started to hit him again, but Jim raised a hand, stopping him in mid-swing. He didn't want to batter the skinny Mex if it could be avoided. Evidence of blood might cause unnecessary speculation.

"No more to the face," he said.

Charlie nodded his understanding and promptly punched Vega in the stomach again. A sharp uppercut, the blow knocked the breath from the man's lungs, and he choked and gasped for air almost a full three minutes before he finally regained partial control of his breathing. He leaned forward with his hands on his knees, mouth gaping, and concentrated on filling his lungs.

"We'll do this all night if we have to," Jim warned. "Look

at me when I'm talking to you, boy!"

Charlie grasped a handful of Vega's hair and jerked him upright while Del pressed the end of his ax handle beneath the man's chin.

"What'd you and your lawyer chat about today?" Jim asked.

Vega swallowed hard and didn't answer.

"Charlie . . ."

The big deputy banged Vega's head against the wall until his tongue loosened.

"We talked about the hearing," Vega blurted out.

"And what else?"

"If I was guilty or not."

Jim smiled. "Are you?"

Vega cursed him bitterly and struggled to free himself of Charlie's bulldog grip. Del cracked him across the knees with his improvised club, glanced over his shoulder at Jim to make sure he approved, and struck him again while Charlie held on to Vega by the hair and bashed his head repeatedly against the wall. It was a comical sight to Jim, who suddenly burst out laughing. They reminded him of two attack dogs, one of whom kept looking back at his master to make sure he was still watching.

"You killed Robert Cates!" Vega screamed. Blood trickled from a cut on his lower lip where he had accidentally bitten himself. He spat crimson saliva in Jim's direction, his body trembling with hatred, pain, and fatigue. "You killed him, you bastard!"

"Why would I kill Cates?" Jim asked softly.

Vega drew a long, slow, shuddering breath and stared past the deputies at Jim. His black eyes glinted in the lantern light, and his mouth tightened beneath the wispy mustache.

Charlie regarded Jim impatiently. "We're wasting time.

Let's finish him off," he said in a rough voice. "You know damned well he told his lawyer everything."

Jim addressed the prisoner. "Charlie here tells me that you made a very insulting remark two weeks ago about me and Arizona Land and Development. Is that true?"

"I was drunk . . ."

"Who else have you shared your opinions with, Paco? Ned Owens?"

"I didn't tell him nothing," Vega said. He wet his lips with quick darts of his tongue. "I don't know what . . ."

Charlie hit Vega in the stomach, and he moaned and slid down the wall to the floor, gasping. Jim shook his head and made a tsk tsk sound with his tongue. The man was lying, and while Jim guessed he should be concerned about it, his interrogation of Vega stemmed more from boredom than necessity. Through Robert Cates or some other do-gooder, Regino Vega had found out about his association with Arizona Land and Development, and it made sense that he would share the information with his attorney. There was no questioning that. Jim needed to shut them both up. The sooner, the better.

He realized he hadn't handled the situation well so far. Given that Vega's trial was probably months away, he hadn't considered the lawyer complication until Ned Owens appeared today, demanding to see his client. He had had no choice except to comply, and suddenly his well-laid plans for getting rid of Vega by means of the system were shot.

On top of that, there was Doc Udall's report. As it stood now, the prosecution hadn't enough evidence against Vega to be sure of a guilty verdict anyway.

It amazed him that Doc had unraveled the fine threads of his scheme so easily. His demand for a coroner's inquest had simply been to confirm that Cates was stabbed. Nothing more. Had he known the doctor planned to perform a complete autopsy, he would have kept him away from Cates.

Doc Udall wouldn't be poking around in any more dead bodies. At Jim's urging, both Nimitz and Carrillo had agreed that it was time Doc retired his scalpel for a fishing pole. As of tomorrow morning, his term as county coroner was finished.

Jim reflected that it would have saved a lot of headaches if he had ordered Vega killed days ago.

"You're right, Charlie," he said at length. "We're wasting time." He thumbed the butt of his cheroot between Regino Vega's feet. "String him up."

Del gaped at him, clearly shocked by the order. "We're gonna hang him? Right now?"

"Right now."

"There are men in this town who would pay good money to see Robert Cates' murderer hanged."

At the sound of the man's voice, Jim spun around, saw it was George Nimitz, and relaxed. Estevan Carrillo joined his partner a moment later, and the three of them stood in the doorway and watched as Charlie shook out a rope.

At one time, there had been a long, narrow window with bars in the Hole's east wall. The window had been boarded up on the outside, but the bars were still exposed on the inside. Upending the empty slop bucket, Charlie used it as a stepping stool, and reaching up, secured one end of the rope directly above the top crossbar.

Estevan Carrillo spoke quietly. "Do your deputies know that you killed Cates?"

Jim shrugged, glancing sideways at him. Both Nimitz and Carrillo had assumed he was the one who had killed Robert Cates, while Christina had merely served as his accomplice. He didn't bother to enlighten them.

"I think Charlie suspects I killed the old man," he said.

"Del's too dumb. He wouldn't suspect he needed to pee if it was running down his leg."

Carrillo chuckled, chubby cheeks swelling, almost obscuring his eyes.

George Nimitz never twitched a lip. It occurred to Jim that in his dealings with the man he had never seen him smile. Nimitz smoothed his beard and watched Charlie Reed prepare the noose. "My advice to you, Jim, is to keep the Cates woman happy," he said, "but don't grow too fond of her. We might have to eliminate her someday."

"As if I'd have trouble keeping a woman happy," Jim quipped. "That's your problem, George. Not mine."

Nimitz gave him a sour look but didn't waste his breath arguing.

Charlie Reed hauled Vega to his feet. "Step up!"

Vega stepped on the upturned bucket, almost lost his balance, and grabbed hold of the rope to keep from falling. Without waiting for further instruction, he slipped the noose over his head and snugged it around his neck, positioning the hard knot behind his left ear. Eyes lifting heavenward, his lips moved silently a moment, and then he glanced around at the faces of the men below him while Charlie tied his hands together behind his back. Vega's gaze lingered longest on the three men in suits standing in the doorway. His eyes were hard and bright and defiant.

Aware that everyone was waiting for him to give the signal, Jim delayed, drawing the withered rose from his buttonhole, slowly plucking loose one fragrant petal at a time. He smiled up at Vega.

"Any last words?"

Surprisingly, Vega grinned back at him. "Make peace with your God, Mitchell. Before this is over, you're gonna need Him. All of you."

Before Jim had time to react, Charlie Reed kicked the bucket from beneath Vega's feet, and the man plunged the short length to the end of the rope. It caught everyone off guard. Del leaped clear of his flailing legs, accidentally bumping his head on the lantern in the process, and the swinging light cast weird shadows on the walls, a play of light on dark, dark on light, with Vega's body lurching in the background. Jim could hear his breath wheezing and his boots clunking against the wall. It made him feel a little giddy. He slipped his watch from a vest pocket and checked the time to hide his discomfort.

Regino Vega fought death for six minutes before he finally strangled. His body shuddered, knees, elbows, and feet drumming the wall with staccato rapidity, and then fell limp and heavy at the rope's end.

Jim leaned against the door facing for support and drew a deep breath. His knees were strangely weak. Relieved it was over, he had started to relax when Vega's body jerked violently one last time, and Jim almost jumped out of his boots. He cast a swift look at the other men to see if they had noticed.

"Ah, man!" Del stumbled backwards and clamped his right hand over his mouth and nose. "Ah, man, look at his pants!"

Jim didn't look. He didn't have to. Del vomited in the doorway, and Jim turned and walked swiftly down the hall. Like Del, he was very near to losing his supper. Beefsteak, mashed potatoes, and gravy. He gagged as he went down the stairs.

Jim was twenty-nine years old, currently serving his second term as sheriff, and yet he'd never witnessed a hanging before tonight. The experience disgusted him. Whatever he had expected it to be like, it wasn't this.

The unfortunate possessor of a weak stomach, Jim began

to feel more like himself only after reaching his office. The hanging had unnerved him in a way he had not anticipated. He recalled that day in the desert when he had killed the Apache buck. His death had been swift and clean, and to Jim who didn't have a very high regard for Apaches, about the same as shooting a deer or antelope. He wondered if killing a white man would feel any different.

Jim suddenly grinned. He'd have to ask Christina.

"What's the joke?" Nimitz wanted to know. He walked into the office, followed by Estevan Carrillo and Charlie and sat down across from Jim.

Jim waved a hand. "Nothing important," he said and looked up at Charlie who was standing by the door. "Did you untie Vega's hands?"

He nodded, his red face showing as much emotion as a chunk of petrified wood. Jim guessed hangings didn't bother some people.

"Where's Del?"

"Cleaning puke off the floor," Charlie replied.

Carrillo coughed, politely covering his mouth, and pursed his fat lips in a way that reminded Jim of a sucker fish.

"Vega hanged himself," Nimitz stated, regarding Jim with a stern eye. "Committed suicide. That's all you know."

"Sounds good to me," Jim said. "Come to think of it, Vega did put the noose around his own neck, didn't he? Not us."

"So you shouldn't have any trouble keeping your story straight," Nimitz said tersely.

"Me? Hell, no, George. I'm a born storyteller." Jim winked at Charlie before turning back to Nimitz. "What about Ned Owens?"

"Take care of him."

"Kill him?"

"That won't be necessary." Nimitz drew a piece of paper

from his pocket, leaned forward, and handed it to Jim. "There are Owens' home and office addresses in Globe, the names, ages, and physical descriptions of his wife and children. I believe if you show that to Owens and have a serious discussion with him, he'll forget he ever heard of Regino Vega and return home."

"Why, you slick rascal!" Jim exclaimed. He gave Nimitz a nutcracker grin and glanced at the paper before holding it out for Charlie to take. "Anybody know where Owens is staying?"

"The Cosmopolitan," Carrillo answered.

Jim nodded at Charlie. "You know what to do," he said and watched him leave. "Now there goes a good deputy."

"George tells me you swore in a new man today," Carrillo said.

"Lane Devens. I figure I'll break him in slow, take it one step at a time. Sort of see how he handles it."

"He's known to be a bit troublesome," Carrillo said, "and a gunfighter besides."

"I thought he might come in handy."

"What we were wondering, Estevan and I, is whether or not you'll be able to control him," Nimitz said pointedly. "This Devens character strikes me as a man who doesn't take orders very well. I'm still not sure why you hired him." Here, Nimitz paused and cast a wise look at his partner before continuing. "Given your remarkable abilities with a gun, I don't see why you'd need another gunfighter on the payroll."

Carrillo barely managed to choke back a snicker.

Jim felt his face and neck heat up. George Nimitz's sarcasm was unmistakable. He looked from one man to the other, puzzled. No one had ever questioned his prowess with a gun before. And, indeed, Jim did possess a quick hand, but he had never proved it in a man-to-man gunfight. Jim assumed that so long as he continued to win the annual

Thanksgiving Turkey Shoot, no one would question it.

With both men watching, Jim dropped his left hand to his side, lifted the pearl-handled Colt from its fancy holster, and carefully placed it on the desk in front of Nimitz.

"If you think you can outshoot me, pick it up," he said.

Nimitz shook his head. "Now you're being childish."

"Want me to tell you the real reason why I hired Devens?"

Jim recounted the events of his first meeting with Devens, emphasizing his wounding of one Apache and the killing of another.

The two businessmen listened and glanced sideways at each other. Jim admitted that his excuse for hiring Devens sounded rather lame when put into words.

He concluded, "I decided I'd rather have him as an ally than an enemy."

Wrong message to convey.

"You're not afraid of him, are you, Jim?" Nimitz asked.

Jim's face flushed. "Now what the hell kind of thing is that to ask me? You think I'm not fit to be sheriff or something? Maybe that's why you called in the cavalry today!"

Carrillo yawned, again covering his mouth with a pudgy hand, heaved himself to his feet, and straightened his suitcoat. "Jim, Jim, Jim," he soothed. "Whatever gives you an idea like that?"

George Nimitz nodded in agreement. "You're a valuable asset. I'm merely concerned that Devens might cause you, us, some trouble. If he does, you know as well as I what will have to be done."

"I can handle him," Jim said, his tone sullen, still insulted.

Nimitz rose and looked down his long nose at him. "See that you do," he said. "By the way, since you are the sheriff, have you found out who started that fire in my warehouse last week?"

Jim frowned. “I’m working on it.”

After the supervisors were gone, Jim leaned back in his chair and propped his feet on the edge of his desk. That Nimitz. What a bastard.

CHAPTER SEVENTEEN

"Why are you so quiet this morning?" Abbie asked. "Cat got your tongue?"

Lane looked up from the cup of black coffee he'd been contemplating, smiled, and shook his head. They were sitting together at a corner table in Rosel's—Lane, his mother, and Abbie—chatting while they waited for their eggs and ham to be served. This impromptu get-together was something Lane wished he could have avoided. He tried to hide his discomfort but knew it must be obvious to both women.

R.J. and Ann Devens had rolled into town early this morning for the purpose of buying supplies and garden seeds and for mailing a letter to Lane's half-sister in Colorado, errands Ann had been forced to put off due to her recent illness. The money Lane had practically crammed down R.J.'s throat had already been put to good use, and by selling a cow and calf they even managed to pay off the doctor bills. Ann was in good spirits.

It had been Lane's idea to treat Ann to breakfast before work, and Ann's idea to eat at Rosel's. "We'll ask Abbie to join us," she had said. Knowing he would only be delaying the inevitable, Lane reluctantly agreed.

Of course Ann had heard by now of her son's new living arrangements. To Lane's chagrin, gossiping tongues made a joke of his privacy. Though he and Ann hadn't discussed the matter, Lane was aware of her disapproval.

Seeing Ann and Abbie together, he realized the two women shared nothing in common. Worse, Lane found himself almost loathing Abbie Maginnis. Her course language, the black paint she lined her eyes with every morning, the way she dressed, with her neckline so low that he could see the dark hollow between her breasts—the very vision he admired when they were alone—all seemed miserably cheap in the presence of his mother.

Not interested in the women's idle conversation, Lane watched Rosel lumber out of the kitchen with a tray of food. Abbie saw her, too, and pressing against Lane, she kissed him on the cheek and stood up.

"I'd better get to work before the old battle-ax starts hollerin'," she said and tied on her apron. "See you later."

Lane watched her walk toward the counter, eyes roving up and down her body, and drew a toothpick from his shirt pocket.

"Well," Ann said at length, "she's interesting."

"You don't have to say anything. I can tell you disapprove of her."

Ann shrugged, too honest to deny it.

"I care about her."

"Enough to marry her and be a good father to her son?"

"She doesn't want to get married."

"And you?"

Lane glanced up at her, his discomfort swelling to painful proportions. This was getting personal. He didn't know if he wanted to marry Abbie or not. They had tossed the idea back and forth in the past, but it had never come to anything.

Ann daintily wiped her mouth with her napkin. "Don't marry a woman you're ashamed to be seen with in public," she advised. "It'll never last."

Her perceptiveness didn't surprise Lane. She knew him very well.

"I don't hold with the two of you living together without the benefit of marriage," Ann went on, "and although I'm not familiar with the Catholic religion, I assume the Church doesn't either."

"It's my decision."

Ann sighed. "Are you happy?" she asked him. "With your new job, your new life?"

Lane rested his elbows on the table and picked his teeth, affecting an air of mild contentment. "Sure, I'm happy," he said. "I've been grinning like a jackass eatin' cactus ever since I got home."

Ann frowned, not sure how to take the remark, then laughed when she saw his smile, covering her mouth with her hand in a way that made Lane think of a shy, young girl. Dressed up in a red and brown calico dress, Ann Devens was almost pretty today.

A dreamy smile lingering upon her face, she gazed out the window and said, "Lane, I'm so proud of you." She reached across the table and squeezed his hand. "A deputy sheriff. Just think of that. And R.J. said you'd never . . ."

When she hesitated, Lane finished it for her. "He said I'd never amount to anything. I know."

"He was wrong."

The compliment left him both pleased and ashamed. He wasn't sure if he deserved her praise. His many fights, his run-ins with the law when he was a boy, his bad reputation in general were not the sort of things that made most mothers proud.

The conversation shifted to a lighter subject after that, and Lane was about to get up to pay for their meal when he spotted a familiar blue-clad figure walk into the restaurant. It was Kirk Mallory.

Gazing over Ann's right shoulder at the lieutenant, Lane felt his muscles tense. Their eyes met and locked for a brief moment, long enough for Lane to catch a glimpse of the man's busted lower lip, and then Mallory was turning and walking toward the counter to straddle one of the tall stools.

Ann noticed Lane's burning stare and twisted around in her chair. "Who is that?" she asked.

"Nobody important."

Thinking no more of it, Ann sipped her orange juice and talked of R.J., her garden, the new patchwork quilt she had begun. Lane only half-listened and kept a wary eye on Mallory. Abbie Maginnis approached the lieutenant with a pot of coffee and a big smile. She leaned toward him, fore-arms crossed on the counter, and they talked quietly for sev-eral minutes. Lane could see Abbie clearly. She touched her tongue to her upper lip, listening to Mallory with a sultry smile curving her mouth, cat eyes occasionally slanting to the side to look at Lane. It was evident to him that the object of their conversation was not the menu.

Anger and jealousy boiled inside him. What was the matter with her? Didn't she know who Mallory was? Didn't she even care?

Red-faced and sweaty, Rosel stuck her head out the kitchen door and roared at Abbie to get back to work. Abbie rolled her eyes and pushed away from the counter. As she walked past Mallory to take care of another customer, he slapped her on the butt and cast a spiteful leer in Lane's di-rection, while Abbie pretended to be offended. The entire display sickened Lane.

"R.J. took in a stray dog the other day," Ann was saying.

Lane peeled his gaze off Mallory to look at her. "Yeah?"

She nodded. "Can you believe that? After all these years,

he suddenly decides we need a dog."

His attention divided between Ann and Kirk Mallory, Lane listened to his mother talk about the new dog, and at the same time, tried to convince himself that what he had just witnessed was nothing to get sore about, that it was Abbie being Abbie, and he'd might as well get used to it. She flirted with all the men. Still, it rankled that she would get chummy with Kirk Mallory. Exactly how chummy were they anyway?

"You won't believe what R.J. named the poor thing," Ann said.

"Named who?"

She frowned. "You haven't heard a word I've been saying."

"Yes, I have."

"I was going to tell you what R.J. named the dog, but if you're not interested . . ."

"I'm interested," Lane insisted. He watched Abbie walk back to the counter and refill Mallory's cup. They were talking again. "What did he name him?"

"He named him Dog! Isn't that awful?"

Mallory was a dog, a dog in a blue uniform . . .

Lane forced a smile. "It fits."

A dog who wore leather cavalryman's gauntlets, only he wasn't wearing them today because they were under Abbie's bed with the dust balls.

"Lane, do you feel all right?"

He lit up a cigarette and immediately crushed it out again in the ash tray, remembering Ann didn't like the smoke, and kept his eyes lowered. His movements were distracted, restless.

"I'm sorry," he said finally. "I guess I'm not very good company today, am I?"

Ann regarded him with affectionate concern. "I feel like I've been talking to the wall. Is there something . . ." She broke off with what she was about to say, and her voice took on a pleasant note. "Why, good morning, Dr. Udall. Won't you join us?"

Lane looked up to see Doc standing next to their table with his hat in his hands, a sad expression pulling his face down like a baggy-eyed hound dog's. A crescent of pinkish-white skin glowed above his upper lip. Lane almost didn't recognize him without his mustache.

"Morning, Doc. Pull up a chair."

Doc declined the offer and said, "Lane, I'm afraid I have some bad news."

The jailer on duty had cut down Regino Vega's body and had dragged him out into the hall. Lane dropped to one knee beside the prone figure, lifted the blanket from the dead man's face, and groaned. All the way to the courthouse, he had fostered the possibility that this was a mistake and Regino Vega was alive and that it was someone else. Lane made the sign of the cross and recited the Hail Mary for his friend, his voice husky and low, dark head bowed. Down the hall, inside the jail, cell doors clanged open and shut, and prisoners could be heard coughing, shouting, and complaining, demanding their breakfasts. Doc Udall, standing a pace behind Lane, waited respectfully for him to finish and thought it curious that this was the last man in the world he'd expected to see knelt down in prayer.

". . . Holy Mary, Mother of God, pray for us sinners, now and at the hour of our death."

"Amen," Doc whispered.

"Amen."

Lane and Doc both looked around in surprise to see a tall,

richly dressed young woman with auburn hair standing near the stairway. She walked slowly toward them.

"Christina, this is no place for a lady," Doc said.

"I had to see for myself if he was really dead."

Out of respect for Regino, Lane covered his face again with the blanket and rose. "Take our word for it," he said coldly.

"He's dead."

Doc shot him a warning look before turning back to the woman. "Christina, you remember Lane Devens. He helped you and the sheriff out a few days ago."

She appeared startled. "Devens?" She studied his face. "I didn't recognize you. You look . . . different." Her gaze dropped to the blanketed body of Regino Vega. "Was he your friend?"

"A very good friend," Doc replied.

"I'm sorry. They're saying he killed himself."

"Like hell," Lane murmured. "What do you care anyway?"

She looked closely at him, and Doc quickly tried to smooth over Lane's callous remark.

"Lane's having a difficult time accepting his friend's suicide," he said. "You understand."

Christina Cates nodded, though she didn't seem convinced, and continued to watch Lane as he paced back and forth.

Feeling those dark, questioning eyes on him, Lane turned his back to her and stepped inside the Hole, as it was called. He looked around him at the dingy walls with a pained expression, seeing the severed rope still dangling from the crossbar, then looked down at the floor, at the bruised, wilted rose petals scattered there, at the bloodstained noose that the jailer had removed from around Regino's neck. He picked up the hangman's noose and stepped outside.

"If it's true he killed himself, how'd he get his hands on a rope?" he asked and pitched the noose at Christina Cates' feet.

Doc frowned at him and shook his head ever so slightly.

Christina glanced down at the rope. "I'm sure I don't know," she said, adding, "If it makes you feel any better, Mr. Devens, I want you to know that I never believed Vega killed my husband."

"I bet you didn't."

Doc cleared his throat. "Perhaps after I've examined Regino's body, we'll find out if there was any foul play involved."

"Like with Cates," Lane said.

Christina met his hostile gaze, lips parted, eyes wide, and for that fleeting instant, she left herself open to his scrutiny. On her face, Lane glimpsed a mixture of guilt, fear, and deep sorrow before the curtain dropped again, and she looked away.

Jim Mitchell rounded the corner, whistling a tune through his teeth, then grew silent when he saw the trio standing together in the hallway.

"Christina . . . Mrs. Cates, you shouldn't be here."

"I had to come," she said quietly.

"Wanted to make sure the man who killed your husband was dead, eh?" Mitchell pulled at his nose, nodding. "I can understand that. He hanged himself. Guess he couldn't live with the guilt."

"You sorry son of a bitch!" Lane burst out. "You know damned well . . ."

"Lane!" Doc's voice cracked like a whip, cutting short his angry words.

Lane looked around at the three of them, realized the futility of it all, and decided he'd better leave before he said something happened that would jeopardize his mission. He needed to calm down and think. He sidestepped Regino's body and was about to brush past Jim Mitchell when that something almost happened.

Already on guard after Lane's outburst, Mitchell saw him approaching and misunderstood. He reached for his gun. Lane caught the flash of movement and reacted instinctively. His right hand swept down and up, and before Mitchell had even cleared leather he found himself staring down the wicked, black barrel of Lane's Colt.

Half-crouched, Lane's alert gaze flicked from the sheriff's gunhand to his face. "Go ahead, Mitchell. Draw." His voice was flinty and hard.

Mitchell managed a weak smile. "You're awful jumpy today, Deputy." He raised his hands away from his holstered guns, palms turned out, and swallowed loudly. "Maybe you'd better take the day off," he said.

Lane exhaled loudly, eased the hammer on his Colt forward again, and dropped the gun into its holster. Glancing at Christina Cates' frightened face, he moved past Mitchell and left. He wondered if the sheriff had sense enough to know just how close he had come to dying.

Doc Udall caught up with him midway down the stairs. He grasped his arm, stopping him.

"Son, you're going to have to get a grip on yourself."

Lane gazed down at his boots and tucked his thumbs into his pockets. "I know. I will." He looked back up at Doc. "I'd better go talk to Luz."

"Regino's wife?"

"Yeah."

"You do that," Doc said. "Afterwards, stop by my office. We need to talk."

Lane nodded and continued down the stairs. Dread accompanied his every step. How did you tell a woman her young children would never know their father?

CHAPTER EIGHTEEN

"You shouldn't have come here," Jim said irritably.

Christina watched him pick up the noose Lane Devens had thrown at her moments ago and pitch it into the Hole, slamming the door shut. He was visibly shaken, as was Christina. She looked down the hall again to make sure Devens was gone. It disturbed her that a man could pray so earnestly one minute and become so deadly the next.

"He's an awful sudden bastard," Jim muttered, glancing at Christina. "I wasn't gonna draw on him."

"Yes, you were."

Jim's face flushed. "What are you saying? That he's faster than me?"

"Just drop it, Jim," Christina said wearily. "He didn't shoot you. That's all that matters." She folded her arms together, the fingers of her right hand clutching her black pocketbook. "He knows, Jim." She lowered her voice. "He knows I killed Robert."

Jim stared at her.

"He was so angry," she said and shuddered, remembering the accusation burning in Lane Devens' eyes, his hateful words. "He blames me for Regino Vega's death," she whispered, adding, "and I blame you, Jim."

"You blame me!" He sounded incredulous. "I didn't kill him!"

"Even if you weren't the one who put the rope around his

neck, you killed him. You arrested him and accused him of a crime he didn't commit."

"And I told you why. I love you, Christina. I want to protect you."

Christina listened to his words. That was the problem. They were just words with no feelings, no truth.

Lying awake last night, she had recalled things she'd not given a second thought about before Vega's arrest. She remembered Regino Vega had stopped by the house one day to talk to Robert. They had stayed in Robert's study for almost an hour, and once, walking past the door, Christina overheard Robert shouting that the county needed a new sheriff. Of course, she thought nothing of it, for by this time her husband and Jim Mitchell had ceased to see eye to eye on almost all issues.

Now Robert Cates was dead and so was Regino Vega. It shed new light on an occurrence that had once seemed insignificant, yet Christina warned herself not to jump to conclusions.

"What'd Devens say to you?" Jim demanded.

"In so many words, he said I killed Robert. And he doesn't believe Vega hanged himself."

"Damn!" Jim took off his Stetson and smoothed his hair, then settled his hat on again. "Are you sure he knows, or are you just being paranoid?"

"I'm sure. Maybe R. J. Devens told him."

"Could have, but I doubt it. Word is, they don't get along. My guess is he put two and two together and figured it out for himself. Did he say anything about me?"

"No."

He nodded, clearly relieved. "Well, don't worry your pretty head about Lane Devens. I'll take care of him and his old man."

Christina feared Jim's promises almost as much as the threat R.J. and Lane Devens posed. She glanced down at Regino Vega's body. Was this how Jim intended to take care of things? If so, she wanted no part of it. She wondered what would happen if she went to Lane Devens and told him the truth about her husband's death and Jim's involvement and about R.J.'s attempt to blackmail her. Would he help her? She doubted it, yet she continued to turn the idea over in her mind.

"Have you talked to Robert's lawyer about the will?" Jim asked abruptly.

Christina's pulse quickened. "Yes."

Greedy eagerness brightened Jim's face. "What'd he say? Did you get everything?"

She hesitated.

"Well?"

"Jim, if I told you I was practically penniless, would you still want to marry me?"

"Oh, for God's sake." Jim's eyes rolled heavenward. "Will you just answer my question? Did you get the old man's money or not?"

Christina's face stiffened. "That's what I thought."

Turning, she started to leave, but Jim grabbed her by the arm and whirled her around to face him, glancing up and down the hall at the same time.

"You didn't answer my question."

Christina glared up at him, her eyes black and stormy. "You're hurting my arm." She jerked free of his grasp and straightened her sleeve. "He left me everything he thought I deserved. Now, are you happy?"

"You'd better hope I'm happy and that I stay that way," Jim said, and he dipped the fingers of his right hand into his suitcoat pocket and lifted something out. Christina recognized the small glass bottle of arsenic. "See this bottle, Christina? It's in the palm of my hand and so are you. Doc Udall knows Robert was poisoned. Reckon what he'd think if I told him I found this arsenic in your house?" He favored her with a cocky grin and a wink. "Go buy yourself a pretty dress, baby. We're gettin' married."

Despite the presence of the troops, the atmosphere in Pennington worsened as the news of Regino Vega's alleged suicide spread throughout town. Fearing for their safety, merchants kept their shotguns handy, and men ignored the ordinance against carrying weapons and armed themselves before venturing into the streets. Sheriff Mitchell ordered the saloonkeepers to close their doors for the day. Only the Congress House Saloon was allowed to remain open, a privilege that merely added to Mexican resentment.

Tempers were short and explosive. Two Mexicans beat a Papago Indian in the middle of Cushing Street for, as they explained to Lane later, giving them dirty looks. Riding back into town from Luz Vega's house, Lane helped break up the fight and gave the bleeding Papago a ride home. On the way, the man told him in bad Spanish that three or four soldiers had walked past while he was being beaten without so much as lifting a finger to help him. According to the Papago, they had hooted and hollered in support of the Mexicans.

Whether this was true or not, Lane didn't know, but either way he disliked the army's involvement. Stationed at nearby Fort Lowe for the purpose of protecting Pennington and the surrounding area from Apache raids, most of the soldiers hadn't seen active duty in months and were bored and spoiling for excitement.

"Hey, you!"

Lane heard the shout and looked up to see two young soldiers loitering beneath the veranda of a dry goods store. The Papago quickly slipped off Lane's horse and limped away, wanting nothing to do with them. Lane shifted the reins to his left hand and pushed his hat off his forehead.

"You talking to me, soldier boy?"

The shortest of the two men, a sergeant, answered him in a belligerent drawl. "Yeah, I'm talkin' to you."

He stepped out from under the veranda and halted a few feet in front of Lane's horse, hip cocked to the side in a cavalryman's pose. Behind him, his comrade squirted a stream of tobacco juice into the dusty street and picked up his rifle leaning against the wall.

"Sorry to say it, but I'm gonna hafta take that purdy gun you're packin'," the first soldier said.

"Then I guess you got your work cut out for you."

This wasn't the response the young sergeant had expected. His close-set eyes narrowed as he shifted his weight to the other foot and tried a different approach.

"Back where I come from, an injun gets caught with a gun gets his ass throwed on a reservation."

"You can try," Lane said shortly.

"Who the hell you think you are? Gee-ro-nee-mo?"

Lane gazed impassively down at him. "The name's Lane Devens."

The soldier beneath the veranda leaned his rifle against the wall again. He bit off a chaw of tobacco.

The sergeant squinted up at Lane. "Devens, eh? Well, why didn't you say so?" His smart-alecky grin evaporated as he stepped to the side and out of Lane's way. "You shoulda spoke up sooner. Hey, ain't you a deputy now?"

Lane didn't answer. He urged the restless buckskin forward, breaking into a trot and then an easy canter, and lifted a hand to his shirt pocket where he carried his badge. He had taken it off on his way to see Regino's wife. The sergeant's question stayed with him. Was he a deputy or not? Could he continue to work under Mitchell, knowing he had killed Regino? He wanted to shove the badge down Mitchell's throat.

As before, Lane approached Doc Udall's office by the back way and was surprised to see two of Mariano Diego's bodyguards standing to either side of the door. Grim-faced, they greeted Lane with curt nods of their heads and a formal, *Buenas tardes*.

Lane did likewise and stepped inside Doc's office.

"And here he is now," Doc said, looking up. "Hello, Lane."

Sensing they had been talking about him, Lane looked from Doc to Diego and shut the door. There being only two chairs in the office, Doc started to rise.

Lane shook his head. "Keep your seat, Doc."

"Where's your badge?" Diego asked.

Lane squatted down to one side of the door and gathered Sister Julia's prayer beads into the palm of his hand, caressing the shiny crucifix between his thumb and forefinger. When he failed to answer, Doc Udall and Mariano Diego exchanged glances.

"Have you looked at Regino yet?" Lane asked finally.

Doc rubbed the bare, pink skin above his upper lip. "Nimitz informed me this morning that he was replacing me with another coroner. A doctor with more youth and knowledge, I believe was how he put it."

Lane looked up at him, started to say something, then changed his mind and gazed back down at the floor. Depressed after his visit with Luz Vega, he didn't feel like talking.

"Ned Owens, Regino's attorney, was paid a surprise visit

by one of the deputies late last night," Diego said. "He threatened the lives of Mr. Owens's wife and children."

Doc nodded. "Ned left this morning for Globe. He told me he was going to take his family to Santa Fe to stay with relatives, and then he'll be returning here to Penny Town. He should be back in two weeks."

"This will be over and done before his return," Diego said.

Doc frowned at him.

Lane cut his eyes over at Diego. "How?"

"You will put an end to it," Diego said. "The way it should have been done days ago."

Lane studied the man's bitter, mask-like countenance, the unblinking black eyes, and got a bad feeling in the pit of his stomach. Doc affirmed his suspicions.

"Before we hired you," he said, "Mariano had talked of paying you to kill Nimitz, Carrillo, and Mitchell. Robert Cates and I talked him out of it."

"And I was a fool to have listened to you," Diego said, "especially when I knew that the district attorney was George Nimitz's brother-in-law. The men who killed Regino Vega and who are stealing the land from the Mexican farmers and ranchers will never see the inside of a jail cell!"

Doc shook his head. "We'll make sure another prosecutor handles this case so there won't be any conflict of interest."

"You don't know anything about it," Diego snapped. "An eye for an eye, and a tooth for a tooth! This is the only way these men will be stopped!" He jabbed his walking stick in Lane's direction. "He's the answer to our problems."

Slipping the rosary back into his pocket, Lane rested his elbows on his knees and laced his fingers together. So that was it. He gazed at his hands for a long, silent minute. His hands were slender and brown and quick, and they, along with his gun, were worth six thousand dollars to Don

Mariano. He guessed he should have known it would turn out this way.

"I'm not your henchman," he said slowly, "and I don't hire out my gun to anybody."

Diego's scowl deepened. "You've killed before. You'll kill again."

"Don't dig up my past, Diego. It doesn't have anything to do with what's happening right now."

"He's right," Doc said. "We can bring Mitchell and the supervisors to justice by peaceful means."

"!Que lástima!" Diego exclaimed, glaring at Lane. "You sit there with a long face and call yourself a friend of Regino Vega, yet you do nothing to avenge his death!"

"I said I'd do this my own way!" Lane flared. "Gino's death doesn't change that. If you don't like the way I'm handling it, you can damned well find somebody else to do your dirty work!"

Doc rose to stand between them. "The two of you cool off," he said. "Arguing won't get us anywhere." He turned to Diego. "Mari, you know as well as I do that if Lane kills those three men he'll have every federal marshal in the territory on his trail. They'd chase him from hell to breakfast."

Diego shook his head. "Not if he is careful. No one has to know he killed them."

"You're talking about cold-blooded murder," Lane said.

Diego allowed himself a sly smile. "Is it not true that you've killed Apaches from ambush, Mr. Devens?"

"That's hardly a fair comparison," Doc protested.

"Isn't it?" Diego asked. He studied Lane's troubled face and seemed pleased with what he saw there. "Think about it, Lane. Imagine how Regino must have suffered before he died. Remember his fatherless children."

Diego left shortly after that. Doc walked him to the front

door, and Lane could hear them talking in lowered voices.

After a moment, Doc returned to find Lane still squatted down against the wall. Smiling, he sank into his own chair and gestured to the one across from him.

"Have a seat."

Lane shook his head and remained where he was. "Diego's right, you know."

"That's what he wants you to think," Doc said. "Two wrongs don't make a right, Lane. The best thing you can do is pin that badge back on and continue your investigation."

"Not today."

"Oh, I forgot." Doc slapped his thigh. "Wild Bill Hickock gave you the day off, didn't he?"

CHAPTER NINETEEN

It was half past three when Lane tied his horse in front of Abbie's house. He opened the door and stepped into the shady coolness, sailing his hat across the room to the sofa. The heat of the day pounded in his temples, and he wanted to lay down for a few minutes but knew it would be a waste of time. His thoughts gave him no rest or peace.

Lane felt rather than heard another's presence and spun around to see Abbie coming out of the bedroom.

"Don't tell me you forgot . . ." She stopped, startled into speechlessness. "Oh, Lane. I didn't expect you home so early."

"Who exactly were you expecting?"

Not answering, Abbie smiled and turned her back to him. "Give me a hand here, won't you?"

He moved behind her and slowly fastened the buttons in the back of her bodice. "Why aren't you at work?" he asked.

"Clumsy me." She laughed lightly. "Would you believe I spilled soup all over my dress?"

"No."

She turned to look at him. "Well, that's what happened. I came home to change."

Lane pushed past her, walked into the bedroom, and glanced around him. The bed was neatly made, everything in place and tidy, but that didn't prove anything. He opened the dresser drawer where he kept his few clothes and began taking out pants, shirts, and underwear and dropping them onto the bed.

Abbie drew up beside him. "Lane, what are you doing?"

"Something I should've already done."

"You're cleaning out your drawer?"

Lane glanced over at her as he stuffed his clothes into a knapsack. "Don't play dumb, Abbie." He slung the sack over his shoulder and strode past her and out of the room.

"Oh, I get it!" Abbie exclaimed. "You saw me talking to Kirk Mallory this morning and now you've got your tail over a rope. Is that it? I can't even talk to another man any more without making you jealous?"

"You do a lot more than talk."

"Is that so?" She stood in the middle of the living room, hands on her hips, and watched him walk briskly into the kitchen, gathering his scattered belongings, then come out again and stalk back into the bedroom. "What are you looking for?" she asked. When he didn't answer, she said, "So you're leaving. Just like that. Have you thought about how Seth's gonna feel?"

"Yes." Lane emerged from the bedroom. "He's a good kid, Abbie. You're the one I can't live with." He paused, gazed at her a moment, then looked away, shaking his head. "I thought we had something. Guess I was wrong."

"Kirk's only a friend. Can't you get that through your thick head?"

Lane reached behind him and pulled the leather gauntlets from his back pocket. "Then tell your friend he shouldn't leave his gloves laying under other people's beds." He tossed them to the floor. "Somebody might get the wrong idea."

"Damn you." Abbie looked from the gloves to Lane's face and tossed her head, flipping a strand of blonde hair from her eyes. "Just because you practically take an oath of celibacy every time you leave this house, doesn't mean I have to do the same. We're not married." She looked him up and down, lifting her chin. "I'm not your squaw."

Lane's eyes blazed with anger. "You know what you are, Abbie?" He fought to keep his voice controlled. "You're nothing but leftovers. Kirk Mallory's leftovers!"

Abbie's hand shot up and out, but Lane grabbed her by the wrist before she could slap him and gave her arm a rough, downward jerk that elicited a gasp of either pain or surprise. He let her go and quickly backed away, opening the door.

"So long, Abbie. Mallory can pay your bills from now on."

He heard her scream an obscenity at him as he walked to his horse, heard the crash of something hitting the wall, and wondered why she even cared. What difference could it make to her whether he left or stayed? She should be happy. Her many lovers could come and go as they pleased now.

Seeing Abbie and Kirk Mallory together this morning had been an eye-opener. Not only had she proved that she didn't love him, but she didn't even respect him enough to hide her unfaithfulness. Remembering Mallory's sneering smile, Lane's mouth drew taut with renewed fury as he strapped the knapsack to his saddlehorn.

Mounting up, he glanced toward the house one last time, his face hard, smoky eyes narrowed beneath the brim of his hat. Abbie was standing on the front step with her arms folded across her chest.

"You're a cold fish, Lane Devens! I hope you rot in hell!"

Lane tipped his hat to her and jerked the buckskin's head roughly around, reining him into the street. It was nice knowing you, too, he thought.

After leaving Abbie, Lane drifted aimlessly around town. He stopped by the Congress House Saloon, daring someone to try to throw him out, and stayed long enough to drink a cold beer. Nobody bothered him. He ate supper in the dining room of the Russ Hotel but didn't check in, returning instead to the saloon where he purchased a quart of whiskey and then left. The place was too crowded, and he felt an urgent need to get away . . . away from Abbie, away from town.

When a reporter for the *Arizona Star* stopped him on the boardwalk and asked for an interview, Lane regarded the man with vast impatience.

"What for?" he asked.

The reporter smiled genially and plucked a pencil from behind his right ear. "Why, to learn more about you, Mr. Devens. Your ambitions, your appointment as deputy sheriff, your feelings about the current Mexican unrest here in Penny Town." He trailed Lane to his horse, so close he clipped his heels. "Anything you feel like talking about."

"I don't feel like talking."

"Because of Regino Vega's tragic death, no doubt," the reporter presumed. "I understand he was a close friend of yours."

"Yes. He was."

"I see . . ." The reporter scribbled something in his notepad. "How do you feel about his arrest?" He looked up at Lane with a falsely sympathetic smile. "Surely you don't believe your good friend murdered Robert Cates!"

Lane tucked the bottle of whiskey into a saddlebag and untied the buckskin's reins. His silence merely served to intensify the reporter's questioning.

"What about Vega's death, Mr. Devens?" he queried, his voice rising as Lane swung into the saddle. By now, several men had gathered around them to listen. "Do you agree with Sheriff Mitchell that it was a suicide?"

The saddle creaked as Lane leaned forward and rested an arm on the pommel. "If you want a story, then write this down in your little notebook," he said. "Gino didn't kill himself. He was murdered." He looked past the reporter to the men beyond and singled out the few Mexicans in the crowd. "The sonsabitches that lynched him will pay for what they did," he promised. "One way or another."

The reporter wrote furiously and plied more questions, but Lane considered the interview over. Leaving, he saw Charlie Reed standing at the corner of the saloon next to a street lamp and drew rein in front of him. The two men regarded each other with undisguised animosity.

"You got a big mouth, Devens."

Lane shrugged. "Unless you were in on the lynching, it shouldn't bother you." He bobbed his head in the direction of the *Arizona Star* reporter. "You can tell him I'm lying, but he won't believe you. Murder makes for a better story than suicide."

"If that's put to print, you're finished," Reed said, his voice deep and rumbling. "Enjoy your badge while you got it."

Lane watched the big man turn and amble into the saloon. He was right, of course. Mitchell would give him the boot, and his investigation would be forfeited. Lane felt he was digging his own grave with his mouth. It made him realize he wasn't cut out to be a detective.

Lane rode out of town toward his parents' house, away from the lights and the noise and the people to where the only sounds were the chirping of crickets and the soft thuds of his horse's hooves on the dusty road. Moonlight bathed the fields. Winter wheat and barley rustled slightly as a soft breeze stirred their drying stalks, a whisper of sound that was soothing to Lane who, after only a few days, had already gotten his fill of town life.

Nearing the Devens homestead, Lane drew up within the

shadow of a few mesquites growing at the edge of the road and gazed toward the house. The soft yellow glow of lamplight illuminated the kitchen window, and Lane could see his mother washing supper dishes. He watched her almost wistfully and took a swig from the quart bottle he'd bought earlier. Ann's face became blurred as his eyes watered from the whiskey. He wiped them dry and swallowed another mouthful of Old Crow.

Lane wasn't sure what force had propelled him home, but now that he was here, he thought about going inside. No, that wouldn't do. For his mother's sake, he'd have to be nice to R.J., and he lacked the patience tonight. Besides, Ann would smell the booze on his breath and be disappointed with him.

The front door opened, flooding the yard with light, and Ann stepped outside and placed a bowl of leftovers on the ground for Dog. Lane saw the big black stray run to her, tail wagging, and bury his nose in the bowl. Patting him on the head, Ann straightened up and turned to go back inside when Lane's horse nickered. Hearing it, she turned and peered into the darkness for a moment before glancing down at Dog. He continued to wolf down his food, undisturbed, and apparently trusting his senses more than her own, Ann went inside and closed the door.

"Some watch dog," Lane muttered.

He stripped the saddle and blanket from the buckskin and staked him where there was a little grass growing in the ditch by the road, then spread his bedroll beneath the mesquites. Digging a rock from beneath his blankets, he sprawled on his back and gazed past the lacy leaves at the thousands of stars beyond.

He thought of Regino Vega. Rosary would be recited for him tomorrow evening in the Church of San Augustín, followed the next day by a celebration of Mass. Lane supposed he would attend each one, for by tomorrow morning Mitchell would surely have read the *Arizona Star* and fired him, and he'd not have to worry about taking time off from work.

Loose-limbed and lightheaded, Lane took a final swig of whiskey, corked the bottle, and tossed it aside before he got really soaked. It didn't take much. His jumbled thoughts turned to Abbie, but strangely enough, it was another woman's face that he saw, a sad, beautiful woman with a low-pitched voice and quiet manners. Killers, he had found, came in all shapes and sizes. He fell asleep thinking about her.

The night air grew chilly. Lane was lying on his side, huddled beneath his blankets, when his eyes suddenly flared open. He lay perfectly still for several seconds before sliding his hand forward, feeling for his gun. His fingers curled around the grip. It took him a moment to remember where he was. Something had awakened him. He lay with his body facing east, and raising his head slightly, he saw on the horizon a strange orange glow that caused a chill to shinny up his spine.

Pennington was on fire!

He rose to his knees, his blankets sliding to the ground, leaving him exposed to the sharp air as he stared toward town in disbelief. He could hear the vibrant clanging of the fire bell, and an occasional whisper of wind carried upon its breath the pungent smell of smoke.

Lane started to rise, then dropped swiftly to his stomach when he heard the sound of horses' hooves and looked toward the road. Five horsemen appeared and rode slowly past him, holding their mounts to a walk. Soft moonlight shone on the fancy silver conchas and trimmings decorating the lead rider's saddle. Tiny bells dangled from the breast strap and tinkled faintly with the horse's movements.

The riders themselves were silent, eerily so, and when they passed from Lane's sight, he grabbed his Spencer carbine, ran to the edge of the mesquites, and knelt down, his eyes probing the darkness for the five horsemen. He didn't see them. Had they left the road?

Lane stared toward the house. Behind him, the buckskin neighed shrilly and snorted, alarmed either by the distant fire or the horses, and the stray dog R.J. had adopted began barking. A light came on in the house, and by its glow Lane caught a fleeting glimpse of someone running past the window, his head covered with a gunnysack, masking his identity.

Shouting, Lane fired a shot at him and then was on his feet, racing across the open ground to the next point of cover, R.J.'s buckboard. Three shots crashed, one striking the side of the buckboard, another sparking against the iron rim on one of the wheels, and Lane hit the ground. He wriggled his way beneath the buckboard and opened fire as two masked men on horseback galloped past him.

A bullet seared the left side of his face and whined angrily as it ricocheted off some object behind him. Yellow flames licked upward from the back of his parents' house. Four of the five riders Lane had seen earlier circled the house on horseback, shooting into the air, shouting, and breaking windows, and Lane saw R.J. step out onto the front step with his shotgun raised. "R.J., get down!"

The shotgun roared, and a horse went down, tumbling its rider. Another rifle shot cracked, and R.J. stumbled backwards. The scattergun slipped from his hands to the ground.

Lane sighted down the barrel at one of the retreating raiders, squeezed the trigger, and saw him throw his arms up as he somersaulted over the rump of his running horse.

Throwing down the empty Spencer, Lane drew his six-gun and rolled from under the buckboard in time to see the last horseman help his wounded comrade swing up behind him and gallop away, disappearing over a rise and into the darkness.

Lane raced across the yard to the house. The whole back of the house and part of the roof were engulfed in flames, and the night sky was alive with flying sparks. Lane had to shout above the crackling roar.

"Where's Ma?"

R.J. stared at him, white-faced and speechless, while his blood spread across the front of his longjohns. Sweat rolled down his face. Lane shoved him out of the way and entered the house, searching wildly for his mother and shouting her name. Smoke roiled within, suffocating him, blinding him, while the intense heat baked his skin as he ran through the kitchen to his parents' bedroom.

Raising his arm in front of his face, Lane kicked the door open. The room was already ablaze. Fire ravaged the entire north wall, melting broken glass, devouring Ann's calico curtains, and chewing away at the wooden bedstead. A glass jar burst, and Lane felt a shard bite his arm.

He found his mother on the floor on the far side of the bed where she had fallen, her hands still gripping a heavy rug with which she'd been trying to beat out the flames. The hem of her nightgown had caught fire, and Lane stomped it out, stooped, and hoisted her over his shoulder. Part of the bedroom ceiling caved in behind him as he struggled through the smoke and heat to the door.

Recovering from the shock of his wound, R.J. helped get Ann outside and lay her small, limp body on the ground. Lane staggered backwards, choking and gasping for air, his lungs burning fiercely. Doubled over with his hands on his knees, he watched as R.J. tried to revive Ann. She wasn't responding.

"Is she breathing?" he asked. His voice, however, was little more than a hoarse croak, and R.J. didn't hear him.

He dropped down beside his stepfather and looked into Ann's face. Cold fear seized him by the heart. Her eyes were open, but she didn't see him. He passed his open palm over her mouth and nose and felt for her pulse, while R.J. waited and watched for his reaction.

Shuddering slightly, Lane closed his mother's eyes.

R.J. stared at him in horror. "She's . . . she's gone?"

Lane nodded. Eyes downcast, he pushed himself to his feet and turned away. His mind and body felt numb. Behind him, R.J. cradled Ann's head in his lap and rocked to and fro, and the fire consumed the rest of the house. Jars and bottles and an occasional bullet exploded with muffled pops. Old, dry pine boards crackled and crashed to the ground, spewing showers of ocher sparks into the sky.

Lane stood with his back to the blaze and felt the reality of it sink in. He swiped his forearm across his face, smearing black soot and sweat and blood, and tried to get a handle on his emotions. Tears stung his eyes and left their tracks in the grime on his cheeks.

A soft tinkly sound reached Lane's ears. He glanced up. On the road, just at the edge of the flickering circle of firelight, stood a lone horse and rider. A gunnysack covered the man's head, and two empty black holes cut into the sack marked his eyes.

Lane's right hand streaked downward for his .45, but the raider was already wheeling his horse around and plying hands, feet, and quirt to the animal's flanks and rump.

"Damn you! Coward!"

Lane emptied his gun into the darkness and yelled until

his voice was a rasp of sound and his body trembled. A gust of wind swirled smoke, dust, and ashes around him and ruffled the scorched lace on the hem of Ann's nightgown.

R.J. buried his face in his hands. "It's all my fault," he wailed. "All my fault."

CHAPTER TWENTY

Lane stood in the front doorway of Doc Udall's practice and dried his face and hands on a clean towel. Smoke blanketed the town like fog over water. He could see tendrils of smoke still rising from the blackened ruins on Main, Meyer, and Congress streets. It was through this downtown area that most of the damage had occurred.

Lane gazed westward, watching men shovel what remained of the daily stage depot into a wagon. He wondered if the same men who had wrought so much destruction here in town were also responsible for his mother's death.

Doc Udall stepped up behind Lane and showed him the flattened slug he'd extracted from R.J.'s shoulder. "This is the fifty-seventh bullet I've dug out of some fool's hide since I started practicing medicine forty-odd years ago."

"You keep count?"

"Hell, son, I keep a collection." He dropped the slug into a Mason jar with the other fifty-six and screwed the lid back on.

"Let's have a look at you now," he said.

"I'm all right."

Doc studied Lane's somber face. His eyes were bloodshot and tired, his hair, lashes, and eyebrows slightly singed, and the bullet wound slanting across the left side of his face still oozed blood.

"Let's have a look anyway," Doc said.

Too weary to argue, Lane followed him into the examining room and sat on the sterile steel table. Doc smeared a greasy ointment on his burns, then carefully cleaned the open gash on his cheek and swabbed on antiseptic.

"A little more to the right and that bullet would have put your lights out."

"Doc, did anybody see the men who burned the town?"

"Not that I've heard, but do you want an old codger's opinion? I think it was the same bunch that's been setting fire to some of these farms and ranches, and I'd bet that they're Mexicans." Doc winked at him. "Mariano Diego'll fight me on that one."

"You think it was the gunnysackers, huh?"

Doc nodded. "Possibly the same devils that killed your poor mother."

But these five men weren't the only guilty party. According to Doc, after the fire bell sounded, the whole town went berserk. Gangs of angry Mexicans trashed and looted white-owned businesses, and whites did the same in the barrio, terrorizing the entire community. One Mexican man, accused of making obscene gestures to a couple of ladies outside the post office two days ago, was taken by force from the city lock-up and lynched. He was still dangling from a telegraph pole at the edge of town.

Doc had been up all night and all morning, mending broken bones and cracked skulls, treating burns, and patching knife and gunshot wounds.

When Doc finished with him, Lane put on his shirt, buttoned up, and tucked in the tail. He reached for his hat. It was light enough now that he might be able to pick up the trail of the men who had attacked his parents' farm.

Thoughts of his mother tortured Lane. Her death left an immense void within him. For thirteen years of his life, Ann Devens had loved him unconditionally. She had understood what drove him; she understood the reasons for his moodiness, his quirks, his many faults. Not since those dark days in the Franciscan Mission School had he felt so terribly alone.

Lane checked in on R.J. before he left and found him awake. He was lying on his back on a narrow cot in Doc's back office, propped up with pillows and naked to the waist except for bandages. His face was unnaturally pale beneath the white stubble of his beard.

He looked up at Lane's entrance and gestured to one of the chairs. "Sit down. I got something I need to get off my chest."

Closing the door, Lane straddled a chair and propped his forearms and chin on the back, his solemn gaze fixed on the scrubbed puncheon floor.

When R.J. spoke, his voice cracked with emotion. "It's my fault your mother's dead."

Lane's eyes flicked up to look at him.

"If I'd known this was gonna happen, I never would've . . ." R.J. paused, shaking his head. He gazed down at his hands clasped together in his lap. "I guess I should start from the beginning," he said. "You see, I saw them do it. I saw Jim Mitchell and Christina Cates dump the body."

"Robert Cates' body?"

R.J. nodded. He looked up at Lane. "I tried to blackmail the woman," he confessed.

Lane stared at his stepfather, stunned, as he explained exactly what he had witnessed late that night and how he had concocted the insane plan to blackmail them. He was certain that Mitchell had retaliated by setting fire to the house.

Lane was standing now, his slim body tensed and perfectly still. He gripped the back of his chair with both hands.

"One hundred thousand dollars," he said, spacing the

words, his voice little more than a whisper. "Was it worth it, R.J.?"

R.J. refused to look at him. "If I'd known they was gonna do something like this . . ."

"If you'd known!" Lane uncoiled like a spring, hurling the straight-backed chair against the wall with such force that two of the legs cracked and splintered. "Who'd you think you were dealing with? For God's sake, R.J., they'd already murdered one man!"

Doc Udall looked in when he heard the commotion, saw the busted chair and the fear in R.J.'s eyes, and said, "Lane, I don't know what this is all about, but he needs to rest."

"You stay out of it," Lane snapped, walking around R.J.'s bed, and Udall withdrew. "You're sure it was Mitchell?"

"Yes, yes, I'm sure." R.J. pressed his thumb and forefinger to his closed eyes and heaved a sigh. "I did this for Ann's sake," he said bitterly. "I just wanted to give her a better life."

"Oh, cut the crap. You never gave Ma a second thought."

R.J. glared up at him. "I loved your mother!"

"You treated her like one of your work horses."

Beads of sweat broke out across R.J.'s forehead as he leaned forward and jabbed a finger at Lane. "You listen to me, and you listen good. I loved Ann enough to bring her half-breed bastard son home and feed and clothe him and send him off to school every day. I would've done anything for her."

"Don't call me a bastard," Lane said, his voice low, restrained. "I know who my father was. He was a better man than you could ever hope to be."

R.J.'s laugh was ugly with derision. "You damned fool. Do you really think your mother would have willingly left me for some filthy injun?" He shook his head and uttered the words

Lane would never forget as long as he lived. "Ann was raped by an Apache buck during her captivity, and you're the offshoot of it!"

His words were like a physical blow to Lane. He reached out, grasping the edge of Doc's desk. His face drained of color.

"All these years, I kept Ann's secret," R.J. continued. "I allowed her to ruin her good name and reputation because she wanted to raise you, because she wanted to protect you from the truth so you'd be proud of who you were." He gave a disdainful snort and scowled at Lane. "How she could even stand the sight of you beats me."

"You're lying."

R.J. regarded him with open contempt. "Go to Fort Defiance. Talk to a General John Bickham. Him and his wife took your mother in and nursed her after the Navajos surrendered, and Bickham helped me find the mission in California. He'll back up my story."

Lane was silent. He passed the back of his hand across his mouth, turned away from R.J., and gazed blindly out the open window at the weedy alley. He felt shaky inside and sick, and his fingers quivered as he rolled a cigarette.

A gray moth fluttered through the window and lit on the sill near Lane's hand. He smashed it flat with his fist.

"If what you say is true," he said quietly, "then who was Niyol?"

"Before the Navajo wars broke out, he worked for the army sometimes. He helped white captives return to their families. Niyol rescued Ann from the Apaches, and she figured he saved her life."

"Is it true he's dead?"

"Killed and scalped by soldiers," R.J. replied.

Lane glanced over his shoulder at him, pain clouding his

face. "And what about the Apache . . . the Apache who raped her?"

"The Mexicans called him *Cuervo*. The Raven. That's all Ann ever said about him."

"Why'd you wait so long to tell me this?"

"Like I said, Ann didn't want you to know." R.J. sighed and rested his head against his pillow. "For thirteen years, since I brought you home from California, you've been a constant reminder of what them red devils did to her."

"I didn't know," Lane murmured.

He walked to the door and had his hand on the knob when R.J. stopped him.

"You remember one thing," he said gruffly. "No matter how I feel about you, your mama loved you. Always did."

"You don't have to tell me that."

Half-dazed, Lane left him and walked through the examining room to the waiting room where he found Doc Udall discussing the night's events with Mariano Diego.

Diego was dressed today in full Mexican garb, from the gaudy sombrero shading his face to his buckskin bolero jacket and breeches and large-rowelled spurs. One of his bodyguards was posted by the door and openly packing a pistol. The vaquero's left wrist was tightly bandaged, and the whole left side of his face was skinned and raw, as if he'd taken a bad fall from his horse. He stared straight ahead, avoiding Lane's gaze.

Doc heaved himself to his feet. He looked at Lane strangely, but if he had overheard R.J.'s revelation, he didn't mention it.

"Lane, will you talk some sense into this stubborn old mule? He swears it was Jim Mitchell and his deputies who started the fires."

"Maybe it was."

Doc threw up his hands. "Estevan Carrillo's stage station is in ashes. So is George Nimitz's furniture store. Why would Mitchell and his ruffian deputies burn down businesses owned by the very men they work for?"

"Do they not have fire insurance on these buildings?" Diego asked loftily. "Of course, they do. Their loss will be minimal, I assure you. However, I believe they would slit their own throats if only to bring more trouble on my people."

Doc knocked the dottle from his pipe. "That's stretching it a bit, don't you think, Mari?"

"Not at all. Even as I speak, they are blaming us for the fires." Diego turned to Lane. His sharp eyes glittered like wet, black stones. "My friend, I am truly sorry about your mother's death. It was very unfortunate." He sounded sincere. "It was the smoke that killed her?"

"The smoke. Her heart. We're not sure."

"And your stepfather?"

"He'll live." Lane fumbled with his hat, put it on, took it off again, agitated, in a hurry to leave. He glanced toward the door, then back at Diego. "I don't guess you know where I could find Mitchell, do you?"

Diego's heavy, salt and pepper eyebrows arched upward. "Ah, I see you've come to your senses." He slipped a calfskin glove from his left hand, one finger at a time. "Perhaps if you had taken care of Jim Mitchell as I suggested, your mother would still be alive, yes?"

"Yes."

"Lane, you don't know that it was the sheriff," Doc objected. "Granted, he's no angel but . . ."

"He killed Regino Vega," Lane cut in. "He killed my mother. Maybe tonight or tomorrow or next week he'll kill someone else, someone you care about this time, and you'll be singing a different tune." He brushed past Doc, heading for the door. "You gotta draw a line somewhere."

Lane stepped outside into the lingering cool of early morning and looked up and down the street. People were milling about, surveying the damage and estimating their losses. The overall mood was grim and subdued as men and women and even children began picking through the charred ruins for anything worth salvaging. Many of the smaller store-keepers had been completely burned out of business.

Diego drew up beside Lane, followed by his bodyguard. "Mitchell is in town," he said, "helping the *policía.*" His tone was sarcastic. "When you kill him, you must also kill Nimitz and Carrillo and the two deputies."

Lane gave him a chilly look. "Don't tell me what to do."

"Someone needs to. Your reluctance to take action has caused enough trouble already."

Lane untied his horse and had his hand on the saddlehorn and his foot in the stirrup when he suddenly froze. His breath caught in his throat, and he held it, listening intently. It was a soft tinkling sound, very near, a familiar sound that grew louder when the horse tethered closest to the buckskin on the hitch rail shook its head. Lane's gaze settled on the tiny silver bells decorating the animal's breast strap. "Diego . . . is that your horse?"

Don Mariano nodded. Yes, it was his horse. What of it? He met Lane's intent stare, then cast a swift glance at his bodyguard, before turning back to Lane.

"It was you," Lane said softly. "You . . ."

"¡Cuidado!"

Diego's bodyguard shouted a warning, shoved him out of the way, and grabbed for his gun. His hastily aimed shot missed Lane by a hair's breadth. In that fleeting flicker of time, Lane drew his Colt and returned fire, smoke and flame belching from the blue-black barrel. The bodyguard fell against the side of the building and painted the whitewashed wall red as he slid down it to the boardwalk. His boot heels scuffed spasmodically against the weathered planks.

Lane swung the buckskin around, keeping the horse's body between himself and Doc Udall's office building, his left hand gripping the reins and the saddlehorn. A bullet zipped past his head as another of Diego's bodyguards rounded the corner of the building. Lane snapped a shot at him, missed, fired again, and saw the man's body jerk as he took a bullet and fell to his knees. His terrible screams shredded the air, and Mariano Diego dove for the man's fallen pistol.

Slapping the frightened buckskin on the shoulder, Lane lunged past him, ducked under the hitch rail, and kicked the gun from Diego's hand as his fingers curled around the grip. Diego scooted backward on his butt, head tilted up to look at Lane, until he felt the wall behind him. He lifted his hands above his head, fingers spread wide.

"What's the meaning of this?" he rasped. "Have you lost your mind?"

Lane gazed down at him, jaws knotting and unknotting, an expression of savage hatred frozen on his dark face.

"Where are the others?" he demanded.

"What others?"

"The other two bodyguards. Where are they?"

Diego's unblinking eyes dropped from Lane's face to the Peacemaker Colt clenched in his hand. He licked his lips. "They will arrive soon. They'll kill you for this."

"Liar."

Lane kicked him in the face, a swift, vicious blow that caught Diego on the cheekbone and knocked the back of his head against the wall. As Lane brought his foot down, he raked his spur across the man's chest.

"At least one of your bodyguards had to stay behind because he was shot last night . . . shot by me."

"I don't know what you're talking about."

"Like hell, you don't. It was you. You and your men set fire to my parents' house. You killed Ann."

The corners of Diego's mouth pulled down in a ferocious scowl. With his goatee and thin, hard face, he appeared evil, like the devil himself. He massaged the red bruise on his cheek where Lane had kicked him and cut his eyes around at Doc Udall as he stepped cautiously out the door.

"Tell this madman to put away his gun so we can talk."

"Lane . . ."

"We'll talk now." Lane stood over Mariano Diego, feet spread, gun outstretched and aimed squarely between the man's eyes. "Why? Why did you do it?"

Diego was silent a moment, and when at last he spoke his words were in Spanish.

"You refused to obey my wishes."

Lane's eyes narrowed. "To kill Mitchell and the others?"

Diego shrugged, then nodded. "I never meant to harm your mother." He met Lane's attentive stare with proud arrogance. "Until last night, my men and I made many night raids without incident. God was on our side."

"Leave God out of this."

"He understood that everything we did was in behalf of those who were too weak to fight for themselves," Diego continued. "Perhaps it was you He did not approve of, Mr. Devens. Perhaps you are the one who is to blame for your mother's unfortunate death."

"You crazy son of a bitch."

"Lane!" Doc eased toward him and held his hand out. "Give me your gun. Let a judge and jury decide his punishment."

"He wouldn't shoot an unarmed man," Diego said softly, his gaze riveted on Lane. He placed his hands palm down on the boardwalk, and with slow, careful movements, began to draw his legs beneath him, preparing to rise. "Mr. Devens is too honorable for that."

One side of Lane's mouth jerked upward in a brief, scornful laugh. "You're a mighty poor judge of character, Diego."

No sooner did he get the words out than Diego shoved away from the wall, making a desperate lunge for Lane's six-gun. His hand closed over the barrel, tipping it up, and Lane heard the hard blast, felt the gun's recoil jar against his palm.

Having never shot anyone at pointblank range, it came as a surprise when the top of Mariano Diego's head disappeared. Brain matter, blood, and fragments of bone splattered against the wall, and Lane felt something wet and warm slide down his cheek. He took an awkward step backward, raised his arm, wiped his face on his sleeve.

Somewhere behind him, a woman screamed, and only then did he notice the faces, white, featureless faces, watching him from behind the glass windows of the hardware store across the street. Doc Udall stared at him in open-mouthed horror.

His body slouching, Lane sighed wearily. He dropped his gun back into its holster. Court was adjourned.

CHAPTER TWENTY-ONE

The Mexican's body hung suspended ten feet in the air like a dirty bag of laundry, hoisted to the top of the telegraph pole by a rope thrown up and over the crossbar where the wires were attached. His head drooped forward, chin on his chest. His face was black. Earlier this morning, someone had been seen squirming up the pole to steal his boots, and the dead man's bare, bony toes pointed toward the ground.

Down below, Jim Mitchell stood with his hands on his hips and watched Police Chief Bill Klarner and one of his underlings prepare to cut the rope where it was lashed to the base of the pole. Klarner had his knife poised over the rope when gunfire echoed across town. He gave Jim a frazzled look.

Jim waved him on. "Go ahead and cut him down 'fore he starts stinking," he said and crossed the railroad tracks to his tethered horse. "I'll check out the fireworks this time."

He saw Charlie Reed waiting for him in the middle of Penny Street, sitting his horse like a gob of melting lard. He lifted his hat and scratched his head.

"What now?" Jim asked.

"A shootin' in front of Doc Udall's office. Are we gonna handle it or leave it to Klarner?"

"We will. Anybody killed?"

Charlie shrugged. Didn't know. Didn't care.

Another shot rang out, and Jim and Charlie spurred their

horses into a run. They met Del Hardy at the corner of Church and Congress streets. Jim ordered him to cut through the church plaza to Udall's office while he and Charlie continued down the street.

By the time they reached the scene, a crowd was forming across the street from the doctor's office, indicating the shooters were either dead or had already cut and run.

"Three of 'em didn't run," Charlie said.

"God a'mighty. Will you look at that?"

Jim dismounted and tied his horse to a drain pipe at the corner of the building. Lane Devens had his rear end propped on the hitch rail nearby, feet crossed at the ankles, his back turned to the ghastly scene. What the hell was he doing here? Jim and Charlie exchanged glances. Ignoring their approach, Devens struck a match on his Levis, lit a cigarette beneath his cupped palm, and shook out the flame. He tossed the extinguished match into the street.

Jim's gaze shifted, and he felt the hair on his scalp start to rise. Lordy, lordy. The sickish-sweet smell of blood invaded his nostrils. Drawn by the scent, blue- and green-bottle flies buzzed happily over the three bodies.

The man sprawled on the boardwalk behind Devens never knew what hit him. The bullet had entered his left eye socket at an upward slant and had exploded out the top of his skull, taking everything in its path right along with it. Another man lay slumped against the wall in a pool of blood, shot once in the chest. Jim saw Doc Udall bend over him, shake his head, and walk past him to the third man curled up in a fetal position near the opposite corner of the building. He was gut shot and slowly dying. Folding up his suit coat, Doc placed it beneath the man's head and examined the purple-rimmed hole in his abdomen.

Jim took all this in with swift, darting glances, never

staring too long at any one body. He focused instead on Lane Devens.

"What happened here?"

Devens flicked the ash from his cigarette. Reaching into his shirt pocket, he drew out his badge and held it out to Jim. "You'll be wanting this, I reckon."

Assuming his resignation was due to Regino Vega's death and last night's chat with the newspaper reporter, Jim accepted the badge with child-like disappointment. He had looked forward to firing Devens himself, making a show of it, maybe rip the badge off his vest with a sharp, witty remark men would remember and talk about in the saloons.

Instead, Jim stood awkwardly next to Devens with the badge forgotten in his hand as he concentrated on not looking too closely at the dead men or stepping in something nasty.

"Say, who is that anyway? Mariano Diego?"

Devens nodded, his gaze still fixed on the ground. "He likes fire so much, he oughta feel right at home about now."

"What d'you mean? You think he's the firebug?"

"I know it."

Surprised, Jim turned to look at Charlie but found him gone, across the street with Del, questioning the bystanders.

His attention shifted back to Devens. He had a feeling the man knew more than he was telling. Devens appeared shaken, his face ashen and drawn, and when he met Jim's quizzical gaze, his expression was one of wary watchfulness. He reminded Jim of a gray-eyed wolf.

Exhaling blue cigarette smoke through his mouth and nostrils, Devens pushed away from the hitching rail and walked to his horse.

"Hey, wait a sec! I'm not through with you," Jim said. "Who killed these fellas?"

Devens reached for the buckskin's reins.

"Hey!"

Irritated, Jim started toward him, then stopped abruptly when he saw Charlie lumbering across the street, gun in hand, his hat flying off his head to land in the dust.

"Stop him!" Charlie yelled.

Lane Devens spun to face the deputy, and Jim spontaneously drew both six-shooters, covering Lane from behind. Off to his left, Del Hardy raised his Winchester to his shoulder.

With four guns trained on him, Devens checked himself and jerked his right hand up and away from his own sidearm.

"Get both hands above your head!" Jim shouted, though he still wasn't quite sure what was going on.

Slowly pivoting his body at an angle so that he could see all three lawmen, Devens plucked the cigarette from his mouth, dropped it on the ground, and lifted his hands. He watched the three men close in on him with little emotion. Jim never took his eyes off him, aware of the danger this one man presented, remembering his deadly swiftness. And if Lane Devens had, indeed, killed Diego and his two toughs, his caution was justified.

"Turn around!" Jim shouted. "Face the street!"

Devens hesitated an instant, and Jim's nerves jumped. He quailed at the thought of what might happen if the man decided to resist. If Devens died, he would most certainly take someone with him.

Doc Udall called out to Devens from the office door, urging him to listen to reason. It worked. Lane reluctantly gave in and turned his back to Jim.

Sidling toward him, Jim lifted Lane's gun, quickly stepped back, and rammed the weapon beneath his waistband. Only then did he relax and flash a wide grin.

"Cuff him, Charlie. We got him right where we want him."

It was too bad about Devens' mother, but murder was murder. That was how Jim looked at it in one of his fits of piousness, and nothing Doc Udall or anyone else said swayed him. Firebug or no, Mariano Diego had been unarmed when the breed shot off the top of his head. A crowd saw it happen, and that was enough for Jim. He was surprised that Udall would try to rationalize the killing.

Charlie and Del escorted Lane Devens to the Hole where, after a violent scuffle, they managed to get him through the door and cuff his hands to the same iron bars from which Regino Vega had been hanged. Devens knew the real reason behind his arrest.

Jim's sunny smile faded a little, however, when he saw the headline article on the front page of the *Arizona Star*.

Charlie nodded his massive head up and down. "Told you."

Jim looked from the paper to Charlie then back down again. The headline itself was enough to fill him with rage and humiliation: NEW DEPUTY SPEAKS OUT, ACCUSES SHERIFF OF BOTCHING INVESTIGATION. Jim crashed his fist against the desk top. He read the article, rapidly the first time, more slowly the second, and paid particular attention to Lane Devens' word-for-word quotations. George Nimitz burst into the office and slammed his copy of the paper in front of Jim, almost swiping his nose.

"What is the meaning of this?" he demanded.

Jim cleared his throat. "Well, George . . ."

"Is he locked up?"

"Of course."

"Get rid of him."

Jim was dumbfounded. “Let him go?”

“Kill him!”

“Oh.” Jim relaxed. “All in good time, George. He won’t make any trouble for us in the Hole.”

“Do it tonight.”

“Now hold your horses,” Jim said. “If we kill another prisoner so soon, somebody’s gonna get suspicious.”

Nimitz scowled. “You can’t keep Devens locked up forever. Half the people who witnessed his shooting of Mariano Diego say it looked like an accident, while the other half is calling it self-defense. Very few think it was outright murder.” He stabbed a bony finger at Jim. “I say get rid of him. Kill him.”

“My, my, my, aren’t we getting bloodthirsty all of a sudden. Are you still taking those liver pills, George?”

Nimitz glowered at him. “This isn’t funny.”

“You think I don’t know that?” Jim exploded. He swept the newspapers off his desk. “Devens is making me look like a damned fool in front of this whole county!”

“You were a fool for hiring him to begin with,” Nimitz said. “Did Del tell you about the questions Devens was asking about the inmate work program?”

Jim nodded. “Last night.”

“What do you think?”

“He was just being nosy.”

Nimitz considered that a moment, brow furrowed, mouth tight. “Perhaps I’m getting too suspicious,” he said at length, “but what if someone such as, say Robert Cates, hired this Devens character to infiltrate your department for the purpose of finding out what your connections are with my company?”

“Cates is dead.”

“I only used him as an example. It could be anyone.”

Jim stared at Nimitz in dismay as the possibility began to sink in and actually make sense. He looked across the room at Del who was standing in a self-conscious pose by the door, alternating between biting his nails and picking his nose.

"Told you I didn't trust Devens," Charlie said.

Jim rose and put on his hat. "Del, get your finger out of your nose and hand me those keys. We'll see what Devens has to say about this."

Upstairs, Charlie, Del, and George Nimitz waited in the narrow corridor and listened to the discontented voices coming from the jail while Jim unlocked and opened the Hole door. Charlie lit the lantern. Picking up his ax handle, Del slapped it against his open palm and peered inside the small, hot room at their newest prisoner.

His eyes narrowing in the sudden light, Lane Devens watched Jim as he stepped inside the Hole, then glanced toward the doorway at Nimitz and the deputies. His hands were shackled to the bars above his head. Sweat darkened his shirt beneath his arms.

Jim grinned at him. "How do our accommodations compare with the Fort Bowie guardhouse? Comfy?"

Devens' jaws locked, and he looked away, not answering. The only sound in the tiny room was the rhythmic smack of Del's club hitting against his palm.

Jim glanced up at Devens' hands, saw his fingers flex and unflex. "Bet they're starting to tingle some, eh? Pretty soon they'll go numb, and you won't even know they're there."

"We don't have all day," Nimitz said.

Jim shrugged. "I was just being friendly." He caught Charlie's eye and nodded, beckoning him inside before getting to the point. "Who hired you, Devens?"

Lane's expression didn't change. "Hired me for wha . . ."

Before he could get the last word out, Charlie stepped in

swiftly and drove a brutal right into the man's face. Devens rolled his head with the punch and spit the blood from his mouth.

"Let's try that again," Jim said. "Did somebody hire you to nose around in my business?"

Devens turned his face to the side, wiped his mouth on his sleeve, and lifted his chin. He regarded Jim with an infuriating attitude of arrogance and bold defiance. When he refused to answer, Jim nodded, and Charlie moved in. Unable to protect himself with his hands, Devens twisted his body to the side before the deputy's fist smashed into his gut so that he didn't absorb the full impact. The blow still left him gasping for air but didn't quite succeed in knocking the insolence from his eyes. Jim wondered what it was going to take.

"Who are you protecting?" Nimitz asked.

Devens shook his head, once each way. "Nobody."

Charlie started to hit him again, but Jim lifted a hand. "Wait a minute." He studied Devens curiously. "It couldn't have been Robert Cates," he mused. "Cates is dead. That leaves one other logical person, someone I've seen you with more than once here lately."

Devens stared at him, waiting.

"Doc Udall."

Devens' left eyebrow twitched upward. "Nice try."

Jim was pleased. Now we're getting somewhere, he thought. "Doc Udall suspected something fishy was going on in this department and hired you to snoop around. Am I right?"

"No."

"Maybe I should take Charlie and have a talk with Udall. Get to the bottom of this once and for all. What do you think, Devens?"

"I think you'd be wasting your time."

Charlie balled up his huge right fist and was about to punch the prisoner again when he got a surprise. Using the handcuffs to lift himself up, Devens kicked out at Charlie with both feet, caught him square in the belly, and sent him reeling against the opposite wall. Before Jim could duck out of the way, Devens kicked again, and his boot heel crashed into Jim's lower jaw. Jim both felt and heard his jaw pop before he hit the floor. Del Hardy brandished his club, giving Jim and Charlie a chance to scramble away.

Nimitz helped Jim to his feet. "That was very impressive," he remarked.

Jim straightened his tie and suit coat and worked his jaw from side to side. Every tooth ached. He glared at Lane Devens.

"I'm not finished with you, fella. Not by a long shot. You and the doctor are gonna wish you'd never crossed me."

"Do me a favor," Devens said. He rested his head against the wall and gazed past his left arm at Jim. "Forget Udall. He doesn't know anything about this."

Jim's eyes narrowed. "Then who does?"

"The man who hired me was killed this morning," Devens replied coolly. "You'll find him at the undertaker's."

"Mariano Diego?" Jim was shocked. "That son of a bitch hired you?"

"If it's true he was your boss," Nimitz said, "then why did he burn down your parents' house? Why did you kill him?"

"We didn't see eye to eye on some things."

"How can you prove he hired you?" Nimitz asked.

"He paid me three thousand dollars up front on Saturday. Check to see if he withdrew that much from the bank."

"I'll do that." Nimitz thoughtfully tugged his beard. "You've been extremely helpful, Mr. Devens. It's unfortunate I can't repay you for getting rid of Diego for me. Any last requests?"

"One free hand," Devens said. The corners of his mouth lifted in a faint smile. "One free hand to tear your ugly face apart, you crooked piece of sh . . ."

As before, Devens didn't quite manage to get that last word out before Charlie tore into him. At a nod from Jim, Del joined in, and the two deputies beat Devens until he sagged bleeding and battered against the wall.

George Nimitz drew Jim aside. "Go to the bank. Find out if Diego withdrew the three thousand."

"If he did?"

"Get rid of Devens. Tonight."

CHAPTER TWENTY-TWO

Pain was a reassuring sensation. Lane realized this after his arms fell asleep. His body ached, yet it was the lack of feeling in his hands and arms that caused him the greatest discomfort. It was as if they had been amputated and flung aside.

Locked in the blackness of the Hole, Lane lost track of time. His senses were practically useless. It was maddening. The walls were so thick he could hear little beyond his own labored breathing or the scuffing of his boots as he shifted his weight from side to side. He wondered if this was how Regino Vega had spent his last hours before his life ended.

Lane knew his own end loomed near. By trying to protect Doc Udall, he had cinched his fate. Faced with the unhappy prospect of death, Lane's state of mind degenerated from anger to desperation. There seemed to be no way out.

If only he had done things differently. If only . . . if only what? If only he hadn't murdered Mariano Diego? It was something to think about at least.

The shooting had been an accident. The trigger on Lane's .45 was extremely sensitive, a hair-trigger. When Diego grabbed for the gun, Lane's finger bumped the trigger. Yet, given the circumstances, who would believe that? Lane wasn't even sure he believed it himself!

Maybe you deserve to die after all, he thought.

Lane sighed and rested his head against the wall. He tried to relax the tightness in his shoulders, tried to imagine it melting away, sliding down his body to the floor. A drop of sweat dripped off his nose onto his chest. He stared into the blackness and watched as shadowy, unreal images floated across his vision.

The metallic snap and click of the unlocking door made Lane jump. Yellow light slanted across the floor as the door was thrown wide and the light washed over him, blinding him.

"Hey, Devens. How you doin'?"

Del Hardy stepped inside and hung the lantern on a nail by the door. He was followed by Floyd Waller, the jailer.

"I've got good news for you," Hardy said. He jingled the ring of keys in front of Lane's face. "If you promise to mind your manners, Jim says it'd be all right to free your hands for the night."

"Night? What time is it?"

"Five-thirty. So how about it, Devens? You want your hands freed or not?"

Lane nodded. "That'd be fine."

Hardy chunked the keys to Waller, stepped back, and drew his gun. He cocked it clumsily, using the heel of his left hand to push the hammer back, and aimed it at Lane. He licked his lips nervously.

About to take off the handcuffs, Waller paused to look over his shoulder at the young deputy. "I thought Mitchell said for you to keep that hogleg holstered."

"He didn't say no such thing."

"Well, watch where you point it."

Sniffling a little, Waller stood next to Lane, raising himself up on his tiptoes, and unlocked first one handcuff, then the other. Lane's nose wrinkled reflexively at the smell of the jailer's ancient body odor and onion breath. He looked up, watched Waller pry the cuffs from around his wrists, saw his arms fall like dead weights to his sides. He winced at the sharp pain that stabbed through his shoulders.

Waller stepped quickly away from him and backed out the door. "He's all yours, Del."

"No problem," Hardy said, though his voice quavered slightly as he slipped the leather strap of a canteen from his shoulder. "Jim said to give you this."

He pitched the canteen to Lane, grabbed the lantern by the handle, and hurried out the door. There was a loud slam, another metallic snap, and Lane was left once again in darkness. Unable to catch the canteen, it had struck him in the chest and fallen to the floor. He felt for it with his foot and waited impatiently for the blood and life to return to his arms. It started with a pins-and-needles sensation. He worked his hands, curling his fingers into tight fists, ignoring the accompanying pain. He bent down to pick up the canteen. Sloshing it, he found it less than half full. He slipped the strap over his head and shoulder and groped around in the dark until his foot struck the slop bucket.

His fingers slow and clumsy, Lane fumbled at the buttons on his pants and relieved his taut bladder. The sound of urine striking the empty bucket was a hollow roar within the close walls of the Hole. Finished, he buttoned his fly, unscrewed the cap on the canteen, and immediately lifted it to his lips. He took a couple of sips of the lukewarm water, swished it around inside his mouth, and spit half of it onto the floor. Slightly alkaline, the water stung the open gash on the inside of his mouth and burned his broken lips. He would save the rest for later.

After several restless circles around his tiny prison, he grew tired and sat in a corner. His thoughts continued to revolve around the events of the day—the death of his mother, R.J.'s revelations about his real father, his killing of Diego and the two bodyguards. The confusion of it all made him dizzy.

Breaking out in a fresh sweat, he dragged a hand down his face and wiped his damp palm on his jeans. His skin felt clammy. A strange restlessness stirred him to his feet again.

He was about to stand up when the first of a series of spasmodic cramps seized his stomach. He fell back to the floor, hugging his belly and drawing his legs up close to his body. Breathing hard, he rested his forehead against his knees and waited. No sooner did the first cramp ease than a second one took its place. He gasped, overcome by the pain that seemed to be eating a hole in his stomach, and writhed miserably on the floor in search of a position that might ease his discomfort. Nothing helped.

Over and over, the spasms continued until Lane could no longer tell one from the other. Time passed and his head began to pound, a skull-cracking throb beating against his temples as if his brain had swollen. He lay with his face pressed hard against the grimy floor. What was wrong with him? He felt sure that he was dying. Lying on his side, wet and quaking, he tried to pray but couldn't find the words. Prayers he once had known by heart deserted him. He managed to slip Sister Julia's rosary from his pocket and held onto it, but this provided little comfort to a man whose innards seemed to be turning inside out.

Eventually, Lane slipped into a delusive, dream-like state. He imagined his blood was seeping through the pores of his skin, standing out like beads of dew on grass. He raised a hand to his head, felt his hair wet with sweat, and screamed. The sound of his own voice startled him, sending a chill through his body. It was the cry of a wounded animal, imitated by the voice of a human.

"Lay low, boys," Lane whispered. "They're out there. The Apaches are out there."

Rosel's Restaurant was packed to overflowing when Christina Cates arrived there a little before nightfall. She made her way to the counter, her gaze scanning the supper crowd while avoiding eye contact with any one person, taking in the red and white checkered tablecloths, the blur of faces, hands gripping forks and spoons lifting to meet open mouths. The constant murmur of voices surrounded her, accentuated by an occasional burst of laughter or the clatter of utensils and plates. Delightful aromas wafted from the kitchen.

Wearing a loose, white blouse, a split riding skirt, and boots, Christina was aware of the disapproval showing in some of the women's faces. She wasn't dressed appropriately for a woman who had just buried her husband of seven years. What a shame! Robert's not even cold yet . . . Is it true he was poisoned? Talk is, he used to beat her . . . Not Robert Cates! Such a fine man.

As if they knew anything about it.

Christina saw Abbie Maginnis standing behind the counter, counting out change for one of the customers. She was a short woman, middle-aged, with a figure Christina might have envied had her mind not been on more serious matters. The name-tag pinned to her dress assured Christina this was the person for whom she'd been searching.

"Mrs. Maginnis?"

Abbie turned to look at her, fanning her face with a note pad. "Yeah?"

"Could I speak with you for a minute? It won't take long."

"I guess so." Abbie regarded her cautiously. "Do I know you?"

"My name's Christina Cates."

"Cates? Oh, yeah . . . I thought I'd seen you somewhere. It's too bad about your man."

"Yes. Thank you." Christina glanced around before continuing. "I assume you've heard about Lane Devens."

Abbie sighed. "Who in this town hasn't? Why?"

"I don't have time to explain everything right now, but I think his life may be in danger. I think someone wants to kill him."

Abbie didn't appear too distraught. "Well, they'll have to wait in line, won't they?"

"No, listen," Christina said, becoming anxious. "You don't seem to understand. This isn't a joke, and I need your help. Lane needs your help."

"And you think I care?" With a rueful, halfhearted laugh, Abbie shook her head. "I'm afraid you got it all wrong, honey.

"But I . . . I thought the two of you were very close."

Abbie rested her elbows on the counter, propped her chin on her hands. "I admit it's kinda nice sleeping with a healthy, good-looking man who hasn't been with a woman in almost a year," she said. A bored expression crept into her eyes. "If you like the serious type, you can have him."

"It's nothing like that," Christina murmured, wishing she hadn't come. "I won't trouble you any longer." She turned to leave.

"Wait a second," Abbie stopped her. "Come here, hon." She lowered her voice. "Look, I don't know what's going on with Lane, but if he's gonna try to break out of jail he'll want his horse. This afternoon, my boy, Seth, took Lane's big buckskin over to the stable next to the Russ Hotel. If you can get word to him somehow, you might tell him."

Nodding, Christina said a polite thank you and hurried out the door. So much for that. She wasn't certain what she'd expected from Abbie. A little cooperation perhaps? Concern?

Christina suspected Abbie Maginnis would have been more of a hindrance than a help anyway.

Christina's decision to try to save Lane Devens had followed a lengthy conversation with Doc Udall this morning. She'd stopped by his office to inquire about R.J. and Ann Devens, and learned for the first time of Ann's death. While she was there, Doc asked her pointblank whether or not she'd participated in Robert's murder. Christina broke down and confessed. It was a relief to confide in someone she knew she could trust.

She and Doc had discussed the situation at length, in which time he explained to her why Jim wanted both Robert and Regino Vega dead. He also told her how Lane Devens had been hired to investigate the link between the sheriff and Arizona Land and Development.

Christina found her earlier suspicions about Jim Mitchell confirmed. Afraid to dirty his own hands, he had used her to get rid of Robert.

R.J. and Lane Devens would surely be next on Jim's list. Warning Doc to keep a close watch over R.J., Christina immediately began making plans on getting Lane Devens out of jail. Thinking Abbie and Lane were lovers, her initial plan had involved Mrs. Maginnis. It appeared now she would have to do this alone.

Christina found Lane's buckskin gelding dozing three-legged in the livery stable east of the Russ Hotel. Lane's riding gear, rifle, and a few personal belongings were piled outside the stall. Not seeing the hostler or stable boy anywhere around, Christina saddled the horse, packed a few provisions she had prepared earlier into one of the saddlebags and led him outside.

It was now dark. Dogs barked and howled, chasing cats up and down the alleys, and beyond that were the people sounds, the plinkety plink of a piano, a woman's shrill laughter, the rumble of wagons and buggies. She heard someone calling a child in for the night. The streets, never altogether safe, were even less so now, particularly those not yet lighted by street lamps. For the sake of discretion, Christina tied a scarf over her head to conceal her identity and sought out these unlit side streets. Leading the buckskin behind her own mount, she rode with Lane Devens' carbine across her lap. While she didn't know how to use it, the fact that she was armed might make someone think twice before giving her trouble.

There were two buggies on the courthouse's west side, nearest the sheriff's office, where Jim's horse was tethered stripping paint off the picket fence with his teeth. Christina had expected either Jim or one of his deputies to be at the jail, but who were the other two? She rode past the buggies, holding her mount to a slow walk and noted that one of the rigs sported red-spoked wheels and red pinstripes across its body. She recognized it as belonging to George Nimitz.

Her stomach knotted with fear. What if she was too late?

Christina left the horses in a shadowy nook in back of the courthouse. She could see light from Jim's office window glowing in the jail yard. Cicadas buzzing in the treetops grew silent as she passed beneath them to the west entrance.

She climbed the steps to the door, drew a deep breath, and turned the knob. It was unlocked.

The door squeaked as Christina stepped inside, and almost immediately a door down the gas-lit hallway opened, and a man looked out at her. It was Jim.

"Christina? What are you doing here? It's late."

Christina walked toward him, felt her blouse slip off her shoulder, and resisted the temptation to tug it back up. "Are you busy?" she asked.

"Sort of. I thought you were still mad at me."

"Jim, I've been thinking." She drew closer to him and slid her hands beneath his suit coat. "Maybe I've been too hard on you. I don't know. I feel so mixed up. Can you understand?"

A slow smile spread across Jim's face, and he cuffed his hat off his forehead. "Sure, baby. I know exactly what you mean."

He bent his head to kiss her, but she stopped him, gently touching her fingers to his lips and glanced inside his office. Estevan Carrillo was leaning forward in his chair, craning his neck to watch them. She looked back up at Jim.

"Not here."

"You sure are pretty tonight, Christina."

"Do you know that house next to the mayor's on Main Street? The one Robert used to lease out sometime? That's where I'm staying now. I moved to town." She smiled up at him. "You can come by whenever you want."

He grinned at her. "Like after I finish up here?"

She nodded and stepped away from him as if to leave, then paused. "Oh, Jim, I almost forgot. Did you find my pocketbook?"

"Your what?"

"My pocketbook. I've been so distracted lately. I thought maybe I left it in the jailer's office yesterday when I was with you." She affected an air of concern. "I hope it's still there."

"Let's go see."

"No, wait. The sooner you get your business attended to here, the sooner we can be together. Let me go look. It won't take but a minute anyway."

Jim studied her, smiling a little. "You're something, Christina, you know that?"

Christina waved goodbye. "I'll see myself out," she said and started up the hall.

Before turning the corner, she glanced back and saw that he'd already returned to his office.

Christina was disillusioned. Lonely, afraid, and desperate, she had made the mistake of letting Jim Mitchell fool her into thinking he loved her. There were times when she had actually enjoyed his company, times like tonight when he seemed sweet and attentive. Fortunately, she was no longer fooled by him. Nor was she desperate.

The door to the jailer's cubicle was open, and a light was burning within. Holding her breath, Christina tiptoed the rest of the way to the door and peered inside. Floyd Waller was stretched out on a cot in the back of the office, arms and legs spread wide. He had evidently fallen asleep while reading, for a newspaper was lying open across his stomach. Drool spilled from his gaping mouth and soaked into the soiled pillow beneath his head.

Christina entered the office, moving quietly, careful not to disturb anything, and looked at the different sets of keys hanging from hooks near the door. Above each hook, a number or letter had been scratched into the wall with a knife, a code of some sort. Christina chose a single key, the H key. She dropped it into her skirt pocket. This was the same key Jim had used to lock the door to the Hole yesterday, and Christina knew the Hole was where she would find Lane Devens, jailed in isolation until his death. Just like Regino Vega.

Christina found a lantern and a box of matches, thinking she might need them upstairs. About to leave, she spotted a rolled-up gunbelt lying on a small desk in the corner of the office. There were a billfold and a handful of change nearby. Christina's gaze lingered on the belt a moment, long enough to notice that the initials LD had been burned into the leather holster. He would want his gun.

She scooped up the billfold and belt, and the sound of the gun grip clunking against the edge of the desk exploded the silence like dynamite. Christina froze, her eyes on the sleeping jailer. Waller stirred fitfully, grunted, and rubbed at his eyes. Christina didn't wait to see if he would fall asleep again, but backed out of the office door, one cautious step at a time, and glanced up and down the hall. It was empty. She fled into the narrow passage leading to the ground floor jail, turned the corner, and climbed the back stairs to the second story.

As she had expected, it was pitch dark upstairs, and she struck a match and touched it to the lantern's wick. Walking past the jail door, she could hear prisoners talking quietly among themselves, some in English, others in Spanish. One man saw the light from Christina's lantern and hollered an obscenity at her, mistaking her for one of the deputies or a jailer.

Christina stopped in front of the Hole, set her lantern on the floor, and pressed an ear to the door. There was no sound from within. She tapped on the door, listened.

"Lane? Lane Devens?"

Still no sound.

What if he wasn't here, after all? Or what if he was already dead? There was only one way to find out. She thrust the key into the lock, turned it and heard the bolt snap back. Quivering with apprehension, she picked up her lantern and opened the door.

The heat and stench trapped inside struck her in the face, and she recoiled from the open doorway. She lifted her lantern higher, letting the light splash into the darkness of the small room. A man was lying on his side on the floor, his back turned to her so she was unable to see his face. His shirt was dark with sweat, his black hair sodden. Christina moved toward him.

"Lane?"

She could see the rise and fall of his ribcage and knew he was alive. Was he asleep? Lifting her skirt, she squatted down beside him and timidly laid her hand on his arm.

Too late, she realized her mistake. Like a sprung trap, Lane Devens flipped over onto his back, his right hand driving forward, steely fingers closing around Christina's throat. She tried to cry out, but the sound was blocked by the pressure on her windpipe. She struggled briefly, striking at him with her fists in the first few seconds of panic before she got a grip on her nerves and remembered the many lessons she had learned from living—and surviving—with her husband. Focus on your breathing, conserve your energy, and above all else, don't resist.

Holding herself still, she squeezed her eyes shut. Her breath rasped beneath the crushing force of Lane Devens' fingers. She could hear his breath above her own, an uneven rush of air hissing in and out through his teeth, could smell the masculine rankness of his body.

Her passivity paid off. She felt Lane's grip on her throat lessen and opened her eyes to look at him, startled at first by the bruises and scabbed-over cuts on his face, the swollen eye, the sick pallor of his skin. He hadn't attempted to rise as of yet, and Christina sensed his helplessness and was emboldened by it even while his hand remained on her throat.

"I'm here to help you," she said softly.

CHAPTER TWENTY-THREE

Lane stared at her. "Abbie?" He slid his hand downward from her throat and pressed his palm between her breasts. "Abbie . . ."

Christina didn't bother to correct him. "We have to get out of here," she whispered and shrank back so that his hand dropped to the floor. "Can you walk?"

"I think so."

She helped him sit up, felt his arm encircle her waist, and supported his weight as he struggled to stand up. He leaned against her a moment, steadying himself, and held his hand out for his gun. Christina hesitated, not sure she could trust him. He didn't wait for her to make up her mind. Prying the gunbelt away from her, he rested his back against the wall, buckled on the belt, and snugged the holster low on his thigh.

Not a word passed between them as they walked out into the corridor. When Christina started to pick up the lantern, Lane shook his head, and she blew out the flame and left it behind.

Lane took the lead, trailing a hand along the wall, feeling his way through the dark. Twice, he had to stop and rest before reaching the stairs. Afraid he would fall, Christina gripped his arm.

All was quiet downstairs. Hugging the wall, Lane lifted his .45 and peered around the corner while Christina kept watch from behind. Lane drew back sharply, hearing Jim Mitchell's sudden, muffled laughter, and glanced sideways at Christina. The whites of his eyes shone like crescent moons in the dim light.

"Is Mitchell still here?" he whispered.

Christina nodded. "Talking with Estevan Carrillo and George Nimitz," she said. "The jailer's here, too. We'll have to be careful." She looked down, watched him press his forearm hard against his stomach. "Can you do this?"

Nodding, he drew a shaky breath and rounded the corner.

Christina was shaking, too, but for a different reason. She followed Lane into the main hall. The jailer's cubicle was now dark and the door closed. They moved soundlessly past the office, past the water closet, and paused again near the center of the courthouse where the four hallways converged. Looking to her right, Christina could see a sliver of light shining beneath Jim's office door. Lane turned left, making for the east entrance.

"Hey, you! Stop right there!"

The jailer's nasal twang echoed up and down the empty hall, and Christina's heart leapt with fright. Turning the corner behind Lane, she caught a fleeting glimpse of Floyd Waller emerging from the water closet at a dead run and saw the metallic glint of the pistol in his hand.

"Sheriff! He's out! Devens is out!"

A gunshot ricocheted somewhere behind them as they ran for the door, and Christina's scream collided with the plaintive whine of a wasted bullet. Glancing over her shoulder, she saw Jim burst out of his office.

"Don't shoot!" he yelled. "He's got Christina!"

Lane unlocked the east door, flung it open, and shoved Christina out ahead of him. Stumbling, she fell to her hands and knees on the steps and picked herself up in time to see Lane fire two shots down the hall before ducking outside.

"This way," she hissed.

Seeking out the darkest shadows, Christina ran along the side of the building, followed closely by Lane. Beyond the rapid crunch, crunch of their boots, she could hear men shouting to one another, and the fear that one of them might find the horses worried her into running faster.

Lane touched her shoulder, then dropped back. "Wait," he gasped. "My God, it hurts."

She turned to see him stagger sideways. He sagged against the brick wall of the jail yard, holding his stomach.

"Come on," she pleaded. "I'll help you."

Lane doubled over. Dry heaves wrenched his body, and visions of Robert Cates writhing in agony on the bedroom floor crowded into Christina's mind. Had Lane been poisoned? There was no time to think. No time to worry or deliberate. Strengthened by her own panic and urgency, she slung Lane's left arm over her shoulders and half-dragged, half-carried him to the other side of the jail yard. A rider pounded past them on the street, and by the light of the gas lamps, she recognized Jim's undersheriff. Dust from his mount's hooves left her eyes and teeth gritty.

Ducking beneath a tree's low-hanging branches, she found the horses where she'd left them. Lane spoke quietly to the buckskin, calming him, and allowed Christina to help him into the saddle.

They left the cover of the trees at a hard gallop and pointed their horses northeast—the quickest and least populated route out of Pennington. A fire bell began to clang, alarming the town of pending disaster, summoning all able-bodied men from saloons and front porches and soft beds. Behind Christina and Lane, someone shouted and emptied his gun at them. Already out of range, the six wild shots merely hastened their flight.

Cutting across vacant lots and through empty yards, they hurdled their horses over an ancient, crumbling wall and swept out of town, following the wagon road for half a mile before slowing down. They stopped and looked back at the twinkling lights and cracker-box outlines of adobe houses and shacks. Dogs barked and howled, competing with the noise of the fire bell, but there was no sound of pursuit.

"You go on home," Lane told her.

Christina looked at him in surprise. "What?"

"Go home."

"Don't order me around," she stated. Her voice was flat and cool. She stared at him leaning forward in the saddle, in too much pain to sit upright, and wondered if he still thought she was Abbie Maginnis. "You might not make it alone," she pointed out.

"I'll make it."

"Where will you go?"

He pointed with his chin to the northeast, indicating the moonlit ridges of the Catarina Mountains.

Christina sighed. "There's food in your saddlebag and your canteen is full."

"I appreciate it," he said softly. "More than you can know."

With a parting glance at Pennington, he reined his horse around and struck out across the open desert, leaving behind him a roiling trail of fine white dust. Christina wondered if he would make it as far as the mountains. She wondered what would happen if Jim ever caught up with him. Gazing toward town, Christina shuddered. The bigger question was, what would Jim do to her when he figured out that she had helped Lane Devens escape?

For the first time, she realized her own life might be in danger. She didn't know Jim any more and couldn't trust him. He was not a man, but a puppet, and as long as Arizona Land and Development pulled the strings, his words and actions would not be his own. He would do whatever George Nimitz and Estevan Carrillo told him to do.

Christina's horse shifted uneasily beneath her weight, eyes and ears directed toward the fading sound of pounding hooves, and Christina made a snap decision. She flicked the reins against her mount's lathered neck and dug in her heels. Gravel jumped beneath the animal's hooves as he shot forward.

Lane heard her coming and reined in, swinging his horse to the side. Christina was sure he'd order her home again. When she caught up with him, however, he turned, and they rode together in silence, glancing over their shoulders every few minutes, looking toward town, looking for the posse they both knew would accompany Jim Mitchell. The moon cast a silvery glow over giant saguaros, palo verde, and staghorn and made the poisonous, white spines of the cholla appear almost luminescent. Christina thought the desert more beautiful at night, not so formidable as during the day beneath a hot and brassy sun. Gradually ascending the foothills and bajadas, they let the horses choose their own pace up the rocky, uneven slopes, not hurrying and no longer looking over their shoulders. The air grew cooler, and Christina remembered she didn't have a jacket or even a blanket to protect her from the chill.

Lane stopped occasionally to get his bearings, and Christina hoped he knew where he was going, for she didn't. The southwestern wall, or front range, of the Catarinas was said to be impenetrable to a horse and rider, yet this jagged wall of stone pasted against the night sky seemed to be his very destination.

A small band of javalinas burst out of the dense brush

near the mouth of a wash where they'd been feeding on prickly pear pads. Christina smelled their strong musky odor as she followed Lane between the eroded banks of the arroyo. Sandy deposits among the rocks were the only indication that water sometimes rushed through here to the thirsty desert below.

They followed the arroyo's course until they reached a dry waterfall. The fall was a yard high, and below it, erosion had formed a little amphitheater filled with thorn scrub and was walled in on one side by solid bedrock. A seep collected in a shady depression no larger than a man's hand where the bedrock and sandy wash coincided.

Lane stepped down from the saddle and leaned wearily against his horse. "I can't go any farther," he said, the first words he had uttered since ordering her to go home. His voice was heavy with exhaustion.

Christina was amazed that he had made it this far. "Will we camp here?" she asked.

He nodded and didn't protest when she began stripping the horses of their saddles and sweaty blankets. Dropping to her knees, she drank from the seep, wet her face, and scraped sand from the basin to deepen the pool. She waited patiently for the horses to drink and slowly rolled her head from side to side in an effort to work out some of the stiffness. Her back ached, and she could feel the sting of cactus thorns embedded in her legs but was too tired to bother with pulling them out.

Lane sat down and rested his elbows on his bent knees, hands dangling between his legs. He watched her tend to the horses.

"You've got a lot of grit for a rich girl."

Christina turned to look at him. Rich girl? Like Jim, he wasn't as smart as he thought he was.

"How do you feel?" she asked.

He shook his head.

Not knowing what else to do, Christina spread his ground sheet and blanket down beside him. "Maybe you'll feel better after you've rested."

"They poisoned me, didn't they?"

She straightened his blanket, smoothing out the wrinkles with great care.

"Look, if you know what's wrong with me, say so," Lane said. "Am I gonna die or not?"

"How should I know?"

Wincing a little, he shifted his position to see her better. "Your husband was poisoned. We both know that."

Christina looked up at him. His face was half in shadow, half out, giving him an ominous appearance that startled her at first. She drew back slightly and sighed. Why play games?

"You have some of the same symptoms Robert had."

"Like what?"

"The vomiting, the stomach pains. But you're not as sick or as weak as he was. Did Jim give you anything to eat or drink today?"

"Some water."

"Was that when you got sick?"

He nodded.

"It could have had rat poison in it. Arsenic."

She watched for a reaction, but could detect none.

"How much did you drink?" she asked.

"Not much. I washed my mouth out with it mainly."

Christina felt a measure of relief. "It probably wasn't enough to kill you."

She helped Lane lie down and covered him with a blanket when she felt him shiver. She pressed her palm against his forehead. His skin was damp and cold to the touch.

Wetting his bandana with water from the seep, Christina gently wiped away some of the dried blood on his face. She saw his eyes cut to the side to look at her.

"Why'd you break me out of there?"

Christina shrugged and gazed up at the stars a moment. "Jim was going to kill you," she said finally. "I felt responsible."

"What about Regino Vega?"

"I never dreamed Jim would frame him . . . murder him. When it happened, I didn't even know about Jim's involvement with the land company." She shook her head. "For what it's worth, I'm sorry. I'm sorry for a lot of things."

"I thought you were in on it all along."

Christina sighed. "I killed my husband," she said, matter-of-factly. "I played right into Jim's hands. That was enough."

Lane closed his eyes, and she was thankful when he didn't say any more about it. She didn't want to talk about Jim Mitchell or even think about him. There would be plenty of time for that tomorrow.

Tired but not sleepy, Christina listened to the crickets serenade her and glanced around. A massive boulder was perched on the slope above them, looking as if the slightest nudge might send it tumbling over the top of them. To either side of the arroyo, saguaros stood at attention beneath the starry sky. Nearby, the horses snoozed on their feet.

"Such a wild place," she whispered.

"I used to come here alone when I was a kid," Lane remarked. Surprised he had heard her, Christina jumped at the sound of his voice and turned to see him watching her.

"Weren't you afraid?" she asked.

"Of what?"

"Apaches."

He didn't answer her, and she wondered if she had offended him. He was, after all, half Indian himself.

Hugging herself to preserve body heat, Christina sat quietly and waited in her own calm, patient manner for Lane Devens to fall asleep. He turned over onto his side once, drawing his knees up, and mumbled something she couldn't understand. Perhaps he was thinking of his dead mother, or the three men he killed this morning, or Abbie Maginnis . . .

When his breathing grew slow and deep and regular, she crawled toward him on her hands and knees. Her muscles were stiff and cold. Lifting the edge of his blanket, she eased her body beneath its warmth an inch at a time, careful not to touch him, and very slowly relaxed.

She tried not to think about Robert, but though he was dead, she could almost feel the weight of his malevolent stare. She felt his hatred, his anger, his jealousy. Was it true that the dead sometimes haunted those they left behind? Could Robert see her now as she lay here beside another man?

She lifted her gaze to the big boulder balanced above them. If it rolled on top of them during the night, there would be her answer.

CHAPTER TWENTY-FOUR

Lane awoke before dawn. As was his custom, he lay perfectly still until he was sure of his surroundings and listened for any unfamiliar sounds. Hearing nothing out of the ordinary, he raised up on one elbow. The world tipped beneath him and spun in sickening circles. Lane gritted his teeth and sat all the way up. Bile rose inside his throat. Its acidic vapor filled his mouth, and he swallowed hard to keep it down.

His nausea subsided after a few minutes, and glancing around, he was surprised to see Christina Cates lying next to him. Her body formed a gentle S beneath the covers. It embarrassed him a little, not so much the situation, but because he hadn't thought to ask her if she needed a blanket.

Careful not to disturb her, he pushed himself to his feet and sucked in his breath when a sharp pain stabbed through his abdomen. He could thank Jim Mitchell for that.

He made his way through the dark to his horse, weaving dizzily across the hard-packed wash, and grasped a handful of the buckskin's thick mane. There was something comforting about the familiar oily, sweaty, dusty smell of the horses. He ran his hand down the buckskin's long neck to its shoulder and felt the muscles quiver beneath his fingertips.

It pained him to think he would have to let the buckskin go soon, but there was no way around it. A man on horseback would never make it up this side of the mountain without ruining, or more likely, killing his mount. The slopes were much too steep, the canyons too rocky and treacherous.

He glanced back at the woman where she lay sleeping and wondered if she would be able to handle the climb. His real doubt, however, lay with himself. Though the pain had dulled somewhat, he could still feel the arsenic gnawing at his insides. But at least he remained among the living. For now.

His gaze swept across the desert, stopped, switched back to a point below and a little to the right. The moving lights startled him. They winked across the distance, three, maybe four miles away, several flickering yellow-orange lights, one behind the other at varying lengths and creeping toward them.

The woman drew up beside him. "What are they?" she asked, her voice hushed.

"Torches. The posse's trailing us."

"In the dark?"

"They got a good tracker. Regular bloodhound." He pointed at the lights. "See the one out in front? He stops and starts, moves slow, walking I bet, hunting for tracks. Probably some reservation Indian they had to sober up with about two gallons of coffee." He shook his head. "Damned good thing."

She glanced up at him. "Why is it good?"

"Slowed 'em down some. They could've run right over the top of us while we slept."

They wasted no time breaking camp. Lane led off, following the narrow arroyo to the main watershed, gradually climbing. The route he chose up this, the dry side of the mountains, was a familiar one. He had hiked through here many times when he was a boy, drawn to the mountains like a bee to pollen. A sullen kid with a chip on his shoulder, he had had few friends back then, and so it was desert and mountain that he turned to for companionship and solace.

But there was danger here, as well. Once, following an argument with R.J., he had stayed away for days, penetrating deeper into the Catarinas than ever before. It was during the *tiempo de aguas,* the summer rains, and the streams were full. Chilled from swimming, he was stretched out on a flat boulder in the sunshine one afternoon when he saw the four Apaches. They passed directly below him, skirting the edge of the stream by way of a narrow deer trail that wound through the trees. He had felt more shock than fear. Flattening his naked form against the boulder, he watched as they rode right past his clothes and shoes piled together by the side of the trail without so much as a glance. He listened to their strange, guttural language. He listened even more intently to their laughter.

Barely fourteen years old, he learned that day what few of the Apache-haters back in Penny Town accepted. Apache warriors were human, after all. They could laugh and joke just like anyone else, something Lane would never have guessed after listening to men like his stepfather. More importantly, they could make mistakes. Lane knew what might have happened to him if one of the warriors had looked beyond the end of his nose and seen his clothing. It proved to him that, contrary to what R.J. had said, Apaches were not all alike. Some were more observant and skillful on the trail than others.

Thinking back on this particular experience, Lane wondered at the skills of the man who trailed them now. Certainly he was a better tracker than most, better than Lane himself, and something would have to be done about him sooner or later.

Dawn found them in the cracked and desiccated streambed of a nameless canyon, the same canyon Lane had explored as a youngster. A fresh, pine-scented breeze wafted down from the high country and whispered through scrub oak and manzanita. Gazing around him at the brush-choked canyon and the mottled gray boulders up ahead, Lane drew to a halt and twisted around in the saddle to look at the woman.

"This is your last chance to turn back," he told her.

She shook her head. "I can't."

"Mitchell probably won't do anything to you."

"Maybe not at first," she said. "Not as long as he thinks I have Robert's money."

Lane studied her a moment, then glanced up at the canyon's northwest slope, trying to think about two things at once. "He wants to marry you for your money?" he asked finally.

"Yes. Only there isn't any. I believe Robert suspected I was being unfaithful to him because he recently changed his will. He left almost everything to his brother." She gazed solemnly down at her hands clasped together over the saddlehorn. "When Jim finds out, he won't have any more use for me."

Her assumption sounded characteristic of the sheriff. Unable to think of anything comforting to say to her, Lane turned his attention back to the problem at hand.

A dim trail twisted up the northwest slope to the ridge, probably the last accessible trail out of the canyon they would find for the horses. Lane decided to take advantage of it.

The slope was steeper than it looked from the canyon floor. Loose earth showered to the bottoms and dust whirled as the horses lunged, leaped, and scrambled up the trail. Ocotillo lashed at their bodies like barbed whips, and the catclaws' hooked prickles snagged clothing and flesh with tiger-like ferocity. Lane and Christina climbed part of the way on foot to save their horses the extra burden.

With the buckskin's steamy hot breath fanning the back of his neck, Lane paused halfway up the slope and scanned the terrain. The light of the rising sun was slowly creeping down the northwest side of the canyon, but the rock ledge he had spotted from the streambed was still in shadows.

"Just a little more," he whispered and wiped the sweat from his forehead.

Mounting up, he felt the buckskin's muscles bunch beneath him for another upward lunge, and once again they were working their way through thorns, stickers, and scratchy weeds and eating the dust of a two-year drought.

The trail passed between a vertical break in the ledge, and it was here that Lane halted and stepped down from the saddle, careful to keep his feet on the broken slabs of rock to either side of him. He directed Christina to do the same. If his vague plan was going to have a chance at working, they mustn't leave any footprints from here on.

Fighting off another wave of nausea, Lane handed his carbine, bedroll, and saddlebags to Christina, slung an extra cartridge belt and the strap of his canteen over one shoulder, and took from his knapsack only those items he decided they couldn't do without. Among these were two pairs of rawhide-soled moccasins. One pair was dusty and worn and reached almost to Lane's knees when he pulled them up over his pants legs. He had bought the second pair of moccasins from an Apache woman at Fort Bowie. They were cut at the ankles and decorated with an intricate beadwork of white, blue, and green. He had planned to give them to Seth Maginnis for his birthday but gave them instead to Christina.

"They won't blister your feet," he told her.

Tying their boots and anything else they didn't need to the saddles, he cut a green switch from a palo verde and lashed it hard across the horses' rumps.

"What are you doing?" Christina cried out.

She started after the horses as they bolted away, but Lane grabbed her by the arm and stopped her. She tore her gaze from the horses to look at him, and the fear in her eyes was manifest and real.

"We'll never make it without them," she said. "We'll die!"

Lane bent down, gathered up several rocks, and hurled them at the horses to hurry them on their way. "We won't die if you'll do what I tell you to do." He tipped his head back and watched the two horses thrash and scramble their way up the trail until he could no longer see them. "Maybe the saints will smile on us today," he added.

"I just hope you know what you're doing."

"Trust me." Lane picked up his Spencer and saddlebags and gave Christina a slow up-and-down inspection that made the color rise to her cheeks. "You're a tough lady," he said with a nod and moved past her, scanning the rock ledge and the lay of the land up-canyon. "You'll do fine."

"What about you?" she asked.

He shrugged. "I'm all right."

Christina seemed to take heart after that. They climbed the vertical crack to the top of the ledge, and Lane explained to her the basics of hiding her trail. They would follow the ledge as far as possible, it being mostly bare rock, but even here it was easy to leave behind some small sign of their passing. Broken limbs and twigs, crushed grass, hair or thread caught on a mesquite—all were innocent slip-ups that any sharp-eyed tracker would use to his advantage. Having told Christina this much, he glanced back once to see her following him closely with her long hair braided down her back so it wouldn't become snarled in the brush.

"Do you think they'll trail the horses?" she asked.

"We can hope so."

But they won't follow them far, he thought. Any man who could trail two riders over rocky terrain in the dark wouldn't be easily fooled. At some point, Mitchell's guide would find a few well-marked hoof prints and know by their depth that the horses weren't carrying the added weight of their riders. He'd backtrack then, searching for sign, and try to think like the man he pursued.

It would afford Lane and Christina some extra time but not enough.

Morning advanced toward noon, and the canyon's northwest wall was by now bathed in sunlight. Sweat stung the fresh cuts and abrasions on Lane's face and blurred his eyes. He blinked rapidly several times to clear his vision and wiped his face, leaving a red smear across the palm of his hand. That damned Reed. Big, dumb ape had fists like mauls. A bright pearl of blood dripped off Lane's nose and splattered on the rock at his feet. He bent down and cleaned it up with his sleeve, at the same time pressing his bandana beneath his nostrils.

Christina stopped behind him and slung the bedroll from her shoulder to the ledge. "Let's rest a minute," she said. They sat in the sparse shade of the weeds and brush over-hanging the rock shelf. Lane held his head back and waited for his nose to stop bleeding, while Christina dug into his saddlebags for the ham and fry bread she had packed there the night before.

"Are you hungry?"

Lane shrugged, indifferent.

"You should try to eat," she said and pressed one of the crisp tortilla-shaped pieces of fry bread into his hand. "It'll make you feel better."

Wiping his nose dry, Lane ate cautiously, afraid his tortured stomach might rebel, and washed it down with a swallow of warm water. He handed the canteen to Christina, saying, "Don't drink too much. It may be a little while before we find any more."

He gazed down into the shadowy bottoms at the white-barked sycamores, cottonwoods, graceful willows, and ashes and followed this trail of green to where the canyon swung gently west, then east. Their ledge ended in the westward bend half a mile up-canyon. Rolling a cigarette, Lane studied the steep northwest wall beneath him and traced with his eyes the different lines of weakness where they might descend into the bottoms. He searched for a route that was rocky enough to hide their passage but not so rough they'd break their necks in the process.

Once he had pinpointed a way down that suited him, he lifted his gaze north to the smoky blue peak barely visible over the cliffs of the canyon, north to the heart of the Catarinas. Two days would get them there. Sure now that he could make it despite being beaten and poisoned, Lane began to feel easier in his mind. Walking had never bothered him.

He knew men who wouldn't walk across the street if they could ride. Men like Jim Mitchell. Mitchell won't walk, he thought. No, he'll hang back and send somebody else up the mountain, the tracker and maybe a deputy or two, send them after the dirty half-breed. But careful with the lady, boys. She's worth money.

Lane wondered if Mitchell would want him taken dead or alive. Alive, he decided. Mitchell would have to gloat over his victory a little. Then they'd kill him, throw him over a horse, and pack him back to Penny Town like a bagged buck. Save the taxpayers the expense of a trial, and it'll be remembered come election day.

"What are you thinking about?"

Lane glanced up to see Christina Cates watching him intently. She had finished eating and was sitting facing him with her head and shoulder resting against the cool, smooth surface of a boulder.

"I was thinking it's about time we got going," he answered.

"Besides that."

Lane picked up his carbine and stood up. "Women always want to know what a man's thinking. Maybe he's just thinking about what he ate for breakfast, but they still want to know."

She laughed gently at his observation. "You didn't eat any breakfast," she pointed out.

Her soft laughter lifted his spirits. It occurred to him that he'd never seen her smile and guessed she had no reason to. Life wasn't very funny right now.

Finished with his cigarette, he ground it out, tucked the butt into his pants pocket along with the burned out match, and held his hand out to her.

"We're going down," he said and helped her to her feet.

A narrow gully ran the length of the canyon wall to the bottom, its bed littered with rocks and gravel, hardpan and sand. The sand they tried to avoid, but there were places where they had no choice. With Christina ahead of him, Lane wiped out the few tracks they made, using his breath to blow fine grains of sand into the little hollows left by heel and toe. Thanks to the moccasins they wore, the footprints were already shallow and ill-defined, not like the sharp cut of a man's boot.

Strong and lithe, Christina reached the bottom without mishap and stood waiting for Lane beneath the welcome shade of a cottonwood.

"I'd hate to be Jim's tracker," she said. "He's got a lot of work ahead of him."

Lane smiled at her but didn't comment. He wished he felt as confident. Even without footprints to follow, the tracker wouldn't have much difficulty guessing which direction they would travel.

When Lane reached the bottom, they drank from the canteen and rested a minute. Mesquite catkins sweetened the air. The only sound was the soft rustle of cottonwood leaves stirring in an almost nonexistent breeze and a Gambel's quail calling an alarm somewhere up-canyon.

"There's water near," Lane said.

"How do you know?"

"The quail."

Boulders of all sizes and shapes crowded the narrow floodplain and channel. Sycamore roots twisted and twined around these natural anchors, securing the trees against powerful flood currents that sometimes ripped through the canyon during summer monsoons. It made for a slow and difficult climb, but at least they were out of the sun and thorny brush and cactus.

Squatting at the edge of a flat-topped boulder to catch his breath, Lane tied his bandana around his forehead to keep the sweat from his eyes and looked through a hole in the treetops at the sheer, towering cliffs rimming the southeast wall. Nearly invisible from his position was an open grove of ponderosa pines growing on the most elevated ridge top a thousand feet or more above him. He would have to climb this cliff tomorrow to check out their back trail.

Shadows stretched long, and the reddening rays of a sinking sun made the canyon blush. They had walked almost nonstop since midmorning, and one look at Christina's drawn face and his own weariness told him it was time to call it a day. They found a string of shallow, rather murky pools of water and made camp.

Lane built a small fire in a hollow beneath the trees, no longer worried about leaving sign. If they had not shaken Mitchell's tracker off their trail by now, they never would.

The tiny pools were alive with agitated fish. Adding more dry wood to his fire, Lane dipped up some of the filthy water in a soot-blackened can, covered the surface with a good layer of charcoal, and let it boil. After several minutes, he skimmed off the charcoal and refilled his canteen with the purified water.

They ate another meal of ham and fry bread and took turns drinking coffee from the can. Afterwards, in the uncertain light of evening, Lane picked up his carbine and walked a short way from camp and scouted around, familiarizing himself with the sights and sounds of their campsite. He limped slightly, his right knee already stiffening up after a few minutes of rest, and he sat on a wedge-shaped boulder jutting over the water and massaged his leg. He gazed down at the rippling reflection of his face.

All day he had struggled to focus his thoughts on the trail ahead and the posse behind, but his sorrow and bewilderment were ever with him, lurking in back of the immediate worries like a deep, dark shadow. Who am I? he wondered. What am I?

Lane looked at his reflection more closely. He told himself his was not the face of an Apache. He lacked the broad, flat features. He was taller, thinner, his face was lean.

Although Lane fully intended to speak with General John Bickham to confirm his stepfather's story, he knew in his heart that no matter how much R.J. hated him he wouldn't have lied about this. Lane understood now why he possessed no memories of his father. There were none.

He touched the ketoh on his left wrist and studied the silver and turquoise ornamentation. Taking it off, he dangled the bow guard over the water but couldn't bring himself to let go of it. Ann would want him to keep it, if not to remind him of Niyol as his father, then to remind him of the man who saved their lives. He tied the ketoh back on his wrist.

Lane understood why his mother had lied to him. She had wanted to spare him the shame, to make him believe it was love that had brought him into the world instead of hatred. What he did not understand was why she had cared. Most women, he was certain, would not have wanted anything to do with him.

So who was Cuervo? Was he still alive? He thought it would be nice to find this man, his so-called father. Stake him out in the desert sun and perform a little operation on him with a sharp knife, maybe cut off his eyelids first so he'd have to watch. The old man wouldn't rape any more women after Lane finished with him.

Laying the carbine across his lap, Lane rested his elbows on his thighs and buried his face in his hands, moccasined feet dangling over the water. Never had he felt so sick at heart.

When it grew darker, and he still hadn't returned to camp, Christina wandered upstream to look for him. Hearing her step, Lane jerked his head around, his right hand closing over the Spencer. Before he could rise, however, she touched his shoulder lightly and dropped down beside him. Lane turned his face away in shame and wiped his eyes on his shirt sleeve.

"Lane, I'm sorry," she said softly. "I'm so sorry about your mother. Do you want to tell me what happened?"

He tried to swallow the knot in his throat and shook his head. "Nothing to talk about." His voice sounded husky.

To his surprise, she slipped her hand in his. "Sometimes it helps to talk," she said. When he didn't respond, she continued. "I had a long talk yesterday with Doc Udall. I told him about Robert. It was a relief to get it all out in the open. I see things more clearly now."

"If you had it to do over, would you still want to kill him?" Lane asked.

She didn't answer immediately. He saw her eyes lift to meet his, lustrous, brown eyes in an ivory face, heart-shaped lips. She was a beautiful girl, or woman, or murderess, or however one wished to think of her. Robert Cates hadn't destroyed her looks. Or her spirit, Lane decided. He found himself admiring her.

"Robert killed my baby," she said finally. "He pushed me down the stairs, and I had a miscarriage." Lane felt her hand tighten around his own, heard her draw a quick breath. "No man will ever abuse me again."

Darkness had fallen around them, but Lane didn't need to see her expression to know that she meant every word.

She looked up at him. "I'm certain Robert would have killed me in time. I couldn't get away from him."

"I know. I don't blame you for that."

"But you do blame me for Regino Vega's death, don't you?" She bowed her head, and sitting beside her, Lane sensed the depth of her sadness. "If only I'd spoken up," she lamented. "I could have saved him."

Lane thought about that. True, she had allowed an innocent man to be accused of her husband's murder, but it was Jim who had actually set Regino up, arrested him, lynched him. She couldn't have prevented his death.

"Mitchell would've killed Regino no matter what you'd done," he said at length, hoping to ease her conscience.

"I suppose so, but the least I can do is clear his name. Doc told me I'd probably get a lighter sentence if I revealed Jim's involvement. What do you think?"

"I think it's too late to do Regino any good."

"But his family . . ."

"Luz and the kids are going back to Mexico Saturday. That's tomorrow, I think. So you sticking your neck out for them won't mean a whole lot. And Luz already knows Regino didn't kill anybody."

"So what do you suggest I do?"

"Leave Penny Town and make a fresh start somewhere else," he said. "If you don't, they'll throw you so far back in prison the guards'll have to feed you with a slingshot. Robert Cates was an important *hombre*."

"In other words, a lighter sentence would mean a long prison term instead of death, is that it?"

Lane smiled in wry amusement. "What'd you think it meant? A wrap on the knuckles? You're broke now, remember? You can't afford a fancy lawyer to get you off the hook."

Christina thought a moment and finally nodded, accepting his argument.

"I've been in a prison for seven years," she said in a soft voice. "I don't want to go back." She fell silent then, still holding his hand, but not so much to give comfort, he suspected, as to receive it. On impulse, he passed his arm around her waist and drew her closer, feeling her body relax against him. Coyotes called to one another in the darkness, and their choppy barks and high-pitched howls sounded wild and strangely haunting. Lane closed his eyes a moment, losing himself in their music and in the warmth of the woman at his side.

CHAPTER TWENTY-FIVE

Lane sat cross-legged on a sheet of bare granite rock and lifted the field glasses to his eyes. From his seven thousand foot ridge-top perch, he could see Pennington several miles to the southwest, barely visible through the morning haze. Isolated mountain ranges jutted up from the flat desert like islands. To his west lay a wilderness of rocks, and one thousand feet below him, the canyon. Like all the canyons of the front range, it cut south toward the Santa Cruz Basin and town.

Lane surveyed his surroundings with a certain amount of adoration. This was his canyon, his territory. Mitchell and the posse were little more than trespassers. That was how he viewed it. He wasn't in town any more. He didn't have to play by their rules any more or obey their laws. He was on his own ground.

He settled the glasses on a point a short distance down-canyon where they had made camp the night before, and from there, slowly searched the length of the canyon, up and down and ridge to ridge.

Mitchell's tracker couldn't be far behind them. He was too good. Lying awake last night, Lane worried about this tracker, whoever he was, and wished he'd step on a rattle-snake or fall and break a leg. Anything to get him off their trail. Tracks or no tracks, Lane's every move yesterday had been easily predictable. Of course they would stick close to the canyon; there was water here, and the canyon provided the fastest route into the high country. Mitchell's tracker would realize this.

Weakened by the poison and concerned for Christina Cates, Lane hadn't put as much effort into shaking off the posse as he should have. He told himself today would be different.

Through the field glasses he glimpsed a speck of movement down-canyon from him on the sunny northwestern slope. It vanished, then reappeared again moments later, a mere dot of black or some other dark color set off against the grays and yellows in the background. He spotted two more moving dots beneath the first, almost in the bottoms, walking single file through the mesquites growing on the terrace above the streambed.

Lane's muscles tensed, and his blood tingled with excitement. This was what he had been waiting for. He lowered the glasses, letting them dangle by their strap around his neck, and glanced sideways at Christina.

"Did you see anything?" she asked.

"Three men in the canyon coming our way," he said. "Maybe more."

"What will we do? Keep going?"

Lane glanced around him at the silent, long-needled pines looming to either side of him and behind and shook his head. "I like it here, don't you?"

"Yes, but . . ."

"I think we'll stay here for a while," he said and laid his Spencer .56 out in front of him on the smooth granite. He placed four extra loading tubes next to the carbine, lining them up in a neat row. "Watch the squirrels for a while, take a nap, whatever you want."

She didn't say anything, and Lane knew she was afraid, though she was careful not to show it. He looked at her, admiring the way the loose blouse had slipped off one shoulder, revealing her tan line. It was a nice touch, strangely provocative, yet still tasteful. Not like Abbie Maginnis. He reached out and touched her sleeve, feeling the fine material between his finger and thumb.

"I hate to spoil the view," he said, "but you'd better put something on over this. That gray shirt of mine'd be best."

"I'm not cold any more."

"Not for the cold. I was thinking how far you can see white. Like waving a flag."

She nodded and shrugged into his shirt. The sleeves reached past her fingertips. She rolled them up to her wrists and buttoned the front.

Satisfied, Lane raised the field glasses again and searched for the dots to see what kind of progress the posse was making.

"Christina Cates." He mouthed her name with a flourish, letting the syllables roll off his tongue and liking the sound of it. "What was your name before you married?"

"Christina McClure."

"Irish?"

"Yes. Lane, can I ask you something?"

"Sure."

"What will you do about Jim?"

"I haven't decided yet. Why?"

"I don't want you to kill him."

He looked at her, suddenly wary. This woman had risked her neck to break him out of jail and had shared his blankets—could she be trusted? Perhaps he had let his guard down too soon, something he never would have done had she been a man.

"You still like him, huh?"

"Jim lied to me, and he used me," she said, choosing her

words carefully. "He's not innocent, Lane, but neither are we. If you kill him, what will you have accomplished? George Nimitz and Estevan Carrillo will buy off the next sheriff just like they bought off Jim, and the small farmers and ranchers will continue to lose out to the land company. Jim's not the root of the problem. The company is."

"In other words, you think I need to pull the weed up by the roots?"

She smiled. "Something like that. But you can't do it without Jim. He knows more about the company's crooked business dealings than anyone, and while I think he'd do just about anything for George and Estevan, I don't think he'd die for them. Jim's not courageous."

"He'd testify against them to save his neck," Lane said.

"I'm sure he would."

Lane nodded, appreciating her honesty. "I'll think about it."

Sheltered by ponderosa pine on three sides, he sprawled flat on his stomach in the shade and watched the possemen through his glasses. They passed in and out of his sight, closer each time, and he began to see details. The man closest to him—he estimated the distance at around six hundred yards—kept zigzagging in and out of the bottoms as if searching for sign. His black head was bare, and he wore no shirt. That would be the Indian tracker. Behind him, another man wearing a large sombrero followed at a distance, stopping often to peer up at the cliffs to either side of him. When the man in the dark shirt whom Lane had first spotted on the slope started to climb down into the bottoms, Mr. Sombrero waved him back up again.

The southeast wall of the canyon was more difficult to see, but Lane was certain he had glimpsed movement there more than once. A man or possibly an animal had crossed an area of open ground high above the canyon floor, directly below the rock cliff rimming the top of the ridge. It bothered him a little since it would be fairly simple for someone on this side of the canyon to circle around behind him. But until Lane fired his first shot and gave away his position, he saw no reason to move.

The tracker was nearing their old camp. Lane watched him closely whenever he moved out of the cover of the trees, observing his mannerisms, the way he walked. Bandy legged, squat-bodied, the tracker wore nothing but a breechclout and knee-high moccasins. A rag tied around his head held the straight, shoulder-length hair away from his face. There was no doubt in Lane's mind that he was Apache.

He of the sombrero fired a single shot into the air, signaling their discovery of the abandoned campsite, and the posseman on the opposite slope started down into the canyon. Focusing the glasses on him, Lane recognized Del Hardy.

The three men's movements were hidden for a time by the trees. Lane waited, relaxed now, in control. The next time he saw them, they should be within firing range.

He wasn't disappointed. The three men moved out into the open, not suspecting there might be a sniper hiding in the trees above them, and the Apache scout squatted on his heels in the sun and took a swig from his canteen. Del Hardy kept gesturing down-canyon, wanting to turn back maybe, tired of fishy smelling water and sleeping on the ground. He and the Sombrero seemed to be arguing, while the tracker ignored them completely.

Lane took one final look at the Apache through his glasses and saw the man's eyes lift to gaze up at the ridge. Lane almost choked on his own astonishment.

"Damn! I don't believe it!"

He felt Christina move up beside him, squirming forward on her stomach. "What's wrong?" she asked.

"That's Crazy Eye."

"Who?"

"Crazy Eye. You remember." He looked again to make sure.

"I thought he was your friend," Christina said.

"He is. Damn!"

He watched Crazy Eye a moment longer. He was still squatted down, eating something and washing it down with water. His crooked gaze remained on the ridge, and then suddenly he was slithering backward into the cover of the trees again, almost as if he had felt the weight of Lane's oppressive stare.

But does he know it's me? Lane doubted it. A true friend, Crazy Eye would never betray him.

Del Hardy and the other man continued to argue. Lane recognized the wearer of the sombrero as one of Mariano Diego's henchmen and decided the world would be a much nicer place without him.

He cushioned the Spencer on his folded jacket and sighted down the barrel at the Mexican who had helped to kill his mother. Allowing for the deceptive downhill angle, he settled his front sight a little below the man's heart.

"Christina?"

"Yes?"

"Cover your ears."

The shot boomed like a clap of thunder, bouncing off the canyon walls and flushing birds into the open sky, and three hundred yards away the Mexican hit the rocks on his back. His gaudy sombrero came to rest upturned at Del Hardy's feet. Stunned, the deputy's mouth fell open as he looked from the hat to its owner to the ridge. Spinning around, he scrambled for cover.

A bullet chipped slivers of rock from the face of the cliff and ricocheted into the cool pines behind Lane. Motioning for Christina to move back, he gathered up the loading tubes and his Spencer and crawled backwards on his hands and knees, away from the cliff's edge, and was struck by a sudden idea.

There was loose rubble all around the edge of the sheet of granite. Choosing two rocks slightly larger than his fist, Lane set one of these on the bare granite and placed the other rock on end so that it rested against the first, turning it so the soiled undersurface faced up. It was a call for help, an indication of disaster, and was one of many stone signals used by the Apaches. While Crazy Eye would know what it meant, most white men would not. For added measure, Lane reached into his pocket, drew out his rosary, and dropped it, too, on the expanse of granite so Crazy Eye would be sure to see it. With any luck, he would recognize the beads as belonging to Lane.

"I always knew you were nothing but a no account sneaking savage."

An electric shock jolted Lane's insides. The voice came from behind, and he recognized it instantly.

Afraid to move, he turned his head a bare inch to the side, enough to see Kirk Mallory's uniformed figure out of the corner of one eye. The thick layer of pine needles covering the ground had muffled his footsteps.

"Hey! Is that the brave lieutenant?" Lane spoke casually. "Nice of you to join the party, Mallory."

"Drop that .56 and unfasten your belt."

The order eased Lane's mind. At least Mallory didn't intend to shoot him right away.

The Spencer was in Lane's right hand, and he let it slide to the ground in an effort to appease the lieutenant but made no move to take off his gunbelt. His eyes searched the deep shade of the pines. Where was Christina?

"Now the belt," Mallory ordered.

"What's wrong, soldier? You don't want to play guns? Hey, I know! Why don't you pretend I'm some old fat Apache woman can't half walk and shoot me between the shoulder blades, maybe take my scalp and show it to the boys when you get back to Fort Lowe." He smiled easily and cut his gaze around to look at Mallory. "That's your favorite sport, ain't it, Kirk?"

Mallory's heavy-boned face lifted in a grin that stopped short of his eyes. "Damned Indian lover. You're a mistake of nature, Devens."

"What makes you say that?" Lane turned slowly to the side to see him better and spotted Christina. She was crouched down several feet behind Mallory and partially hidden by the thick undergrowth. Lane focused on the cavalryman's face. "What makes you think I'm a mistake?"

"You're a half-breed," Mallory replied. "You never should've happened."

Though he never looked at her directly, Lane saw Christina creeping forward, saw the stout piece of wood gripped in her hand like a club.

"All right, Kirk." Lane gestured with his eyes at Mallory's army issue revolver, still pointed his way. "You got the drop on me. Now what?"

"First, you tell me where the woman is."

"Christina's my concern. Not yours."

"Christina, eh? I didn't know you two were on a first name basis." He gave an ugly laugh. "Does she know your pa's a dirty injun?"

Christina lunged forward, lifting the club, swinging it hard at Kirk Mallory's head a split second before he heard her and wheeled around. He raised his arm barely in time to fend off her attack, and the club glanced off his shoulder. Christina swung again, aiming for his head, but Mallory was too strong for her. He grasped the end of the club and propelled her backwards, throwing her to the ground.

Lane never remembered drawing his gun, but suddenly it was in his hand, and with Christina out of the way, he fired just as Mallory spun to face him. His first shot caught the lieutenant below his left armpit. When the man still attempted to lift his gun and aim, Lane cocked the hammer and fired again, thumb and forefinger working reflexively, urged on by a surge of adrenaline. Mallory's body jerked with the impact of each bullet, and he fell dead on the soft carpet of pine needles as Lane's third and final shot ripped through his throat.

Punching the empty cartridges from his .45 with shaky fingers, Lane reloaded and veered around Mallory's bleeding body to Christina. She looked up at him with large eyes as he helped her to her feet.

"You all right?"

Lips pressed tightly together, she nodded and brushed the dirt and leaves from her skirt. The color began to creep back into her face, but whatever she was feeling or thinking was quickly tucked out of sight.

Lane found dried beef in Lieutenant Mallory's warbag, and he added it to their own scanty supply of food, as well as an extra canteen of water. He collected Mallory's personal belongings and pried the gold academy ring from the lieutenant's thick finger and pocketed it.

Seeing Christina's questioning look, he explained: "To send to his wife."

“I’m sorry you had to kill him,” she said.

“Christina, don’t waste your sympathy on the likes of Kirk Mallory. Save it instead for the Indian women and children he raped and murdered throughout his Army career.”

CHAPTER TWENTY-SIX

Lane and Christina left quickly, for they had no idea how many more men might have accompanied Crazy Eye and the lieutenant into the canyon. Lane thought it best to let Crazy Eye figure this out for himself. Once his friend found the rock signal and the rosary, he'd know what to do.

They continued up-canyon, winding their way through tall pines, aspen, and nearer the rim of the canyon, immense boulders. The going was steep and treacherous. White and Douglas firs began to mingle with the pines, and the air grew cooler, thinner, and moist. Yellow columbines and pink wild roses nestled within the forest's lush undergrowth. A startled white-tail deer bounded into the trees, flashing its tail with every leap.

The higher altitude coupled with the lingering effects of the arsenic took its toll on Lane's stamina, yet he pushed himself and Christina hard, stopping only briefly at noon to eat and fill their canteens from a freshwater spring. Covering only about a mile of ground per hour, it wasn't until later that afternoon that he reached his destination. The place at which he chose to stop provided ample concealment, good water, and a panoramic view of the country around them. Ancient rock drawings and metates where Hohokam Indians ground acorns into flour could be found among the giant granite blocks and monoliths.

High above their heads was a hole in one of the rock formations fifteen feet high and between twenty and twenty-five feet wide. The first time Lane laid eyes on this natural aperture several years ago, he dubbed it Window Rock. He called the little grassy hollow below it Window Rock Camp.

Lane walked out to the tip of a sharp jag overlooking the canyon and felt the cool wind ruffle through his hair. It dried the sweat on his skin and left him chilled. Christina drew up behind him and pointed in the direction of Pennington.

"Look. You can see the old mission from here. Isn't it pretty?"

Tiny in the distance, the mission's twin towers gleamed white against a lavender backdrop.

There was nothing left for them to do now but wait. All along the way, Lane had left stone signals to guide Crazy Eye to his Window Rock Camp, and he looked forward to talking with him. He was curious to know how his friend had come to be involved in the search.

At dusk, Lane built a small fire in a sheltered nook between the boulders. They ate supper, and later Christina steeped herbs she had gathered from the forest in hot water, and with her back turned to Lane, she bathed the many scratches and cuts criss-crossing her arms and legs.

Kneeling beside Lane, she touched the inflamed skin around the bullet wound on his cheek. He flinched.

"It's infected," she told him.

She wet a clean rag in the hot water and gently bathed the wound, brow furrowed in concentration, or concern, or pure disgust—Lane wasn't sure which. His beard must have scratched her hand, for she rasped a forefinger across the black stubble on his chin.

"You need to shave."

"It's too bad you didn't think to bring along a razor when you were breaking me out of jail."

"And some soap, and my hairbrush, and a fresh change of clothes," she added.

"Yeah, and a soft feather bed to sleep in."

Their faces inches apart, she smiled at him and arched an eyebrow. "Anything else?"

"A bottle of Madeira wine and two of those fancy goblets like you see in the wish books. No, three. Crazy Eye might want some." He grinned.

She laughed, shaking her head. "Abbie said you were the serious type. I don't think she knew you very well."

Lane's gaze sharpened. "Abbie? You talked to her?"

"Yes." She watched his face closely. "Abbie told me where to find your horse."

"What else did she tell you?"

Christina glanced at him coyly. "Just woman talk. Nothing you'd be interested in, I'm sure."

Lane knew she was playing with him, and while he rather enjoyed it, he felt uncomfortable when he tried to imagine what these two women could have talked about. Abbie probably told Christina about the birthmark on his butt. No subject was too lewd for Abbie Maginnis.

"What attracted you to her?" Christina asked suddenly.

"To Abbie?" Lane shrugged. "I don't know. Different things. I guess I just needed her, or thought I did. You get lonely sometimes."

"I know the feeling."

"Do you?" He touched her hair, brushing it from her cheek and feeling her dark eyes watching him, searching his face. "Is that what made you turn to Jim Mitchell?" he asked.

"I suppose. He was nice at first. He told me he understood what I was going through and cared about me, told me everything I longed to hear, and I foolishly believed him." Christina leaned back, withdrawing from Lane emotionally as well as physically he sensed, and set aside the herbal concoction she had prepared.

"You'd think I'd finally learn not to trust so easily," she said.

"Do you trust me?"

She lifted her gaze to meet his, features shadowed by the gentle sweep of her hair. "I would like to," she replied softly. "I've never believed that all men are cruel. My father wasn't."

"I'll prove it, Christina."

She watched him, silent, reserving judgment, and Lane knew it would take more than kind words and promises to gain Christina Cates' trust. He must *show* her. It was suddenly important to him that he prove himself to her, prove that not all men were like Robert Cates and Jim Mitchell. Yet remembering her request that he not take Mitchell's life, he worried that he wouldn't be able to meet her expectations. The man had killed his best friend, a deed that should not go unpunished.

Sitting in the inky shadows of the jumbled boulders, out of the moonlight, Lane rested his carbine across his lap, and he and Christina rested quietly. He had doused the fire, and the mountain air had grown cold with nightfall. Christina started to rise to get their blankets when Lane grasped her wrist and touched a finger to his lips. They sat motionless, staring into the night.

Lane heard it again, a soft, low whistle. Pursing his lips, he answered the call and within a minute the Apache scout, Crazy Eye, appeared, moving silently among the rocks. When he leaped down into the tiny hollow that was their camp, Lane was on his feet, and they clasped each others forearms in greeting. He saw Crazy Eye's leathery face crease in a broad grin.

"Our paths have crossed again," he said, speaking softly in Spanish.

"You are alone?"

"Not quite."

Crazy Eye left them and returned a moment later shoving a red-haired deputy in front of him. Wild-eyed and bedraggled, Del Hardy shifted his gaze back and forth from the Apache to Lane. Crazy Eye had gagged him and bound his hands tightly behind his back.

"Is he the only one?" Lane asked.

Crazy Eye nodded. "The others are waiting." He gestured toward the southwest, down-canyon.

"Cuántos?" Lane asked. How many?

Crazy Eye held up four fingers. "The one with the yellow hair I have met before. He wears a star on his chest and talks loudly. His friend has eyes that are like the stones of ice that sometimes fall from the clouds."

Lane nodded. That would be Jim Mitchell and Charlie Reed.

"What about the others?"

"Nakai-yes," Crazy Eye replied, speaking this time in Apache.

Mexicans. More of Mariano Diego's followers, no doubt. Christina tugged on Lane's sleeve, wanting to know what was being said. He quickly translated and turned back to Crazy Eye.

"Will you lead me to their camp?"

The Apache nodded, and his left eye took an aimless stroll to the outer edge of the socket, as it often did when he had strong feelings.

"Like old times," he said with a smile.

While Crazy Eye gathered wood and started a fire, Lane lashed Del Hardy's feet together and jerked the gag from his mouth. He squatted on his heels near the deputy and quietly smoked, eyes fixed on the young man's sunburned face.

Hardy squirmed uncomfortably beneath his unwavering stare until he could no longer stand it.

"What!"

Lane blew a generous stream of smoke into the deputy's face and shook his head. "Hardy, you're so slow it's pitiful."

"Yeah?" Hardy looked him in the eye, trying to appear tough. "Say that when I ain't all trussed up, and I'll show you who's slow."

Lane sighed wearily, scratching his forehead with his thumb, the cigarette still smoking between his fingers. He glanced over his shoulder at Christina. "Should I tell him the truth?"

She stared at him, puzzled, then saw his wink and nodded. "By all means."

He turned back to Hardy. "When I say you're slow, what I mean is that you haven't learned to see past the end of your nose. Savvy?" When the deputy only looked at him, he continued. "Your boss tries to kill you, and you don't suspect a thing."

"Jim?" Hardy scoffed at the very idea. "Jim wouldn't do that."

"All right," Lane conceded. "So he hired somebody else to do it for him. Same difference."

"You're off your rocker!"

"Am I? Tell me something, Hardy. You had a bad feeling about trailing me into these mountains, didn't you? Like maybe Jim was throwing you to the dogs, right?"

"Well, sort of, but . . ."

"But you didn't listen to your gut feeling," Lane went on. "Now that Mexican fella I shot this morning . . ."

"Herrera."

"Herrera. Yeah. You two didn't get along so good, I bet."

Hardy frowned. "He kept ordering me around like he was in charge."

"Questioning your authority?"

"Heck, yeah. Every time I turned around."

"You know why? Because he was the man Jim hired to kill you."

Firelight flickered across Hardy's slack-jawed face, revealing the shock in his eyes.

"Herrera was just waiting for the right time to do it. If I hadn't killed him . . ." Lane left the conjecture dangling and shrugged.

"He would've killed me!"

"Bushwhacked you," Lane said positively. He was on a roll now. "Herrera was smart. He knew better than to confront you face to face."

"You think so?"

"Are you kiddin' me? All anybody's gotta do is take one look at you and see you're not a man to be trifled with."

Hardy fought to hold back his smile of pleasure, but it broke through in spite of the effort. "You'd better believe it," he said. "But look here, Devens. About Jim hiring Herrera—why would he want to do a thing like that?"

Lane bobbed his head in Christina's direction. "Mitchell told her he didn't trust you any more, that you were gettin' too greedy, and he was gonna have to put you away. Nimitz and Carrillo were in on it, too."

Hardy moaned miserably. "It's because I blabbed," he said. "I told you about the work program, remember? Jim got real mad about that."

"You did the right thing by telling somebody," Lane said, and he poked a finger against the young man's chest. "You know in your heart that what Jim and the supervisors have been doing to those prisoners and the small farmers and ranchers is wrong, don't you?"

"Yes, but . . ."

"And you know the murder of Regino Vega was wrong, too, but you had to go along with it because Jim was your boss, and you respected him. You didn't want to lose your job."

Hardy nodded. "That's the honest-to-God truth."

"I know it is," Lane said. "That's why I'm gonna give you a chance to redeem yourself and maybe even pay Mitchell back if you want to."

"You mean you're not gonna kill me?"

Lane feigned surprise. "Kill you? Hell, no. I like you, Hardy. You've got the makings of a mighty fine lawman."

Not holding back now, Hardy grinned with gratitude.

"Here's what I want you to do," Lane told him. "I want you to turn all this over in your mind, and in the morning you tell me what you think oughta be done about Mitchell and the others."

Hardy appeared dumbstruck. "You're asking for my advice?"

Lane smiled. "You're the one wearing the badge, aren't you?"

"Yes."

"In the morning then. We'll talk."

He started to rise, but Hardy stopped him, holding up his bound hands. "Aren't you gonna untie me?"

Lane hesitated, thinking it over, and glanced toward Crazy Eye squatting by the fire. "I can't untie you, Hardy," he said finally. "Crazy Eye thinks you're too dangerous. But when he's not looking, I'll loosen your hands a mite so you'll be more comfortable."

Flattered by his sudden and unexpected rise to importance, Del Hardy accepted this without argument.

Later, out of the deputy's hearing, Christina slipped up beside Lane. "You're terrible," she said in a lowered voice. "You know Jim didn't hire anyone to kill him."

"You know it, and I know it," Lane agreed, "but he doesn't."

Nodding, Christina was silent a moment, then, "Just remember what we talked about, Lane. About Jim. Too many lives have been lost already."

"I know," Lane said, but he refrained from promising her anything, knowing it would make him appear even worse in her eyes should he break it.

Long after Christina and Del Hardy had fallen asleep, Lane and Crazy Eye remained awake, catching up on each other's lives and discussing plans for Jim Mitchell. When Lane questioned why Crazy Eye had joined Mitchell's posse, his friend's face took on a bitter cast as he explained what had happened.

A week ago, following the incident with Sheriff Mitchell in the foothills, he and his nephew rode into their mountain hideout only to find that his family had been captured by soldiers and taken to Fort Lowe, near Pennington. When Crazy Eye arrived at the fort to reclaim his wife and children, he was immediately arrested and charged with desertion from the United States Army.

"Two sleeps ago," he continued, "Lieutenant Mallory comes to me and says if I will track down this bad man who stole someone's woman, the army will let me and my family return to Mexico." Crazy Eye gave an elaborate shrug. "I did not know that you were this bad man until this morning."

He drew Lane's rosary from a small leather pouch and handed it to him with the solemn reverence of a man who respected another's religion, no matter how different it was from his own.

Lane cupped the beads in his palm, watching the silver cross flash in the firelight. It was good to have it back.

Reaching out, Crazy Eye gripped Lane's shoulder. "Something else troubles you," he said. "What is it?"

Lane glanced up at him and frowned. "Did you ever hear of an Apache warrior named Cuervo?"

"Many times. Why do you ask?"

"I was told that Cuervo is my real father."

Crazy Eye stared at him, his plucked brows lifting in astonishment. "You know this to be true?"

Lane replied that he was almost certain.

The Apache scout considered this in silence and pushed a twig into the fire. Sparks crackled, spewing into the chilly air.

"This warrior you speak of has passed over to the death side," he said gravely. "I am sorry."

Lane was uncertain how he should react to the news. His feelings were mixed. He was disappointed at not having a chance to confront the man but was glad Cuervo was dead. It saved him the trouble of hunting him down.

"How did he die?"

Crazy Eye shook his head and touched the amulet dangling around his neck. "It is not wise to speak of those in the spirit world."

Lane understood his friend's reluctance to speak of Cuervo. It was the belief of the Mescaleros that to mention the name of the deceased, particularly in front of his relatives, might cause the ghost to linger among the living, spreading sickness and death. Everything possible was done to encourage the ghost to enter the afterworld without delay and to remain there.

Even knowing this, Lane pushed Crazy Eye to tell him more.

Crazy Eye drew a heavy breath. "Ten, perhaps eleven winters ago, your father was badly wounded by blue soldiers and taken prisoner," he explained. "It is said that when he recovered, he was sent far away to where the sun sets, to a rock in the big water."

"Alcatraz Island?"

Crazy Eye nodded. "He died there of the white man's sickness."

Lane digested this information. Dying in prison of small pox or consumption could not have been an easy way to end one's life. He was not sorry.

"This man who was my father," Lane began, careful not to say his name, "he was Mescalero?"

"No, Chiricahua."

"What else do you know about him?"

The scout hesitated, obviously uncomfortable, and Lane sensed it was due only in part to superstition.

"I did not know him personally," he said at last, "but it is said that he was very brave in battle and much feared by even the boldest warriors of his own band. It is said he was very cruel." Crazy Eye paused, reluctant to continue, and avoided Lane's attentive gaze. "This led to his banishment by the *nant'á.*"

Cuervo then had been an outcast, a man so cruel—even by Apache standards—that even his family could not tolerate him. Lane wondered if perhaps this explained his own penchant for violence.

Crazy Eye borrowed paper and tobacco from Lane and tried unsuccessfully to roll a cigarette. Lane rolled it for him and lit it with a burning stick from their fire. Inhaling deeply, Crazy Eye choked a little when the tobacco's sharp bite filled his lungs.

"I saw him only once," he said after a moment. "You are like him in some ways. You are tall like him. You are quick to anger and quick to act." The skin around the scout's eyes crinkled in a smile. "But your mother's heart beats inside you," he said, and reaching over, he grasped Lane by the arm and pushed up his sleeve. With a dirty fingernail, he traced the blue vein extending from the bend of Lane's elbow to his wrist. "Your blood is good blood, strong blood. I believe it is men like you, men of mixed blood, who will someday form a bridge between the white man's world and the *Ndé's* world."

"I'm not so sure I want to be the bridge," Lane said. "People walk on you."

Crazy Eye laughed at this and dumped more sugar into his coffee. "No one walks on Lane Devens," he mused.

CHAPTER TWENTY-SEVEN

Late Saturday morning, Charlie Reed told Jim he was certain he had heard gunfire on the mountain.

"I didn't hear a thing," Jim said.

"You were too busy working your jaws."

"Mingo and Pete are teaching me Spanish. Say, you don't suppose our boys tangled with Devens, do you?"

"We could find out."

"And walk?" Jim was aghast.

"Your legs ain't broke," Charlie replied tersely.

Jim dismissed his concern with a joke and a laugh. "If you heard a shot, it was probably Del shooting at shadows. Probably shot himself in the foot. Either way, we'll find out what happened before too long."

It took three days.

They were camped in the canyon bottoms among the boulders and heavy brush—Jim, Charlie, and the two possemen, Domingo Vargas and Pedro Armendariz. Time passed slowly for the four men. Each morning, Charlie led the horses to a small seep a short way from camp, let them drink, and then staked them out to graze on the grassy southeastern slope. He made the fires, cooked the meals, and cleaned his already clean gun until it was time to bring the horses in again. His routine never varied. Jim told him once that he was about as unpredictable as a rock.

Leaving Charlie to do all the work, Domingo Vargas and Pedro Armendariz played poker with Jim and taught him dirty words in Spanish. They laughed at his jokes and his clumsy efforts to speak their language. When he started calling them Mingo and Pete, they grinned at each other in amusement.

Jim wasn't fooled. He had seen them in the city lockup more than once and knew their reputations. Neither would hesitate to slit his throat. Both men had worked for Mariano Diego at one time until he fired them for drinking and fighting, yet they remained loyal to their former boss. Though not loyal enough to blister their feet chasing down his killer, Jim noticed.

Jim finally induced Mingo and Pete to build him a lean-to out of one of the tarpaulins, promising them all the free drinks they wanted once they got back to town. While the others slept in the open at night, Jim bedded down in his lean-to. It was here that he thought about Christina Cates and wondered where, when, and how the romance had gone awry.

Jim had felt sure he was getting somewhere with her, and she double-crossed him in the worst way. He still couldn't believe it. She was in the mountains somewhere, alone with a murdering smoky-eyed wolf, doing God only knew what. She'd come crawling back to him sooner or later, he was certain, begging him to take her back. She needed him. He'd make her wait and worry a little while, let her see how it felt to be rejected before he forgave her. Later, they'd get married and move into one of those fine, big houses over on silk-stocking street. He would be set for life, living high on Robert Cates' money.

Jim worked the complicated situation out in his mind and was pleased with the outcome. An optimist, he never considered the possibility that he might have oversimplified matters.

Trouble stole into their camp a little before dawn, Tuesday morning.

Jim slogged his way out of sleep and lay quietly on his back, trying to figure out what had awakened him. He gazed sleepy-eyed up at the white canvas tarp sagging above his head. Nearby, one of the horses nickered. There was the dull click of a hoof striking against stone, and a crackly snap, like popping leg joints, almost as if one of the horses was walking around. But that was impossible; they were all tied to the picket line. It took a minute before the meaning behind these sounds registered in Jim's mind.

Mingo and Pete! They were stealing the horses! Jim grabbed his boots and gunbelt.

"Charlie, wake up!"

He had expected it to happen, knowing Mingo and Pete would grow tired of waiting at some point and light a shuck for town.

Buckling his belt, he stumbled out from under the lean-to and cast a swift glance toward the horses. They were gone.

"Pete! Mingo!"

Jim crashed into the weeds and brush, stumped his toe on a root, and fell flat on his face. Swearing, he started to push himself to his feet when a strangled cry reached his ears, and he dropped back to the ground. Lying belly-down in the stickers and horse manure, he lifted his head and searched for movement in the uncertain pre-dawn light.

"Jim?"

It was Charlie. Though Jim couldn't see him, he sounded close. His words were hushed.

"Jim, if that's you, speak up before I blow your head off."

"What in the hell's going on?" Jim whispered.

"I don't know. Somebody got Pete. Mingo, too, I think." There was a pause. A twig snapped, very near, and Charlie's voice suddenly raised in warning. "Jim, look out! Oh, shit!"

Gunfire exploded from the brush less than six feet from Jim's hiding place, half a dozen shots all at once, and a bullet kicked grit into his eyes and mouth. Ears ringing, he scrambled away on his elbows and knees, clutching both six-shooters in his hands. A series of high-pitched screams chilled his blood. They seemed to come from every direction.

Scared to the point of panic, Jim jumped to his feet and tore through the mesquites and catclaw, unmindful of the thorns that raked at his clothing and flesh. He glanced wildly around him, saw a shadow flit through the scrub several yards to his left, and threw a shot in that direction.

He fired at every shadow, boulder, and stump, running, stumbling, thrashing his way through the brush-clogged bottoms, leaving behind him the strong smell of turpentine as he crushed the little resinous bushes underfoot. The unearthly war whoops had ceased, yet Jim knew he must be surrounded by a raiding bunch of marauding Apaches. And he was alone.

His breath ragged, Jim staggered and fell, cracking his kneecap on a rock. The sudden sharp pain sliced through his numbed senses. He groaned softly and sank to the ground. Sweat dribbled down his face, and he licked the salt from his upper lip and tried to think what to do. Every muscle in his body quivered from exertion and fear.

Charlie, Pete, and Mingo must all be dead, he thought. I'm the only one left.

Something struck Jim in the back. He flinched violently and twisted around, lifting his guns. He saw nothing, heard nothing. Crouched down near the dry streambed, he searched the boulders behind him with wide eyes.

He felt it again—something struck him squarely between the shoulder blades. Flinching, gasping, he spun back around and stared into the brush. They were closing in on him! He was completely surrounded!

A bird twittered off to his left, on the opposite bank of the streambed. His nerves already jangled, Jim whirled around and fired a shot at the sound before he realized it was harmless.

He felt the sting of another pebble. It struck him in the side of the neck this time, and he cowered in the lee of the boulders, too scared to run.

"Damn you! Damn all of you!" His hoarse shout echoed between the canyon walls. "Stop playing games, you red bastards!"

He caught a movement out of the corner of one eye. Swinging around, he saw an Apache buck slink out of the mesquite scrub less than five yards away. Jim leaped to his feet and hiked up both revolvers. Teeth gritted, he squeezed the triggers. The disheartening snaps of the hammers falling against the firing pins made him sick to his stomach. In his panic, he had forgotten to reload his guns! Jim sank to his knees, letting the fancy pearl-handled revolvers slip from his hands, hollow eyes fixed on the Apache. His brain and reflexes were frozen.

Holding his rifle on Jim, the Apache straddled an uprooted tree that had washed downstream during a past flood and moved soundlessly toward him. He was out of the shadows now, and with the morning light growing stronger, Jim could see him more clearly. The warrior was stripped to the waist, and a heavy bandolier slanted across his bare chest. He wore a sidearm; it was tied down low on his right thigh in much the same way as a white man might wear it. His pants were dusty and washed out and blended perfectly with the gray-beige backdrop, and the legs were stuffed into knee-high moccasins.

The Apache stopped a few feet in front of him. Almost reluctantly, Jim lifted his eyes to look up at the savage face, sure any minute now he would breathe his last, and couldn't have been more shocked than if he had beheld the President of the United States.

Lane Devens' face broke into an amused smile, even, white teeth gleaming against tawny skin. The first light of dawn cast a glow on his cheekbones and nose.

"I counted twelve shots," Devens stated casually. "Time to reload, Sheriff." He slipped a cartridge from his gunbelt and tossed it to Jim.

"Devens, I . . ." Jim paused, struggling to his feet. He looked around him, finding it difficult to speak. "Where are the others?"

"What others?"

Jim gaped at him. "The Apaches! I heard them!"

"You heard me and Crazy Eye," Devens replied, and he grinned. "The imagination's a tricky thing, ain't it?"

Too stunned to reply, Jim watched him set his carbine aside and draw his Colt. Devens ejected five live cartridges into the dust at his feet, leaving only one chamber loaded, and dropped the gun back into its holster.

"We each get one shot," he said. "Load your gun, Mitchell. It's just you and me."

Only now beginning to comprehend what was happening, Jim bent down, picked up one of his guns and the cartridge, and hesitated, looking at Lane Devens. This wasn't how it was supposed to end. Devens should have died, killed by the arsenic, but here he was, standing barely four feet away from him. He appeared much too healthy for Jim's comfort.

He forced a shaky laugh. "This is all sort of sudden. I mean, don't you want to talk it over first?"

"Load your gun, or I'll do it for you."

Jim took a faltering step backwards. This couldn't be happening to him. He was trapped. There was no way out. Or perhaps there was . . . Looking past Devens' left shoulder, he saw the familiar stocky figure of his deputy emerge from the scrub and almost shouted with relief.

But something was wrong. Del Hardy was smiling.

"There you are, Devens! I took the horses and . . ." His voice trailed off when he caught sight of Jim. The smiled faded.

Without taking his eyes off Jim, Devens spoke quietly. "Hardy, you go on back to camp and see if Crazy Eye needs any help. We're almost finished here."

The deputy started to back away.

Jim stared at him, his features distorting in anger and disbelief. "Del!"

"Yeah, Jim?"

"What the hell's the matter with you? Do something!"

Del Hardy laughed a little nervously, buckteeth shining, crazy tufts of red hair sticking out from beneath his hat.

"Do something!" Jim shouted. "Shoot him!"

"Can't do that, Jim," Del said, and lifting a hand to his mouth, he began chewing his fingernails.

Jim wanted to cry. He laughed hollowly instead, and without thinking about the consequences, he turned and fled.

Jim ran for his life, arms and legs pumping, boots crunching the dry, curled mud of the streambed. He fumbled at the loading gate on his gun as he ran and tried feverishly to thumb the single cartridge into one of the chambers. Devens dove into him from behind. The force of his attack threw both men to the ground, and all the air was knocked from Jim's lungs as Devens landed heavily on top of him. Straddling his back, Devens grasped a fistful of Jim's hair and jerked his head up. Drawing his Bowie knife, he pressed the blade's cold steel edge beneath Jim's nose.

"Little girls don't wear mustaches."

Eyes bulging, Jim squirmed as Devens scraped away at the stiff hairs of his mustache, and he felt the raw bite and the warm wetness of his blood trickling into his mouth. The taste of it was brassy and strong, the smell even stronger.

The last thing he remembered before the blackness enveloped him was Del Hardy's voice: "Devens, I'd sure hate to have you for my barber!"

Lane and Del Hardy dragged the unconscious sheriff to camp where they tied him and left him beneath the lean-to. Crazy Eye had already bound the two Mexicans' hands and feet and was bent over Charlie Reed, preparing to dig a .56 slug from his thigh. The undersheriff was sorely displeased with the circumstances.

Hands on his hips, Hardy gazed down at Jim Mitchell and shook his head. "He ran scared, Devens." The deputy was disillusioned. "All this time I've been taking orders from a coward."

"Looks that way," Lane agreed. "What do you figure we oughta do with him?"

Hardy's freckled face brightened. "I've been thinking about that. There's a new deputy U.S. marshal lives over in Wilmot. A real square shooter. He ran against Jim last election and hates his guts. I bet he'd be tickled to make some arrests."

"And maybe help send Mitchell and the supervisors straight to the Yuma Territorial Prison," Lane added. "Are you still willing to testify against them?"

"You bet I am."

Lane struck a match on his jeans and lit a cigarette, eyeing the deputy closely over his cupped hands. "Don't double-cross me, Del. It wouldn't be healthy."

This marked the first time Lane had threatened him in any way, and his words were all the more meaningful.

Hardy frowned. "Heck, Devens, if I was gonna double-cross you, I'd have already done it."

Lane saw no other choice but to trust him.

He had had ample opportunity over the past two days to work on the deputy, turning him against both the sheriff and Charlie Reed. Already angry at the two men for sending him after a man who had just shot down three people, Hardy wasn't difficult to convince, and he confessed to Lane that he "knew derned well something didn't smell right." There was no doubt in his mind that Jim Mitchell meant to have him killed.

As it turned out, Lane discovered that Hardy knew nothing about Mitchell's attempt to frame Regino Vega for murder, nor was he aware that his boss had poisoned Lane while he was in jail.

Deciding to keep Christina's role out of it, Lane had explained to the young deputy that Mitchell had stabbed Robert Cates with Vega's knife, then planted the weapon at the crime scene. The deputy was shocked.

"I thought Vega was guilty," Hardy said. "Devens, I did some rotten things for Jim, but I never killed nobody."

Lane believed him. Hardy was dumb and easily corrupted, but he wasn't a killer.

Leaving Crazy Eye and the deputy to watch over the four men, Lane walked up the canyon to Christina. She was seated in the grass among the lippia and white sagebrush with her knees drawn up, hugging her legs close to her body. She raised a hand and brushed a strand of hair from her face, tucking it behind her ear. Not wanting to startle her, Lane called her name softly.

Christina's head jerked around, and relief flooded her features. "Lane!" She quickly rose and started toward him. "Are you all right?"

He nodded. "It's over, Christina. Almost, anyway."

"What about Jim?" she asked. "Is he . . ."

"He's fine. Nobody was killed."

"Thank goodness!" She gazed up at him, dark eyes searching his. "It wasn't easy for you, was it?"

"No. No, it wasn't. If he hadn't run . . ." Lane paused, reconsidering. "The truth is, I probably would have killed him anyway if it hadn't been for you. He's no good, Christina."

"I realize that. But by allowing him to live, you've ensured the downfall of Arizona Land and Development . . . and you've proven yourself to be a better man in the process."

He cocked an eyebrow at her. "A man to be trusted?"

"Perhaps." She smiled. "So what now?"

"We'll take Mitchell and Reed to Wilmot. Hardy says there's a good U.S. marshal there." He shrugged. "We'll see what happens."

Christina thought about this in silence, her head slightly bowed, and when she spoke again her voice was gentle.

"What about you?"

Lane looked at her. "Me?"

"Yes, you. Have you made any plans?"

"Soon as we get to Wilmot, I'll buy you a train ticket out of here," he told her. "And then . . ."

"And then?"

Avoiding her inquiring eyes, he shuffled his feet uncomfortably. "And then I'll miss you."

"You could visit me," Christina suggested. "Trains run in both directions."

He shrugged. "I never liked trains much. Too damned

noisy." He met her hopeful gaze, felt a smile spread across his face, as uncontrollable as the sudden giddy feeling in his head. "But I wouldn't mind traveling by horse. Where are you planning on going?"

"California," she answered, without hesitation. "San Francisco, I believe. I've been there once, a happy time, and I'd like to go back. Robert left me a small sum of money, enough to live on until I decide what to do."

Sensing a change in her, Lane asked, "You aren't afraid, are you?"

She laughed softly, shaking her head. "No. For the first time in years, I'm not afraid. I'm looking forward to being on my own . . . at least for a little while." Stepping toward him, she rested her palms against his chest, face tilted up and alight with anticipation. "Promise you'll come and see me, Lane."

"I promise," he said.

Slipping his arms around her waist, he held her close, feeling the softness of her hair against his cheek. He cared for Christina Cates very much. There was evolving between them a trust and understanding that shared hardship had served to strengthen, and he found himself already dreading her departure.

Drawing back slightly, Christina favored him with a warm smile. "At least we'll be together during the ride to Wilmot."

"That's why we're gonna take our time getting there," Lane said. He grinned at her and winked. "The first man to complain about the slow pace gets his leg broke."